Through a Shattered Image

Linda Widrick

This is a work of fiction. Names, characters, places, and incidents either are the product of the author's imagination or are used fictitiously, and any resemblance to actual persons living or dead, business establishments, events, or locales, is entirely coincidental.

Through a Shattered Image
COPYRIGHT 2017 by Linda Widrick

All rights reserved. No part of this book may be used or reproduced in any manner whatsoever without written permission of the author or Pelican Ventures, LLC except in the case of brief quotations embodied in critical articles or reviews.

eBook editions are licensed for your personal enjoyment only. eBooks may not be re-sold, copied or given to other people. If you would like to share an eBook edition, please purchase an additional copy for each person you share it with.

Contact Information: titleadmin@pelicanbookgroup.com

All scripture quotations, unless otherwise indicated, are taken from the Holy Bible, New International Version(R), NIV(R), Copyright 1973, 1978, 1984, 2011 by Biblica, Inc.™ Used by permission of Zondervan. All rights reserved worldwide. www.zondervan.com

Cover Art by *Nicola Martinez*

Prism is a division of Pelican Ventures, LLC
www.pelicanbookgroup.com PO Box 1738 *Aztec, NM * 87410

The Triangle Prism logo is a trademark of Pelican Ventures, LLC

Publishing History
Prism Edition, 2017
Paperback Edition ISBN 978-1-5223-9770-0
Electronic Edition ISBN 978-1-5223-9761-8
Published in the United States of America

Dedication

To Keith, my husband and biggest fan. Thank you for the thought-provoking ideas you plant in my mind and for believing that I can do something with them.

1

Karina flinched when someone touched her shoulder. Her breath quickened and her heart raced with sudden fear—the kind of fear that causes a person to jolt in their bed from a deep sleep, their thoughts all askew.

"I'm sorry to startle you. Are you finished with your juice?"

Karina shuddered and then breathed a sigh of relief when her eyes focused on the flight attendant who waited in the aisle.

AJ said I'd be safe. I need to be less jumpy. People will notice.

"I am. Thank you." She handed him the plastic glass.

"Care for some fresh coffee?"

"That'd be great," she answered.

"Cream?" he asked as he poured it for her.

"Yes, please. And honey if you have it."

She pulled the seals from the creamers and emptied them into her mug, swirling a package of honey into it. The warmth felt good as she swallowed the smooth liquid.

Her throat was heavy.

Heavy with emotion.

Weary of the questioning.

Karina was grateful no one was assigned to the

seat beside her. The extra cost for first-class tickets discouraged travelers in this tough economy. At least something worked to her advantage.

She didn't want to talk.

Didn't want to think about what to say.

Didn't want to think about what *not* to say.

A familiar ping sounded over the speaker.

"Hello, folks, Captain Stevens here. We're in for some turbulence as we make our way over the Blue Ridge Mountains this morning. I'll skirt around it the best I can, but please fasten your seatbelts until we're through it. At this time, we're on schedule to get you into Syracuse by eleven forty-five where it's currently twenty-eight degrees with an expected high of about thirty-four. Thanks for your cooperation. Thank you for flying with us."

Karina cringed at the announcement of the brutal temperatures awaiting her. South Beach rarely dropped below the mid-fifties, and when it did, the coat and boots came out.

She reached for the tablet in her bag and pushed the headphones to her ears. The plane bounced as it maneuvered through the turbulence. If the plane fell from the sky and she blended in with the dust of the earth, would it matter? Would anyone miss her? She thought back to the day her parents' single-engine plane went down. Reliving the memory still brought with it a weight of pain. If she joined them soon, she'd tell them everything that happened to her, particularly during the last twenty-four hours.

Karina pulled the courtesy blanket around her a little tighter and tried not to worry. The tablet came to life when she tapped the icon to view the video clip that she hadn't watched yet. Despite her misgiving, she was glad she downloaded and saved it before the order came to remove all traces of the case from the web—one of the many back doors that AJ strategically shut to keep her safe. If anyone searched for her now, all details about her since that day in the elevator would be nonexistent.

Breaking news tonight on News Channel 7. Let's go live to Marisa Crawford, who is covering the story for us from the Miami-Dade Courthouse.

The scene changed from the studio shot to the attractive Latino reporter who stood at the steps of the familiar courthouse. Several reporters stood at attention, the call letters of their stations wrapped around their microphones in hand.

Thank you, Stacey. It's been a long day in the courtroom for prosecutors, defense attorneys, and family members of slain, prominent attorney, Vic Trebari. Trebari, as you recall, was murdered early last year. He was the lead prosecuting attorney in a case that sparked a statewide debate over the misuse of funds that were earmarked for a special Fair Trade project under the Florida Department of Agriculture and Consumer Services division in the state's capital. To recap, the department works in tandem alongside coffee farmers in Central America to ensure a fair price is paid in exchange for organic beans that are imported to Florida's east coast. The FDACS assures sustainable farming techniques are taught and utilized by the growers as part of the state's cooperative extension program. As we reported previously, like a chain reaction, things went awry when the misappropriation of these funds forced the struggling coffee farmers to convert their crops from coffee to poppy, resulting in a surge of heroine production.

Karina could almost narrate the story herself. The reporter provided the background of the case as footage continued with video clips from the courtroom to candid, still shots of family photos of the decedent.

...and while that case is still ongoing, after days of deliberation in the courtroom, late last night, the jury came to a verdict, convicting Edward DeFresnio of the murder of Vic Trebari. Sheila Trebari, the widow of the deceased, was clearly shaken, although much relieved, when the verdict was announced.

Karina pulled a tissue from her pocket and dabbed at the tears that fell as she continued to take in the report.

While this new development provides Trebari's widow and family a sense of justice, the courtroom battle is far from over. Prosecuting attorneys will resume on Monday as the search continues for other accomplices in the case. We tried to reach Karina Rubenski, the emergency room nurse who took the stand two weeks ago, but she's been unavailable for comment. One thing is certain. Her testimony clearly proved to be the nail in the coffin that moved the jury toward the final verdict against Edward DeFresnio. More on this as details become available. Now back to you, Stacey.

The video panned out across the courtroom steps. Karina's eyes were drawn to the far left of the screen where two figures stood in the distance at the edge of the frame, half inside, half outside the camera footage. While their features were difficult to distinguish, they appeared to be deep in conversation. One man was in uniform. His stance was vaguely familiar.

The seatback shifted as someone behind her braced themselves to stand. "Interesting story. I caught that on the news earlier," the woman offered.

Karina dropped her head, hoping her hair would cover her eyes. She waited until the woman made it into the aisle. Then Karina pulled the earphones from her head and clapped her tablet case shut. The woman probably meant no harm. Still, she must be cautious. AJ warned her, and for now, he was the only person she was supposed to trust. He was the one who could strip her of her life to give her another that was worth living—or so he said. *Everything will be taken care of for you. We'll get you settled in a new place, and no one will find you. It's the only way we can guarantee your safety.*

Well, she understood a lot about guarantees. Nothing was ever really guaranteed. Slick words were designed to deceive the trusting public.

Some assurance.

Already, she doubted her choice to leave her past behind to step into the new life AJ planned for her.

The plane rose and fell abruptly as it hit another pocket of turbulence. She gripped the armrests and held her breath. No doubt this rough patch of air space was the first sign of an ominous new beginning.

One she claimed no power—or wherewithal—to control.

~*~

Scordino glanced around the concourse one more time. How had he lost her, especially after he'd gotten so close? Mariucci would kill him.

The reflection of a 747 in the tall glass window to

his side caught his attention. He slicked his fingers through his hair—his attempt to appear unobtrusive. Passengers were boarding, yet there was no sign of her. He'd managed to follow her from Miami to Atlanta, and one hour ago was the last he'd seen of her. The trail was growing cold.

Dozens of flights were taking off, creating a spider web effect all across the country. She could be on any one of them by now. If not for his extra wait for the tram at the last concourse, he might've spotted her at the gate.

But now, he didn't have a clue which direction she'd gone. He cursed under his breath into the newspaper in front of him. Certainly, a woman like her should be easy to spot. Her wispy, shoulder-length hair draped nicely across her white collar. She was dressed in a pair of dark jeans and a black jacket that complemented her frame. He knew her style. He'd studied her meticulously over the last few weeks. The details of her life were imbedded into his mind: where she lived, what car she drove, her parking space number at Miami General, and yes, even her preferred spot in the courthouse parking lot.

He and Mariucci had waited as long as possible. But now, Scordino feared they'd waited too long. If tipped off, she'd definitely make a run for it. He was inches away from having her in his clutches last night. If only Patrick's blunder hadn't sparked the chain reaction.

Scordino rolled up the newspaper and stood. He reluctantly reached for the phone in his pocket.

Mariucci wouldn't be happy, but there was no alternative. It was time to move to plan B.

~*~

"One iced caramel macchiato, light on the macchiato." The barista slid the drink across the counter.

"Thanks, man," AJ answered. "Tomorrow. Same time."

The warmth of the morning wrapped around AJ as he stepped outside the South Beach Drive Starbucks and headed for his unmarked car. His phone vibrated at his belt. The sun was too bright to read the caller ID. He clicked the accept button. "AJ Lang speaking."

"Everything's ready to go."

"Fantastic. I really appreciate your doing this. She's extremely fragile, and she's on high alert, as well she should be. You saw her photo so you know who you're looking for?"

The silence from the other line made him wonder if he hadn't lost him.

"I did. And, of course, I'm up for it. Did you think I'd lost my touch?"

"Just making sure, buddy. It's been a while," AJ reminded his colleague.

"Worry not. I've got this. Discretion is my middle name, and when it's all over, I'll remind you every day how successful it was."

AJ laughed in spite of his concerns. "Good deal. She's going to call me after she arrives. Let me know after you've made your first contact."

"You've got it. Talk with you then."

"Later, man." AJ ended the call and tucked the phone back in his belt. Karina should be landing shortly. He hoped she was going to be OK.

Life for his witness was about to change forever.

2

"Whew! It's chilly outside." Karina pulled the door shut as she entered the private hangar.

Marci looked up from the stack of log books she was reviewing at the front desk. "Good morning, Leah. It *is* cooler in Watertown than Toledo. But you'll adapt to this Tug Hill region of New York."

The bookkeeper's reference to her as *Leah* quickly brought her mind to the present. And she'd never even been to Toledo. She hated the deception she was forced to live in. But it was something she'd better get used to. The name *Karina* needed to vanish, just as she had. From now on she would only think of herself as *Leah*.

"I sure hope so. How long did it take you to adjust to these brutal temps?" Leah walked behind the counter overlooking the lobby and pushed her purse inside a cabinet.

"About two years. But I'm from Fort Lauderdale. My blood was thin."

Leah shot her a sideways glance. "That's comforting."

"Give yourself a chance. You've only been here a week. Besides, it's supposed to warm up nicely today. Fifty-five makes one feel alive." Marci chuckled at her own joke.

The light that danced in her co-worker's eyes might've convinced Leah if she didn't know better. But fifty-five may as well have been twenty-five. Cold was cold, no matter how you packaged it.

In the short time since she'd arrived in the upstate, Leah made more adjustments than she thought she was capable of, yet she had countless more to make. She traded her spacious Florida home for a quaint cottage in the center of Lowville, New York, forty minutes from the Watertown hangar. The ride to and from work every day incited good, think-tank sessions. But sometimes the extra time to think had the opposite effect.

At times, she was certain she'd made the biggest mistake of her life by joining the Witness Security Protection Program.

She settled into her seat and turned on her computer. As she waited, a Learjet touched down in the distance with smooth precision. A rumble followed. The plane slowed to taxi down the runway before her.

"That must be Phillip," Marci announced without looking up. "You haven't met him yet, have you? You'll like him. I'm going to the kitchen to make some fresh coffee. Tom will be here shortly, and I expect Charles will call with an update soon as to when he'll return."

Marci didn't even give Leah an opportunity to respond as she whisked her way out of the room. From the sound of it, the lively redhead who was training her on the front desk was already highly caffeinated this morning.

So far, everyone at PRZ Aviation was quite pleasant. She hoped she'd feel the same about the owner.

Leah glanced around at her surroundings while waiting for her computer to boot and install updates. PRZ was the picture of understated elegance. Even the lettering on the tall glass entrance door seemed to reluctantly boast its title. Comfortable furniture was arranged in the lobby with aviation magazines scattered on low tables. Photographs in handsome silver frames graced the adjacent walls as beaming students posed beside the plane that carried them on their first solo flight as the caption indicated. Their smiles appeared laced with promise—like her smile had once been. Panoramic windows made up the perimeter of the stilted building.

She glanced outside to see the Learjet come to a halt about fifty yards down the tarmac. The pilot, wearing a long trench coat with a dark scarf around his neck, moved down the cabin steps. Someone must've called him, because he stopped to talk on the phone. Leah noticed his tall frame and the way he engaged himself in the conversation.

Leah's attention moved back to the screen in front of her where a program was waiting for a password to continue. She clicked the *OK* button and decided to grab a cup of coffee while it continued to boot up. The dark roast was still dripping when she entered the break room, but she hijacked a cup anyway, and doused it with a healthy dollop of half-and-half and a tinge of honey.

As she rounded the corner to head back to the lobby, she ran head-on into a distinguished obstacle— the tall gentleman on the tarmac she'd seen earlier.

Her left hand flew in front of her to brace for the impact, and her right hand whisked to the side, as she gripped the cup firmly to keep the liquid from spilling. There was little she could do to remove the heat from her face when the gentleman caught her hand that landed on the lapel of his coat.

"I am so sorry!" Leah exclaimed. "I wasn't paying attention where I was going."

"It's my fault. Evidently I wasn't watching either." The man chuckled, and they each stepped back a foot. She pulled her hand away in embarrassment. "Are you OK? Did you burn yourself?" he asked.

"I'm OK." Leah glanced down and spotted the stain on her sweater. "Layers do have their benefits."

"You must be the new customer service rep." His voice was smooth and relaxed, and his emerald eyes held hers. She had the impression from her brief contact with his torso that beneath his coat, he was rather fit. His hair was full, dark, and neatly styled, and his face was clean-shaven. Even so, she imagined he looked good with rugged stubble as well.

"Yes, I am. I'm Ka... My name is Leah. Leah Merrins."

"It's great to finally meet you, Leah. I'm Phillip Zellmer." He offered his hand.

She complied. "Thank you. It's a pleasure to meet you as well, although my apologies for the impact."

"It really wasn't so bad," he said as he straightened his scarf. Leah noticed the pale line that circled his ring-finger where it appeared a band of gold might've recently been. "Our first aid kit is in the kitchen, and we do have a good supply of burn cream. Plus, we offer a pretty decent health care plan that you can sign up for after your probationary period."

"Thanks. I'll try not to become a liability."

"Well then, I do hope you'll like it here. Let me know if there's anything you need."

"I will. It was nice to—"

"Mr. Z! Welcome back. How was your trip?" Marci bounded around the corner.

"Not bad. But it's always good to be home."

"Looks like you've met our new rep."

"Yes. She's already made quite an impact on me." Phillip's lip curled into an impish smile.

Leah's face grew warm.

"Great. We've lots to go over, Leah. Come see me when you're ready to talk," Marci chattered on, apparently oblivious to what was going on. She moved past and walked toward the front desk.

"It was nice to meet you, Mr. Zellmer," Leah said as she politely excused herself and followed Marci.

"You can call me Phillip."

She glanced back and noticed him watching her. She gave a brief nod of recognition before continuing on her way.

"So, today we're going to plug the info into the new database we talked about yesterday." Marci didn't miss a beat. "Why don't you get settled, and I'll bring the rest of the logbooks to you."

Leah returned to her station, and for the next thirty minutes the two worked together. The pilot's logbooks, according to Marci, were stored at PRZ for safekeeping. She explained that the new software program enabled their pilots to better track flight times, which integrated with PRZ's own maintenance logs and appointment trackers. Once the database was loaded, all calls and rentals would route through the software to make scheduling a breeze. Automatic payment processing would deposit funds in real time and achieve a healthier bottom line. Mailers could be generated quickly and efficiently. From what Leah understood, the nuts and bolts of her everyday existence would revolve around this handy-dandy database.

Leah continued to load the information after Marci returned to her office. Soon, it seemed effortless. Data in. Enter. Save. New record. Over and over again. Of course, it was nothing like her busy nights in the ER, but it was something…and she was safe.

A few hours later, she returned to the break room for another cup of coffee. Leah took a deep breath on the way to her desk and willed herself to relax while waiting for a new record to reboot. The mug was warm to her lips, and she blew into it hoping to heat her face by the rush of steam that escaped. The swirls of moisture evaporated into nothingness as it mingled with the rest of the air around it.

That's how she was supposed to be. Like a vapor blending into its surroundings, one that's so unobtrusive, it's gone before anyone even recognizes it existed to begin with.

She sipped the hot liquid, letting it sink deep into her soul to sooth the uneasiness that lingered. A tear trickled down her face as she remembered the past she'd vowed to leave behind. Everything about Karina Rubenski had been stripped away, and in its place, the shell of a person took form. Now she was only a mask—a façade named Leah. Her whole life was planned for her. Sure, she made a few choices along the way. But deciding on whether to have her groceries bagged in paper or plastic didn't account for much when she considered the big picture.

AJ's voice echoed in her memory. *The change will be tough, but the program is the only way you can be protected, Kari.*

He was right. Everything about the change was tough. But there was little choice.

AJ made the arrangements for her housing and

presented her with some job options. She spoke with him when first arriving and hadn't heard from him for a couple of days. It seemed as if he'd already passed the torch to Richard, her locally assigned case manager. AJ assured her that she'd be well taken care of by Richard. Her on-call CM was a reserve member of the Special Operations Group for the US Marshal's office. For security purposes, he was to only be a telephone contact for her. He seemed nice enough from what she could tell over the phone, even though his voice sounded altered, somewhat muffled, as if changed through a filter.

In her first conversation with Richard, he'd urged her to get out again and function like normal.

Whatever that meant…At least for Leah Merrins.

Well, that was a difficult thing to do after weeks of seemingly endless testimony that landed DeFresnio behind bars. The fact that DeFresnio's face was only one of the three on the elevator that day complicated her life greatly. And like a glitch in her usual photographic memory, she could not recollect the faces of the other two. That simple fact haunted her every waking moment since the day it happened.

Marci's and Phillip's voices from the hall jolted her back to the present, and she snatched up her purse to retrieve a tissue. Her hand brushed something heavy, and she opened her purse wider. A cell phone. And it wasn't hers.

"How's it going?" Marci asked.

Leah forgot the tissue, stuffed the phone back down into her purse, and faced her co-worker. "Not bad. I have a few more entries to go." She quickly returned to character. "Oh, by the way, Charles called this morning. He's still in Jersey. Plans to be home by the weekend and back at work Monday."

"Fantastic," Phillip answered. "Bet he and Sarah are enjoying their new granddaughter."

"I imagine so," Leah replied. The office manager that conducted Leah's phone interview hired her the following day, right before his daughter brought his first grandchild into the world.

"Yeah—all seven pounds and thirteen ounces of her," Marci piped in. "He's probably already a doting granddad."

Tom walked in the side door and joined the conversation. "Something going on?"

"Nope," Marci answered. "I'm muddling through on the audit, and Leah's been working on the database program that we're gearing up to implement."

Phillip moved in behind Leah, leaning slightly over her shoulder. "You'll show me how it works?"

Leah exited the data entry page and opened up the main menu to give him a brief overview. "We still need to get each terminal linked before this is fully operational, but we'll be able to search our clients by entering their contact information into the search link. Scheduling is cross-referenced by name, by the actual date a plane is requested, or by the particular aircraft the client is requesting. We can access the client's payment history by clicking onto this dollar icon, to verify that he or she is in good standing." Leah pointed to the right quadrant of the screen in front of her with her lightly polished nail.

"Sounds like that'll work. So if John Doe wants to rent a Cessna on a particular day, all the information is accessible on the same page to see if that plane is available, and if not, it'll list alternates?"

"Right. This system is dashboard driven, and

prevents double booking of any aircraft. If you're attempting to double-book, a warning icon will appear that won't go away until you acknowledge it. When you do so, a pop-up provides you with additional options." Leah turned her head slightly and found Phillip's attention on her instead of the computer.

"Impressive," Phillip said, quickly shifting his gaze back to the screen. "This may be hard to get used to. This way of doing things, I mean."

His presence unnerved her, but she forged ahead. "I suspect you'll wonder how you managed to live without it."

"I'm beginning to think so."

"Sounds like she'll be able to give us a client list at the touch of a button, Mr. Z. Then you won't be able to deny how important it is to host that anniversary party we talked about." Tom razzed him, breaking the invisible spell that hovered between Leah and Phillip.

Phillip straightened. "Oh, so you have ulterior motives?"

"Just one of the side benefits," Marci informed him. "Besides, you know you need to do an open house. You're simply too stubborn to admit it."

"I concur." Tom threw in his two cents.

"Seriously, you too?" Phillip asked.

"Our boss doesn't think it's necessary to host a tenth anniversary open house," Marci explained to Leah. "The rest of us are convinced we should. Phillip has skirted the issue for months. With all the clientele in one database, it'll be easy to access and determine if it's even worthwhile."

"Don't let them corrupt you with their way of thinking, Leah." Phillip flashed a smile at her. Just as quickly, his eyes grew intent and a sudden reserve slipped behind them. "Nonetheless, if you can bring me a client list and an accurate count that I can't ignore, I'll take a look at it and reconsider."

Tom and Marci let out a whoop.

Phillip picked up the message slips that were waiting for him and tapped them on the counter. He gave Leah a glance she wasn't able to decipher and then disappeared around the corner. She pushed aside her discomfort and nodded her head in agreement.

"I'll fill you in on the open house later," Marci announced as she headed back down the hall with Tom on her heels. The front counter became quiet again, and Leah returned to the task at hand.

The banter helped, at least a little. Apart from the interaction at work, her social life was nonexistent. She missed her friends, her church, the stately home she'd inherited on South Beach, and her entire life. If her parents had still been alive, she would never have left them, especially after they'd gone to great lengths to adopt her when she was merely a week old. The homesickness was overwhelming, but doing anything about it was futile. There was simply nothing that she could do to get them—or her life—back.

Situations got confusing. In her short time here, well-meaning people at work would ask questions, simply trying to be polite. They only wanted to know her better, but it was during these times she felt like a perpetual liar, taking on the mantle of Leah's manufactured background rather than her own. Was it wrong to live in deception like this when it was in a controlled setting such as the WITSEC Program? The thoughts plagued her mind and confused even the simplest issues.

Condemnation gripped her, pressing into her like

a vice, one crank at a time. Had she allowed fear to become such a part of her that she'd given the mastermind himself a key to her heart? Had God condoned her decision to join WITSEC with the lie she would be forced to live?

Probably not.

The foundation of deception had been laid, and she cringed at the thought that her future was now in the hands of a diabolic master. The consequences she now faced were clearly of her own making, decisions made out of fear and not trust.

She brushed a tear aside as another wave of homesickness flooded her. It wasn't that she didn't feel accepted here. Marci, Charles, and Tom welcomed her as one of them. And the owner of the hangar...well, he wasn't quite what she'd expected.

Pushing herself onward, she plugged the last entry into the database and backed it all up on a flash drive. What a far cry from working the night shift in the ER. But at least it was a job that kept her mind occupied, although on what, she wasn't sure.

Time to embrace the uncertainty. She still had a lifetime to go.

~*~

Frank Mariucci sat back in his tall, leather chair with a U.S. map unfolded across his desk. He eyed Scordino and vowed to pull him off if he couldn't produce the results necessary to eliminate the complication. In doing so, his own hands would be crippled in the process.

"You still have no clue where she could have gone?" Frank leaned forward, his elbows pressing into the map.

Scordino lifted his hands and let them fall. "Sir, with all due respect, are you aware of the number of flights that depart from Atlanta every hour? I could not have done anything differently. I simply had and still have no idea which direction she disappeared to. There was nothing else I could've done."

"If our faces surface in her memory, you and I are both history. DeFresnio, bless his soul on death row, is proof of that. The composite sketch of her recollection of him was uncanny. We must find her before she remembers us."

"So, what do you want me to do, Frank?" Scordino slammed back in his chair.

"Chill, Scordino."

"You jest!"

Mariucci glared at Scordino. "Patrick—do you think he'll talk?"

"No. Patrick's been with us long enough that we can safely say he's loyal. Besides, his uncle is one of us. Blood always runs thicker than water, even with stakes as high as these. With the steady paycheck he collects from us, why would he stop? There's no way he'll go back to collecting chicken salary from the police department after he's been eating steak with us for so long. Miami-Dade can't begin to give him the financial benefits we've provided. He'll make something up and fudge his way out. At least he chose to stay in the department as an insider. We won't lose that benefit. We won't lose Patrick."

"How's he doing?" Mariucci polished his cufflink with the sleeve of his suit coat.

"As of this afternoon, he was still in fair condition. But he's being heavily guarded, so there's no way either of us can get in to visit him."

"What about Sam Canali?"

"Canali said he would go, as an old friend. But if you ask me, that might lead to a little meddling from the feds. Not sure I'd recommend it."

Mariucci pushed back the map and casually leafed through the photos Scordino provided. This woman was definitely their witness. In a way, it surprised him that Scordino spotted her at the first airport, let alone followed her as far as Atlanta. Scordino was more of a liability than an asset at times, but for once, he had done well—except for the fact that he'd been so close and then lost her. And now, time was slipping by.

"Did you send the flowers yet?"

"Today, sir." Scordino squirmed.

"Who did you indicate they were from?"

"I sent it as a canned get well from his friendly neighborhood investment institution."

"Very good. Surely that will generate a follow-up call from him. By the way, you didn't leave a voice message on his cell phone, did you?"

Scordino continued to fidget. "Nope. Nothing's traceable. I called from a secure line."

"Great. That's what I thought. For now, keep checking out Atlanta's departure flights for the first three hours she was missing. Follow any and all leads. Go from there."

Scordino nodded. "Anything else?"

"Call me when you find something."

"Yes, sir."

"And shut the door behind you."

At least the man listened. The short, stocky Italian walked out the door, shutting it behind him. With as much money as they paid the underling, Scordino really couldn't afford not to follow orders.

He leafed through the photos again, etching the woman's image into his memory one more time. Then he closed his eyes and drew a deep, satisfying breath.

3

Leah pulled the trench coat a bit tighter around her frame, hoping to keep the wind from biting her in fury as she walked from the house to the car. AJ said it would be cold in Lowville, but hearing his words and experiencing them firsthand were polar opposites. The morning sky was overcast, and a thin mist hung in the air.

When people spoke of New York, she'd always pictured the extremes—the glitz and glamour, the scum and slums—of the city. The Tug Hill area was neither. It seemed to meet somewhere halfway, as did a good portion of middle-class America. Rolling farmland provided plenty of hay for the numerous dairy farms that lay nestled in these Adirondack foothills. Small towns dotted the outskirts of Lowville, most of which remained nameless except to those who lived there.

Sidewalks lined the residential streets that wound their way throughout the main part of town. The stately homes held a certain charm and character about them that spoke of days gone by. Most had been restored, while some begged a talented hand to give them yet another chance. She was grateful for her accommodations in the center of town. The brick bungalow was small, but it was all she needed, and it was comfortable.

The Chopin tone chirped from her purse on the floorboard. She reached for it, knowing only a handful of people had this number. A sobering thought, really, to think that apart from her coworkers, only Richard, AJ, and the checkout lady at the grocery store were aware of her existence. If she added the drivers that thoughtlessly passed her on this misty morning, it would raise the count by only a few.

She smiled at the caller ID and pressed the button that connected it to her Bluetooth. "Hello?"

"Hi, Leah. How are you?" True to his word, Richard hadn't forgotten her. His phone calls, although few, gave her something to look forward to.

Between her phone and his voice adapter, the echo sounded as if he was in a faraway tunnel. The rain, falling heavier now, didn't help.

"I'm OK. On my way to work."

"I figured as much. Thank goodness it's Friday, right?"

"Yes, but it's not like it brings a sense of relief. I don't have anything else exciting to do. I made it through my first two weeks though, so I suppose that's exciting in itself."

"Congratulations! How are you liking this weather?"

"Is it always this miserable in March? The lion seems crueler as the weeks go by. Please tell me the adage is correct, that the lamb will soon appear to end out the month." She maneuvered around a bend in the road.

"Don't worry. You'll see his wool one of these days, although he's probably running a little later than your taste. By May, it'll be beautiful."

"That's two months away…" Her voice tapered as her thoughts jumped to her future. "Hopefully, I'll be gone by that time, one way or another."

Richard's deep sigh was evident even through the voice adapter. "What's that supposed to mean? You're beginning to sound morose."

"Sorry, that came out wrong. What I meant was, maybe by then the case will be resolved, and I'll move on. I'm anxious for this to be over. Spending my next two months waiting for better weather is about all I've got going on right now." She pushed back a tear, hoping to stop the flow that welled beneath the surface.

"I understand."

He sounded like he really did. "I know you do."

"I talked with AJ a few minutes ago."

"Oh? How's he doing?"

"Good. But still no leads on the cell phone you sent."

"That's too bad. Wish I'd discovered it right off. I can't believe it was in the bottom of my bag all that time before I found it. If I'd mailed it to him sooner, he might've honed in on a critical lead already."

"Maybe. Maybe not. These guys are pretty ruthless, and they've covered their tracks well."

"Evidently so. I hope they slip up soon."

"I'm sure they will. Tell me. How's the job?"

"All right," Leah answered as she turned her wipers up a notch.

"People there easy to work with?"

"Yes. They're pleasant. Small place. It's not nearly as stressful as the emergency room."

"I'll bet. So, that's good, right?"

"Maybe in some ways—" Her voice choked. Another tear made its way to the surface at the thought of all she'd left behind. Her emotions were on edge. For days, she'd done well to keep them at bay. She'd even surprised her own expectations by being lighthearted at times. Perhaps it was the atmosphere at the hangar that lent itself to one's carefree mood. She supposed the job was a godsend, at least for now. But suddenly, it was too much. The façade she sported at work and elsewhere concealed any thoughts or emotions that belonged to the real person who resided deep within. When she talked to Richard, Leah disappeared and Karina emerged.

"Hey, you OK?"

"Yeah," she mumbled.

"Listen, I know this is difficult for you," Richard said. "If there was anything in my power that I could do to get you your life back, I'd do it in a flash. Believe me. But it's not possible. Not without completely jeopardizing the case. And you wouldn't want it that way either. You must hang in there. Pour yourself into something. Make new friends. And when you need to talk, call me. Don't let it escalate and strangle the life out of you. You weren't meant for that."

"You're right." She pulled a tissue from her purse and still managed to stay on the road. "It's just so hard."

"I understand. But you're gonna make it, Leah. Don't you ever let go of that."

She breathed in deeply, willing herself to absorb his words. The other end of the line was comfortably silent as she gained her composure. The tears diminished, and she wiped her eyes and took another deep breath. He was right. She must hang on. Making friends was critical to her wellbeing. She hadn't been to church since she'd left Miami. "Do you know of any good churches in the area?"

"Community Fellowship is right outside of town.

Locals call it the *Barn Church* since the original building was restored from an old barn years back. There's also Mount Hope Assembly that's not far from you. Both are good Bible-believing churches."

She nodded and wiped her nose. The thought of walking into a church gave her a sense of hope. There's a chance she could meet people her age and get involved. Hopefully, she would be able to sense the presence of God even in the shell of a person she was forced to become. "I think I'll give one of them a try this weekend."

"Check out their websites."

"I will. Are you…are you a Christian?" She hoped it was OK to ask.

"I am."

The fact that he was, comforted her. She wondered where he attended. Not that she should entertain the idea of ever meeting him. Besides, she had no clue what Richard looked like, and even if she did, he would guarantee it never happened. Richard seemed private, a trait that no doubt served him well in his job with the marshal's office.

"Thanks for the info."

"You'll find one to suit your needs. If not, let me know, and I'll ask around."

"I sure will."

"So what's your plan tonight? Or is that a premature question?"

Her spirit lifted as a smile touched her face. "My biggest plan might be to order pizza and run to Kroger for some excitement later on."

"Kroger?"

"Don't laugh. You'd go, too, if you had nothing better to do. My social life stinks."

"Hang in there. With your charisma and charm, it won't be long before your calendar is full, and you won't have time to talk to me. Then I'll be the lonely one."

"Yeah, right."

"You'll begin to love it so much up here, when the case is finally resolved—contrary to what you might think—you won't even want your old life back."

"Try me," she challenged.

Richard's muffled laugh warmed her. "Remember, be yourself. The tangible you is who we need to protect—your physical person. But while that's happening, the intangible you can blossom. That's your character, your inner spirit. That's who you really are. Don't ever lose that, no matter what name you're forced to answer to."

Leah let the words wash over her. "Thank you. I needed that."

"You're welcome. I need to run. Call or text me later if you need to talk."

"I will," Leah promised.

"Enjoy your day at work."

"You, too."

They said good-bye, and Leah slipped the phone back into her purse. She breathed out a sigh, the kind that happens after a good cry when emotions are spent and hope is in sight for a better day ahead. As she drove into the outskirts of Watertown, the hard rain stopped and all that was left was a thin mist that was quickly dissipating.

Perhaps it was possible to focus more on who she was deep inside instead of on the person who made up her outer shell. If she struggled, and that was a given, Richard would be there, and she could be honest with him through and through. Living her life in a cave of fear would stifle every bit of life that was left in her. At first opportunity, she'd take his advice, get involved with a good church and hope to make new friends in the process. Sure, she would need to be on guard to avoid questions from new acquaintances that she didn't want to answer. Somehow, she needed to find a balance.

How she'd do that without being a perpetual liar, God only knew.

~*~

"Phillip wants to talk to you about the open house. He finally agreed to it."

Leah jumped at Marci's abrupt announcement a few hours after she arrived at work. She pushed aside the phone messages she'd unconsciously been doodling on.

"Why me?" Leah asked, puzzled.

"He suggested you head it up. He thinks you have good taste. Besides, I'm still swamped with prep work for next month's audit."

"Phillip hardly knows me. How would he know about my taste?"

"It doesn't take long for him to figure someone out. He's more observant than you might think."

The thought unnerved Leah. She couldn't afford for anyone to be observing her, no matter who it was. "What's he looking for?"

"Something nice. Talk to him." Marci left for her office with a cup of coffee in hand.

"Anything going on?" Tom asked as he walked into the room with a stack of flight plans in his arms.

"Nothing much. David left with the Beechcraft. Otherwise it's been quiet."

"Thanks for covering for me."

"Not a problem."

"Killer coffee," Phillip exclaimed as he strolled in with a steaming mug in his hand. He lifted it in a slight cheer. "Who made it?"

Tom pointed to Leah. "She's in your line of sight. Nabbed the job right out from under me."

"And rightly so. As weak as you make the coffee, you'd think we were on a strict budget here."

"Don't even go there." Tom put up a hand to stop Phillip before he had a chance to further voice his complaint.

Leah laughed at their banter.

"So, how are things in the reservation and rental world?" Phillip pulled up a tall stool across the counter from them.

"Good. Here are a couple of messages for you." Leah slid the slips to Phillip.

He shuffled through them, and a smile played at the corners of his mouth. "Thanks."

"That guy with the Piper for sale keeps calling but doesn't leave a message," Tom informed him, coming out of his self-imposed pity party. "He called twice before nine."

Phillip took a swallow of his brew. "Annoying, isn't it?"

"You're telling me."

"I'll call him today and get him off our backs. There's another one I'm more interested in anyway."

"What is that, three Pipers now?"

"Soon to be. It's a good plane. Has some advantages over the Beechcraft. Ever been in a small plane?" Phillip asked, turning to Leah.

Leah hesitated as memories flooded her. "Not...not to speak of."

Certainly not to speak of.

In the past, she'd spent several weeks a year on short-term missions, flying in and out of remote villages with her adoptive parents, delivering medical supplies to those in need. If they'd have stayed home instead of going to that last trip to Haiti, none of this would've happened. She wouldn't be living under the guise of an alias. There wouldn't have been financial business to take care of in the Connor Tower that day. No estate to settle. No elevator encounter. No DNA that would gather onto the fallen document. No one on death row whose accomplices were likely searching for her even now.

What a chain reaction her life had become.

"We should remedy that sometime."

Phillip's voice brought her mind back to the present. She needed to get a grip. Had to remember what Richard spoke to her about just this morning.

"Oh, by the way," Phillip said as he stood to his feet, "did Marci mention that I wanted to talk with you about the open house?" he whispered the dreaded words with a touch of humor.

"She mentioned it a little while ago."

"Is now a good time?"

"Sure."

"Great. Can you stop by my office in a few minutes?"

Leah nodded as he turned to leave. She stepped down from her stool and went over a few details with Tom. Soon she was rapping at the slightly open door.

"Come on in and sit down." Phillip pushed back a

folder and extended his hand to the chair across from his desk.

"Nice upholstery." Her eyes were drawn to the fighter-jet tapestry print that covered the chair he offered her. She hadn't noticed it before.

"You like that? Thanks. I thought it fit perfectly in here."

"It does."

"So, by now you know our tenth anniversary is coming up." It was more of a statement than a question. Phillip tugged at the knot of his tie.

"Yes, I've heard the hoopla," Leah smiled.

"I suppose they finally won. Your co-workers say it's expected of us to throw a celebration, so I guess if I can't beat them, I'll join them."

"Seems like your best option. What were you thinking?"

"Something nice. We'll invite seasoned clients as well as young students and their families. You've seen the client list. Perhaps we should make it open to the public as well. What are your thoughts?"

Leah shifted in her seat. It seemed awfully stuffy all of a sudden even though it was cool outside. She pushed her growing apprehension aside and forced her confident exterior back in place. "Opening the guest list to the public seems fitting. It depends on your objective. Do you want to thank clients in the past and present for making PRZ a success, or are you using it as a solicitation for more clients in the future?"

"I suppose a bit of both would be appropriate. Any ideas on tying the two together?"

"The lobby would make a lovely display area to serve cold cuts, hors d'oeuvres, that kind of thing. You could emphasize the elegant edge and cater to the guests' fascination of private aviation. Add some hands-on educational displays with high-quality print ads out on the tarmac for young aviators or mechanic wannabe's. Toss in a few promos such as personalized pens, coffee mugs, maybe a couple of door prizes. Raffle off a few hours of flight time. Let them tour a number of freshly-detailed planes to get it into their system—that sort of thing."

Phillip lifted his brow. "I like it. I guess most pilots catch the bug when they're young. What a great way to build upon their future dreams. I knew you'd be perfect for the job."

Her eyes met his briefly then shifted when he pulled out a navy pen from the pocket of his pressed shirt. He picked up a note pad and flipped through his desk calendar. "Saturday, May twenty-first sound good?"

The light scent of spice and musk distracted her, but she caught herself quickly. "Yes, that's fine." She was certain she'd no pressing plans for that date—or for any other in the near future.

"Then it's settled." He jotted it down and lifted his eyes to meet hers as the tip of his pen held its place. "Is it too much trouble to ask you to take care of everything? Coordinate it, order the food, and do whatever else needs to be done, or delegate it out?"

"I'd be happy to do that."

"I'll jot down some places in town that I have accounts with. I'm sure you'll come up with something nice. If you find items elsewhere, ask Marci to cut you a check, or we can reimburse you whenever needed."

"Fair enough," Leah replied as he continued to make notes. The roar of a plane coming in for a landing distracted her. She watched it touch down. When she turned back to Phillip, he was watching her.

"This ought to do it." His gaze shifted, and he tore off the sheet and handed her the list. "Whenever you need to leave to check things out, please do so. As long as Tom and Marci are aware, they can cover for you. They're partly responsible for this anyway. And keep track of all your time after hours on this stuff. I'm not looking for a freebie."

"You got it."

She noticed that look again, the careful reserve that slipped behind his eyes. She knew little of him personally but wondered what caused him to become so guarded. What was it that triggered the intense, personal emotions of a man as successful as Phillip Zellmer?

"By the way, you're doing a great job. I hope you like it here."

"Thank you. I do."

"Very good." Phillip stood, prompting Leah to stand. "Thanks for heading this up. I really appreciate it."

"You're welcome. It'll be fun to put together."

"Please let me know if you have questions, or if you need anything at all."

"Sure thing," she assured him as she started toward the door.

"Oh—and be careful out there." Phillip's voice caused her to turn back to him at the doorway. "The traffic in the hall gets pretty congested at times."

She forced a laugh, but the heat that rose to her face made her cringe. She turned quickly and headed back down the hall, eager to get to the safety of the other room.

~*~

Phillip sat at his desk for a long while after Leah disappeared around the corner. He closed his eyes and blew out a slow breath in a futile attempt to corral his thoughts.

When he'd given her the list of job options, he hadn't expected her to choose the aviation assistant. He'd only thrown it in at the last minute to round off her choices. *What was I thinking?*

Not that he was disappointed.

He'd certainly had no regrets about seeing her on a daily basis. He was just ill prepared for it. Before he'd actually met her, it hadn't seemed like much of a problem. But the moment he ran into her that day in the hall, his challenge hit him head-on.

Since that time, concentrating was difficult. He tried to brush it off, but the more he tried, the more his mind fought with him. In his years of working privately as an on-call case manager for the Special Operations Group of the US Marshal's office, he'd never struggled like this.

Some of the cases he'd been assigned to involved hardened criminals who'd been given immunity for their testimonies, resulting in protection by WITSEC.

But Leah was no criminal. She was the furthest thing from it, which in this case, was to her disadvantage, if one could call it that. A person with little or no feeling or emotion could have adapted much easier. She was only an innocent bystander.

Phillip unlocked the bottom drawer of his desk and pulled out the unlabeled manila envelope. AJ assigned him the case after she'd had another close call. Finally, albeit reluctantly, she agreed to join. He worked on the sidelines to prepare things for her arrival. But the only thing he hadn't prepared was his heart.

The photograph he reached for was a good one. Yet it did her no justice. It had been nearly three years since someone affected him like this. It was no secret that he lacked interaction with women these days. How on earth was he even to act around this one?

Of course, the exception was the little woman of his life—his pride and joy, Jessica. He smiled at the thought of her. At the tender age of three and a half, she had no recollection of Daria. It saddened him to think of it. And Jess was the splitting image of her mother. Beautiful beyond words.

He would never forget the day he lost his bride.

He was the one who created the dream in her to fly. With Phillip's wings a permanent fixture, Daria wanted to take lessons as well. She received her private pilot's license and proved herself as capable as any pilot Phillip had ever seen, all bias excluded.

But within moments of her last takeoff, it had been clear that Daria was in trouble.

"Tower, this is Beech One, I have a problem."

"Roger that, Beech One. What's the issue?"

"I'm losing altitude. Engine one is losing power."

"Tower to Beech One, turn around and bring her in if you're able. All other airspace is clear. Copy that?"

"Roger. Electronics dimming…" Her voice faltered.

"Bring it up. You can do this."

"I'm starting to nosedive—"

"Hang tight, Beech One. Ground squad en route."

"Phillip!"

"Oh…no…Daria…"

The sound that followed was more than Phillip could bear. He replayed it in his mind again, those last words she'd spoken to the control tower. The conversation that echoed from the intercom in his office that fateful spring morning was etched in his memory forever. In a split second, he found himself rushing to the tarmac, screaming, crying out toward her, begging her to be OK.

He remembered coming out of his oblivion, his face on the pavement next to hers when the emergency crew pulled him away. He'd been cold, shivering as if it was the middle of winter. Dark gloom had threatened to suffocate what was left of his existence. The days after had been a blur, and from what he comprehended, the future held only the promise of a blur as well.

During the past three years, he tried to go on. He really did. But at times, it seemed impossible. The loneliness deep down inside took up residence without any indication it would ever leave. His intention to hide it from those about him worked most of the time, at least that's what he chose to believe. He was certain he would never look at another woman the same way he looked at Daria. But to his surprise, over the last couple of weeks, something stirred deep within, noticeable the first time he laid eyes on Leah. It confused him and scared him half to death.

He also understood how complicated things could get. It was dangerous to mix a client relationship with a personal one. These two paths of his life were not meant to cross.

As her CM, he needed to guard his words—needed to keep her at arms' length, which he was finding more difficult to do each day.

As her employer, he'd no choice but to turn the other way and forget any inside knowledge of her. It was critical for him to avoid personal interaction. But that was hard to do, especially when the assignment he'd just given to her required the very interaction he was supposed to avoid.

He was most definitely between a rock and a hard place.

He'd never seen her angry, but he imagined her deep brown eyes might set him afire with their intensity if there were a valid cause. No matter what, he couldn't let that happen. His dual role must never be exposed. But as quickly as he thought it, his resolve to distance himself from her began to fade.

Confusion and anger ate at his mind for allowing himself to even think of Leah in a personal way. Fear tugged at him, reminding him that if he allowed thoughts of Leah to creep into his consciousness, his precious wife's image would vanish, leaving only a smoky haze in its trail.

Losing the memory of Daria was not an option.

But he was young, only thirty-eight. Could he recover? And did he even want to? He was convinced that he must find a way to go on for Jessica's sake. Whether he'd enjoy it or not, only time would tell.

He ran his thumb across the edge of the photograph of the one who stirred him now. With the doubts and feelings that rushed through his consciousness, perhaps he had removed the golden band too soon.

~*~

Mariucci slammed the phone down, cursing

Scordino under his breath for not being able to come up with anything definitive about Karina's whereabouts. Why did he make it so hard? He drummed his fingers on the desk, contemplating what to do next. It seemed as though she'd all but disappeared from the face of the earth. But somehow, Karina Rubenski was going to mess up. Someone of her caliber wouldn't be able to forsake her privileged life so easily.

He leafed through the folder, memorizing the informative details. She'd been an employee of Miami General for nearly seven years. On numerous occasions, he'd called her department from a secure phone to speak to her at work, or at least to someone who might disclose her whereabouts to him. He tried her at home and drove by her house multiple times. He even disguised himself and visited the church she attended, hoping to learn something. Warm handshakes and welcoming smiles didn't help. All he'd gleaned from the Sunday morning expedition was the small textbox at the bottom of the bulletin where her name was listed among other prayer requests. At least it appeared he wasn't the only one searching for her.

He recalled her features distinctly from the day they'd shared the Connor Tower elevator. He supposed most of the people she met remembered her. She'd been dressed in a royal blue satin tank and creamy pencil skirt that perfectly complemented her curves. He guessed her to be about five feet, seven inches, give or take a bit for the sleek heels on her feet. The poise and confidence in her seemed natural, as if she'd grown up with the finer things in life. Too bad their paths hadn't crossed under different circumstances. He might have enjoyed entertaining someone like her, albeit the obvious age difference between them.

No, she was not difficult to look at, and — certainly — she was not easy to forget.

They must find her. Time was running out, and luck didn't seem to be on their side.

Even then, he was hopeful. It wouldn't be long before Karina Rubenski slammed into a dead end. So long as they were there when she rounded that last corner.

If his hunch was right, they were closer to that corner than they'd ever been before.

4

Crystal Robbins adjusted her Bluetooth.

"Are you positive no one's home, dear?" her husband, on the other end of the phone, asked.

"Relatively. It's as quiet as it was the last time we tried."

"Are there still newspapers on the front porch?" Michael asked.

"Yes, a couple, along with today's paper. I wish you were with me, honey. Do you know how long you'll be tied up?"

"Grant should have things under control shortly, so my guess is an hour or so."

"I hope so. Your moral support would come in handy right now. Maybe it's good if there's no one home. You know, as many times as I've rehearsed my speech in the last few weeks, I'm not sure that I'll be able to speak when I see her face-to-face."

"I hear ya. But you're tough, babe. You have a two-year-old, right?"

"Yes, we do." Crystal laughed as she knocked on the door again. In the reflection of the door's sidelight, she noticed a dark SUV as it slowed then passed by and moved on through the posh Miami neighborhood. Something seemed odd about it. Tension mounted in her neck, but rubbing it didn't ease the pain. Her nerves were on edge. The entourage of emotions should be commonplace by now. Gripping the stucco pillar at the front entrance, Crystal steadied herself and forced a deep breath. This was not the time to be paranoid.

"Grant's hoping to sign the deal today. There'll be a lot to do after the fact, but if he can at least get the contract signed, we can buy some time before closing. After we're home, I'm confident that the rest will fall into place."

"You're a good brother to come to his rescue at such short notice."

"It really isn't that short. He's been in negotiations for this takeover for a while. But when they're ready to bite, he needs to move on it. Hey, why don't we meet for lunch at that little place by the hotel in a bit? I'll text you after I'm finished here."

"Sounds wonderful. Get us a seat if you're there first?"

"I will. Be careful, OK?"

"Of course. I wasn't assigned to the graveyard shift because I was a coward, and remember, I'm not out of practice." She glanced around and noted the absence of the SUV.

"I never said you were. By the way, did you get someone to take your place this Sunday for the Wiggle Giggle Club?"

"My mom's going to experiment with her ventriloquist voice."

"To be a fly on the wall... Should be interesting."

"I know. I'd love to observe Mom in action, trying to bring Professor Nelson to life with the kids. I think it'll be therapeutic for her."

From criminals to cribs and drugs to diapers, coordinating the Sunday morning Wiggle Giggle Club was the polar opposite of Crystal's role in downtown Dallas. How greatly her life changed in two short years. Teaching toddlers was a productive way to incorporate her love of ventriloquism into lesson plans for the active group. The kids loved Professor Nelson. The commitment to develop a story line for the weekly class kept her well-practiced in the creative art form.

"I better run. Might try to walk toward the back or chat with a neighbor. If nothing happens before long, I'll go to the restaurant and wait for you."

"Good deal. Love you."

Crystal tapped the Bluetooth and brushed against a string of foliage that fell from the colorful basket hanging from above. She reached up and touched the soil. Even if Karina was on vacation, someone was looking after the house and watering her plants. The soil was damp but not soggy.

The bench nearby looked inviting. There'd been little time to think since she and Michael arrived in Miami on their search. She sank into the floral print for a few minutes of reprieve. The decorative cushions didn't disappoint her. The scent from the flowers above evoked memories of her childhood.

A childhood without a sister.

When her mother invited her to brunch in February, life had changed forever. At first there was shock, then anger, learning she had a sister—an identical twin at that—who was unaware she was even a twin at all. Like she herself had been unaware all these years.

To be angry was her right. What a gutless, insensitive, uncaring thing to do.

Yet she must forgive.

Her mother changed. The constant fatigue in her eyes had lifted, making it difficult to remember the strain on her face. She appeared more beautiful at forty-six than she ever had. It took courage for her to come forward after so many years, and it caused Crystal to respect her mom even more.

But the grief was unbearable when she thought about what she'd missed out on as a twin. Empty dreams continued to replay on an emotional loop since the day she learned of her sister's existence. Empty dreams that could never be fulfilled.

They'd have walked hand in hand to the bus stop each day, sitting together on the army-green seats, their hair blowing in the wind. They'd have primped each other for high school prom and sipped sodas at the mall after school while whispering secrets like the ones Crystal still kept locked inside. They'd have shared their heartaches, calmed each other's fears, and triumphed over their accomplishments.

They would have been best friends.

In counseling sessions with Crystal and her mom, the pastor's wife said healing was a process, and it would take time. They peeled through layers for weeks. Finally, forgiveness had taken root and soon grew and even flourished.

It was Michael's idea that they fly to Miami for the weekend to the Rubenski's last known address to shed some light on Karina's whereabouts. It gave Crystal hope, although her long distance inquires had been futile. Her mother asked to come along, but Michael was right—if Karina were found, she'd probably be more receptive to a sister than the birth mother who'd given her up. Besides, Michael needed a break from the law firm and the timing was perfect for him. Her mom was babysitting Trevor, and according to last night's report, things were going fine.

The sound of a car made her jump to her feet. How

long had she been sitting here? It was the same SUV she noticed earlier, which now slowed as it neared the house.

The sound of a garage door opening at the house next door prompted her to glance at an elderly neighbor as he walked to the end of his driveway. He stooped and picked up the newspaper, then spotted her.

"Karina?"

The single word, although soft-spoken, was unmistakable…and a little unnerving.

The man started walking toward her.

5

Leah stretched out on the sofa, wondering what to do. The skylights overhead told her this Saturday was too beautiful of a Saturday to be wasted by sitting at home.

It amazed her how guarded she had to be while living this far north, in order to protect herself from the dreary moods of the weather. It was much easier to be optimistic when the sky was bright than when it was hidden and overshadowed with gray. She'd taken the blue canopy for granted in Miami. Today, though, as she peered through the skylights and glanced at the thermometer on the back deck, a smile skirted her face. It was sixty-two degrees and barely noon. She jumped to her feet. Within minutes, she was wandering in and out of the Main Street storefronts, something she'd wanted to do since her arrival. The charm of a downtown district, no matter the location of the city, always held an attraction for her.

She ducked in and out of a few consignment shops, priding herself on finding another pocket watch to add to her collection. She wandered into an old five and dime, amazed that the franchise was still around. When she spotted *The Coffee Loft* some forty-five minutes later, she was ecstatic. She always made time for coffee.

The barista glanced up from cleaning the counter as she walked in. "Hey there. What'll it be for you?"

"Any recommendations?"

"The Café Latte is killer today," he said.

"That sounds great. A large, please."

"A Lofty. Got it. And your name?"

"Ka—Leah."

"OK, Kaleah. I'll bring it to you shortly."

A small table was available at the front window. She breathed in the aroma of the freshly ground beans as she watched people enjoy the day outside. The familiar sound of the barista's tools of the trade stopped, and Leah looked up as he brought the frothy cup to her.

"Hope you enjoy it." She took one sip and was convinced she would.

Something about the rich brew caused her to ooze with creativity. Like a best friend, it wrapped itself around her. She came alive with confidence, ready to face any challenge that lay ahead. She pitied those who didn't embrace the private ritual.

She pulled out a notepad and pen from her purse. The open house was only a month away, and plenty of work still needed to be done. This was a perfect time to review the plans and finalize others.

Admittedly, the assignment was a lifesaver, and helped to keep her mind from growing weary and bored with her lack of social activity. Why Phillip chose her to organize the event was beyond Leah's comprehension, but for him to presume she had the ability to do so brought her a sense of satisfaction. Still, she struggled when the planning required her to be near him. The educated, professional side of her handled trauma cases with ease. Yet her confidence as a mere customer service rep frayed at the edges every time he was near. She fingered the pen in her hand. Even the doctors she'd socialized with in Miami hadn't affected her like this distinguished, understated pilot.

She lifted the cup to her lips and closed her eyes.

"The Coffee Loft—home of Lowville's finest latte."

Phillip? Was her creative imagination getting the best of her? She looked up to see her boss standing beside her with a large cup of coffee in his hand and a newspaper under his arm. She regretted the thoughts that were running through her mind seconds prior and hoped her façade wasn't evident.

She swallowed and tried to hide her surprise. "Good morning."

"How are you, Leah?"

"Fine. You?"

"Not too bad. May I join you?"

"Of course." She brushed aside her uneasiness as she moved her purse and keys from the tabletop and pushed her notes to the side.

More casual than she'd ever seen him, his sweats and t-shirt only emphasized the fact that he was ruggedly handsome. And he hadn't shaved. She forced her eyes from him and picked up her latte, reminding herself he was off limits. As was she.

"Is this the part where I ask if you come here often?"

At least he was good at breaking the ice. "My first time. Where have I been?"

"They opened not long ago. Do you live around here?"

"Yes, down the street. You?"

"Yes. See that cantaloupe-colored two-story, right down there?" He referenced the house with the lift of his finger.

She nodded. She lived within eyesight of the restored home. She admired its character and charm every time she passed by. It would make a perfect bed and breakfast. She had no idea they were a stone's throw from one another.

"Next time go for the Guatemalan."

"Sounds serious."

"It is. Don't try it after—about now." He laughed, glancing at his watch.

"Thanks for the warning."

"It's hard for me to get a good cup of brew anymore—unless I'm at work, of course. I'm thinking about getting a Keurig for the house."

Heat rose to her face at the hidden compliment. She'd assumed the role of coffee duty since Tom's playful refusal to make it anymore.

His eyes met hers briefly. "You go by Kaleah?"

"Pardon me?" Her heart skipped a beat.

"The name on your cup."

"Oh! No, it's just Leah. He misunderstood."

"I figured as much." He glanced at the notepad she'd been writing on. "You doodle on weekends, too."

A sudden panic seized her. She hoped her scrawling wasn't a dead giveaway to the thoughts that dominated her mind moments before. Her eyes fell to the sheet in front of her. She sighed in relief when the ballpoint scrollwork gave nothing away, apart from the intricate doodlings of the face of a pocket watch.

"It may sound strange to you, but I didn't realize I did that."

"Aah, you're a true artist." His warm laugh was as smooth and rich as the latte she was drinking.

"There's a stretch. An artist is one thing I'm not."

"I beg to differ. You scribble on my message slips at work more often than not." He took a swallow of his coffee.

She grew uncomfortable, wondering what other secrets her pen may have revealed.

"Don't worry. It's a nice touch. So, what's the pocket watch all about?"

"Old timepieces intrigue me. Something I like to collect."

"Cool collection. Is your doodling something you conjured in that imaginative mind of yours?"

"No, I saw it in a museum once and I couldn't get it out of—oh never mind." She stopped short.

"The one you're wearing is unique. Is it significant?"

She reached down to the long chain at her neck and fingered it absentmindedly. The face of it was a watch that opened into a locket. "This was given to me on my twenty-fourth birthday." She hoped it was OK to say that.

He gestured toward her to take a closer look. "May I?"

It was safer for her to remove it from her neck to avoid any more space from closing between them. He obviously meant nothing by it. Polite conversation is all it was. Still, she could take no chances. She needed to keep her distance. He was her boss. She pulled it over her head and dropped it into his palm and hoped he wouldn't discover the tiny device behind her photograph if he opened the locket. One touch of the silent alarm was all it took to link her to Richard, alerting him that she was in a precarious situation.

He eyed it briefly and popped open the latch. "You had long hair."

"I did."

"Very nice. Then and now." He handed it back to her.

"Thanks." She slipped the chain back over her head.

"How are the open house plans coming? Amidst your doodling it seems you're working on a plan."

Relief filled her as he returned to the subject of work. "Things are going well. I picked up a few items at the party store last night. And I've come up with a preliminary menu."

"What's on the menu?"

"Have a look." She offered her notes.

He reached for the notepad. His jaw clamped firmly as he focused on the words before him. Then a smile turned up the corners of his mouth. When he raised his eyes to meet hers, there was a sparkle in them.

"Swedish meatballs, pistachio shrimp with mango dipping sauce, and cheese and walnut stuffed mushrooms in phyllo? Wow. When can I get a sample?"

She laughed in spite of her nervousness. "I need to make a practice run first."

"You're going to cook this stuff yourself? I thought you were hiring a caterer."

"I was going to, but I wasn't able to find anyone with a menu that offered more than prepackaged-looking smidgens, and that didn't seem to fit the bill."

"Prepackaged-looking smidgens?" He chuckled as he shook his head.

"Well, yes. You know. The stuff you buy at those wholesale clubs that anyone can get their hands on. I think we're all jalapeno-poppered-out already."

Phillip leaned back and his eyes met hers. He picked up his cup again and gave her an agreeable nod. "You are so right. I can hardly wait to see what you come up with."

"You'll want to keep an open mind."

"Evidently, you're not kidding." He looked as if he were trying to hide a smile.

"I'm not."

"Where'd you learn to cook like that?"

The uneasiness reappeared. WITSEC could not take her love of cooking and entertaining away from her. Still, she had to avoid the possibility of any unintended exposure.

He must have noticed her discomfort and spoke before she said anything. His voice was quiet and humorously guarded, and the twinkle in his eyes wrapped her in warmth. "Listen, if Julia Childs is your mother and you're trying to keep a low profile, your secret's safe with me."

She relaxed at his humor. "She is the one who taught me to make a killer poached salmon with chilled cucumber sauce."

"A recipe handed down. I rest my case."

The next few minutes turned into an hour before the last swallow of coffee was down. She didn't notice that the brew had grown cold. This man—even though intimidating—was quite pleasant to talk with when she let her guard down.

Oh no. What had she done? Letting her guard down was the one thing she promised herself she'd never do. Especially not with him—he was her boss!

And she was...well, it was hard to know who she was anymore. What was she thinking?

His sauntering in here had been a coincidence. Still, she should have been more careful. She reprimanded herself for the brief moment of pleasure she'd experienced and vowed it could never happen again.

~*~

Scordino breathed a sigh of relief as he disconnected his cell phone and waited for Mariucci to arrive.

It was a good living, this occupation. Sure, there were risks to be taken, but that was to be expected when the rewards were as high. That's what investment firms were all about. A glimmer of hope flickered for the first time in days.

Even if no monetary value had been placed on the woman, he would still be obliged to be a key player in the game. He was in too deep. She'd seen both of them. He'd do it to save his hide, and his alone, if necessary.

What luck he had today. He must thank Sam Canali for the tip the next time he ran into him.

But why on earth the girl ventured back here, he couldn't figure out. Not when she was being sought after. Maybe she was simply tired of living her life in hiding. He turned the stereo to his favorite classical station and leaned into the comfort of his seat while he waited for Mariucci to arrive.

If all went as planned, Karina Rubenski would never have to live in hiding again.

6

"Karina?"

The neighbor approached, and Crystal couldn't help but notice his expression. He seemed surprised, almost relieved. She walked toward the driveway to meet him.

"I can't believe it! It's so good to have you back." He reached out as if he would embrace her.

Crystal's lip quivered, and she hardly knew what to say. Tears formed in her eyes. The thought of being mistaken for Karina was new to her—something most twins experienced every day of their lives.

She composed herself. "I'm sorry...I'm not Karina."

The man's brow furrowed, and the arm he'd extended stopped midway. "Excuse me?"

"My name is Crystal Robbins. I'm Karina's twin sister. I really need to find her."

"Wait a minute. Karina's a twin?"

"It was news to me, too. We were separated at birth. Neither of us had any idea the other existed. I haven't been able to contact her by phone."

The man lowered his head, so his expression was hid. Finally, his eyes met Crystal's. "I'm Albert Stewart. My wife and I haven't seen Karina for some time now. But if you'd like to come in for a bit, we'd be happy to tell you all we know."

"I'd appreciate that, Mr. Stewart. Maybe I should move my car first."

"You can, but the house is vacant, so it won't be in the way if you leave it. And please, call me Albert."

Crystal shook his hand, grateful for his kindness.

The two walked across the grass that divided the properties. The SUV that circled earlier was gone. Within minutes, she met Sylvie, who had the identical reaction as Albert. After the ice broke, they settled into the living room, where Sylvie brought in cool glasses of tea.

"We talked about Karina this morning," Sylvie offered.

"So, you're close to her?"

"Yes," Albert answered, "we were."

"Were?"

"We've been close to the Rubenski family ever since they moved in, when Kari was probably two or three years old," Albert said with an unmistakable sadness in his voice.

"There's no denying—you are identical. It's amazing you never knew each other, yet you carry yourselves in much the same way." Sylvie's voice was soft-spoken and smooth. "The visible differences are few. Kari is a beautiful young woman as well. Your hair is long, but Kari's comes to here, more or less." She held her hand to the top of her shoulder. "I guess it should've been obvious that you weren't her. Kari's hair could never have grown that long in this short of a time."

It brought tears to Crystal's eyes to imagine the tangible details of her own flesh and blood, her own mirror image. "I...I'm speechless."

"Well, it's obvious your intentions are honorable, and it's a good thing you're identical. Otherwise we would say very little to you." Sylvie cleared her throat and threaded her fingers together in a nervous gesture.

"Given the situation," Albert added, his expression grave.

"What situation?"

The Stewarts were quiet for a moment.

"Your sister has been reported missing," Sylvie finally spoke. "We haven't seen hide nor hair of her for six or seven weeks now."

"Missing?" Crystal tried to process the word.

"Yes. It's been about that long since the end of the trial."

"What trial?" Crystal's ears perked, and her senses zoomed to high alert. She looked at Albert, then Sylvie, certain the confusion was evident on her face.

"You didn't see the news? Where are you from?" Albert asked.

"Dallas."

"Around here, it's been big news," Albert said. "You're aware that Dr. Walt Rubenski and his wife Doris were killed a few years ago, right?"

Crystal took a deep breath as she squeezed her eyes shut. She shook her head. The research she'd been able to obtain was sketchy.

"Walt was a well-respected physician. He and Doris donated a lot of their time and money to people in poverty-stricken areas. Many times, Karina would accompany them. A few years ago, their small plane went down during a medical mission in Haiti. Karina was devastated. Since their death, she's tried to keep things together, and she's done quite well, really. Such a wonderful young woman. She was an emergency room nurse at Miami General, and an amazing one at that. She's one of the reasons I'm still here, she and the good Lord anyway. She took care of me in the ER when I had a heart attack last year. Even prayed with me. She was like that. Real Christian-like. Not enough words to express how much we loved her."

Crystal's throat tightened.

Was?

Albert picked up his tea glass. "Kari got thrown into the spotlight after the murder of a prominent attorney. She was an eyewitness. Vic Trebari was one of the finest in all of Florida, they say. One of his cases involved a scandal over the misuse of funds from the Florida Department of Agriculture and Consumer Services division in Tallahassee. Evidently, a key player in south Florida came forward and spilled the whole truth to Trebari. At least, that's what the prosecutors are putting together. But there are a lot of missing pieces. Before Trebari made his move, this key player was killed, and Trebari was permanently silenced as well, in his private office in the Connor Tower here in Miami."

Albert looked at Sylvie and she continued the story. "Meanwhile, Kari happened to be in the Tower for an appointment with her attorney, unrelated to the case. Three men got onto the elevator with her. A paper dropped out of her folder and grazed the shoe of one of the men, who we later found out was a guy by the name of Edward DeFresnio. But the big break? It just so happened there was a smudge of blood on the man's Italian leather shoes. Karina didn't see it at the time. She just stuffed the document back into her folder without realizing the bloodstain was there until she got home and pulled the papers out to review them. That night, the news broke about an attorney who'd been stabbed in the Connor Tower that day, during the same time she'd been in the building. She had an eerie feeling—given the unexplained bloodstain on her document—as she recalled the moment in the elevator, the man's face, and those shoes. She went to the authorities, turned in the paper, and gave a description of the man who was standing beside her."

Crystal took in the words, visualizing every detail.

"The DNA belonged to none other than Vic Trebari, the slain attorney," Albert said. "The sketch they came up with led them to DeFresnio. They got a warrant and discovered his shoe also carried traces of Trebari's DNA. With the evidence they needed, they were able to place DeFresnio at the scene. He was convicted of murder and is now on Florida's death row. The big problem is that Kari reported there were three men on the elevator that day, but she couldn't recollect the faces of the other two. It wasn't long after the trial that she disappeared. We've been keeping our eyes on the house ever since. It's not like her to leave without saying anything. She always told us when she was going out of town for any length of time."

Defeat threatened Crystal, mocking the very mission that had become her soul's quest. "In your opinion, do you think she's OK? Any clue as to where she might've gone?" she spoke quietly, measuring her words.

Albert stared out at the lush landscape.

Sylvie cleared her throat and brushed a tear from her eye. "No idea. That's why we were breathing a sigh of relief when you showed up."

"It doesn't look good." It was the first time Crystal allowed herself to form the words. But speaking them also made them more real—something she didn't want to think about.

The worry also settled over Albert's sea-blue eyes.

"I know. With the other guys unidentified and at large, it makes us quite nervous for her."

"She's probably running for her life." Crystal's voice wavered, despite her best attempt to control it. Either that or she was in protective custody.

"Can I get you something to eat, perhaps a sandwich?" Sylvie spoke through a sea of tears.

Was it lunchtime already? Michael would be wondering about her. "Thank you, no. I need to keep moving. Will you please call me if you see or hear anything more?"

"We'd be happy to. If Kari had any idea you were looking for her, she'd be thrilled and excited to meet you, too."

The thought gave Crystal comfort. She reached for a pen and paper in her purse and jotted down her home and cell numbers. "Is there anything else you can tell me about her, like where she hangs out or any hobbies she has?"

The two were silent a moment, but it was Sylvie who replied. "She was very active in church. She attended that nondenominational church—what's the name of it, Albert?"

"Calvary, I think. She invited us to a Christmas play this past December. It's on University Ridge, on the west side of town."

"The play was excellent, too," Sylvie added. "You can check out Miami General. We tried and got nowhere, but it's worth a shot. She also loves antiques and is especially fond of old pocket watches. She treasured Mr. Rubenski's collection. She was always adding to it."

Crystal's mind raced ahead with a plan. She'd search antique shops in the surrounding areas this afternoon. "If you think of anything else, please give me a call. Thank you both so much for your time." She pushed off the chair.

"It was our pleasure," the two agreed in unison as they rose. "We can only hope you'll find her, and that she's all right."

A tear moved down Crystal's face, and she brushed it aside. "Thank you. It was so good to meet you both."

The Stewarts embraced her, and after brief good-byes were spoken, she returned to the rental car, more eager than ever to turn over the tables that seemed to be covering the one she searched for.

She only hoped she would get to her sister before anyone else did.

~*~

Crystal hurried to the car, eager to call Michael with an update. In some ways, she was so close to Karina. But in reality, she was farther from her than ever.

She backed out of the Rubenski driveway and drove toward the entrance of the subdivision and glanced at the GPS app in her phone before turning onto the main road.

"Call Michael." She spoke to her phone. She was relieved when he picked up on the second ring. "I've got some new info. Good news, bad news. Which do you want first?"

"Good." Michael was eager to hear.

"OK. We definitely have the right house. I talked with a neighbor."

"Fantastic, honey. So what's the problem?"

Suddenly, there was a thud from behind.

"What in the…" She glanced in her rearview mirror. A black vehicle was on her tail.

"Crystal, what was that?"

The thud was constant now, as if they were pushing her. She fought to keep the car from hitting a telephone pole on the shoulder, gasping for breath as she slowed to a stop along the side of the road.

"What a jerk!" Crystal's anger intensified. "I've just been hit, honey. Some bozo tailgated me and literally pushed me off the road."

"Are you all right? Are you hurt?"

She tried to gather her thoughts. "I'm OK. They're backing up now. They better not think of leaving the scene. I gotta go. I'll call you back after I give them a piece of my mind."

"No! Wait. Keep me on the phone. I want to be sure you're all right."

"I'll be fine, Michael. I need to catch them before they make a run for it."

"I know you're fine. You can handle it. You always do, but keep me on the phone. It's only wise."

Crystal glanced in her rearview mirror. "OK, stay with me. They stopped now. Looks like they're getting out of their vehicle to talk to me." Michael always worried too much. When she was working full-time, it was even worse. Crystal dropped the still-connected phone on the seat. She might not appear tough on the surface, but she was still a cop, with or without a gun. She reached for the door latch.

Two men approached, now at the rear of the car. Something was wrong, and suddenly she knew it was no accident at all. Dread overwhelmed her, and her professional skills took a temporary leave of absence.

She grabbed the phone that she'd carelessly tossed onto the seat, while fumbling for the door locks.

"Michael, something's not right."

"Calm down. What's the matter?"

She couldn't find the locks. In an instant, she'd lost complete control of her senses. It wasn't like her at all. She'd been off guard—a professional failure as well as a personal one. The words spilled out of her mouth. "Westward Road. Black Cherokee. Two men. Something's wrong. I need help."

"I'm calling the cops, and I'm on my way. Can you get a description of them?"

Her words were short, but calculated. "Both white. One tall. One short. The lock. I can't—"

She found the lock and struggled to press it. At the same time the man outside the passenger door lifted the latch. She panicked and hit it again as his eyes locked onto hers. But the door was already opened. There was no escape. Crystal screamed, kicked, and fought. In an instant, the cell phone—her connection to Michael—was abruptly disconnected.

~*~

The sky darkened about Leah as she headed home from the grocery store later in the afternoon. What a difference a few hours made—a big switch from the blue skies of Saturday morning.

Trees swayed with the breeze as she drove through the residential part of town, taking a shortcut she'd learned the week before. Anticipation grew within her when she passed Community Fellowship. She looked forward to church the next day. The people were friendly, and the pastor and his wife seemed to be genuine enough. She still hadn't established any close relationships, but it was a start.

A trash can lid blew across the road as a gust of wind gave way to the coming storm. Up ahead, lightening shot down in a jagged force that compelled the thunder to rumble a split second later. She hoped to be home before the rains began, but at this rate, she was certain to get wet.

As she rounded a corner near the edge of town, she sensed the dread. She searched the rearview mirror for any oddity, but the road was deathly quiet behind her. For every beat of her heart, there suddenly seemed to be two. What on earth was wrong with her?

What triggered this reaction in her? Was someone following her, out of her line of sight?

Her right hand reached into the backseat and confirmed she was alone. She normally made a habit of checking it before she got into the car, especially since the trial. She fingered the gold chain at her neck, tempted to alert Richard to her sudden unease. Yet there was no rhyme nor reason for her discomfort. She couldn't just call him on a whim, a notion fueled by her unruly emotions.

And then she felt the urgency to pray—not for herself, but for someone else who might be in danger. It happened to her a lot, it seemed, this nudging. But this time, it was different. She couldn't put her finger on it. As she continued on her trek, the rain began to pound on the roof of her car.

Lord, I have no idea what's going on. Why do I feel like I feel sometimes? Is it just me, or is there a reason You're tapping me on the shoulder? Whatever the case, I can't brush it off. If there's someone who needs Your help right now, I ask You to be their comforter. They may not be in a position to pray, but You know their name, and You know the number of hairs on their head. You see each sparrow that falls to the ground, and You care. The battle they find themselves in is no surprise to You, and Your might is much greater than the circumstance they are facing. I ask You to be a shield to them, and redeem their life from destruction.

When Leah finished praying, she had the surest sense that the rain outside was more than just a spring shower. Rather, it was healing rain that sang in chorus with the prayer of faith she offered for one she did not know.

As she drove up to the small brick house a short time later, she found there were still words on her lips, but they had turned to words of praise.

And then peace settled over her once again, and she ran into the house unafraid.

7

Phillip walked off the tarmac as the first plane left for the morning. The blast of the engines gave him a thrill he never tired of. As he climbed the stairs to the office, his phone vibrated.

He read the display as he breezed past the counter, and nodded to Leah, grateful she was busy on the phone. He shut the door when he got to his office.

"Morning, AJ. What's up?"

"We have a little issue here, man. I'm holding a report that your witness is here—in Miami. What's going on?"

Phillip's eyebrows furrowed as he dropped into his chair. "What are you talking about? That's impossible. She's here."

"She was spotted on Friday evening with a gentleman, probably in his mid to late thirties at a trendy restaurant on South Beach. I hate to break it to you, but my sources are good."

"And I'm telling you it's not possible. I'm keeping my eye on her. She couldn't have slipped away."

"When's the last time you had contact with her?" AJ asked.

"I spoke with her this morning."

"Well, she was here at eight thirty Friday night, and she made it back before you missed her."

"I don't mean to second-guess you, but that's highly unlikely."

"Can you prove it?"

"I saw her Friday afternoon, and I ran into her

Saturday morning as well." Phillip's mind was spinning out of control with the possibilities.

"Listen, don't get me wrong, but my sources are reliable, Phillip. They know what they saw. It's possible your witness got lonely, jumped a plane for a quick visit to Miami on Friday evening, and caught the red-eye Saturday morning. And if that's the case, then it's a serious mistake on her part, and a very dangerous one at that. Karina knows the rules. She needs to stick with them, no matter how difficult it is."

"I know, AJ. It would be a mistake, and it is possible, but it's just not likely. I can assure you I'll find out and get back with you later tonight."

Phillip ended the call, flustered. It couldn't be true. For her to board a flight on Friday after work with a connection to Miami for an eight thirty dinner was impossible. The chances of catching a red-eye for Saturday morning was implausible. It made no sense.

What time had he run into her at The Coffee Loft on Saturday? He remembered glancing at his watch and looking at the timepiece that hung from the chain on her neck. But for the life of him, he didn't remember what time it was. All he recalled was what she looked like and how quickly the hour had flown.

Still, what if it was true? Who was it she'd been seen with? But wait, didn't she mention she'd picked up supplies for the open house the night before?

AJ, good friend and colleague that he was, had no idea just how closely Phillip was watching the witness. His dual role was a challenge, greater now than ever. Most certainly, AJ would get a charge out of his dilemma when the dust settled.

Phillip opened his office door and walked back through the hall. He filled a mug with coffee and made a casual appearance at the counter where Tom and Charles were deep in conversation.

"Hey there," he greeted them, resting his free hand on Charles' shoulder. "Glad to have you back, Gramps. How's it going?"

Charles laughed at the teasing. "Great, Phillip. Tom and I are recapping what all happened last week while I was out."

"How's the grandbaby?"

"She's the cutest little bundle of joy, and I miss her already."

"I'll bet. Bring her in sometime when they're visiting so we can all meet her."

"Will do."

"How was everyone's weekend?" he asked, aware that Leah was off the phone.

"Good," Tom answered. "Parents are here from Philly right now. Kept me hopping the whole time."

"I can imagine," Phillip said as Charles excused himself to take care of a ringing phone. "Yours, Leah?"

"It was good, thanks."

"How are the open house plans coming?"

"Not bad. I picked up a few more things."

"What did you come up with?" Phillip tried not to sound like an interrogator.

"I finished planning the menu. That was my biggest accomplishment."

"A hurdle has been crossed."

"I think so."

"If you bring me your receipts, I'll cut a check for you." He promised he would get proof. This might be his only chance.

"No worries. I'll hold my receipts until I'm finished and get them to you all at once."

She wasn't making this easy. "I'd prefer to get you reimbursed right away. It'll be easier for Marci to stay on track that way." He hoped she didn't catch the fact that no budget had been set yet.

"OK, sure." Leah reached under the counter and retrieved a couple receipts from her purse. She handed it to him but she looked puzzled. "So...what is my budget?"

"Honestly, I guess I worded that wrong. I'd like to have an idea on where we're at before I get hit with the bills all at once in the end. You know, break it to me gently." He forced a laugh, trying to brush it off. "I'll be back in a few minutes."

When he walked into the hall he took a cursory look at the top receipt.

The Party Experience in Watertown. Friday evening, seven thirty.

Perfect. His mission was complete. Relief flooded him, but he still wondered about it. AJ's sources were good. But someone had obviously made a grave mistake.

He walked into the bookkeeper's office and tried to sound casual. "Marci, will you please cut a reimbursement check to Leah for this?"

"Sure." She took it and put it with her next batch of payables.

"May I wait for it?" Since he'd insisted on the receipts right away, there was an obligation to produce a check immediately.

"Yes, of course." Marci put aside what she was working on. Within minutes, the check was in his hand.

He scrawled his signature and walked back to give it to Leah who was already on another line. He waited at the counter until she was off the phone and continued to wait while she typed in a quick profile notation.

Leah removed her headset and looked up at Phillip.

"Here you are." He handed it to her.

"Thank you."

"Everything else going OK?"

"Yes. Invitations are set to go out next week. Here's what it looks like." She showed him a sample.

"Very nice." Phillip was impressed. He was certain they would get plenty of attention. He tucked his hands into the pocket of his pressed trousers. "You're doing a great job."

"Thanks. It's kind of nice, actually. Keeps my mind occupied so I don't get too homesick. For Toledo," she added.

That's right. Her application said she was from Toledo. "Aah, you really didn't like Toledo all that much anyway. You just weren't aware until now." He winked at her in jest.

"Putting words in my mouth?"

He glanced at her softly defined lips as she spoke. A slight flush crept into her face, and he realized he'd stared for too long. He pushed himself off the counter. "I suppose I need to get back to my work—and I'm sure there are plenty of other things you want to tackle today." He was relieved when her phone rang again before he said anything he would regret.

~*~

AJ twirled a pencil between his fingers as he gazed out his office window. The Miami sky darkened as low-hanging clouds moved in from the west. It seemed like a long Monday already. The sound of a vacuum cleaner in the distance spilled through the hall.

He flipped the pencil on end and dialed Phillip's number on the desk phone with the tip of the eraser. He got to the point of his call. "The plot thickens."

"How's that?"

"Long story." AJ spun his chair around and propped his feet on the windowsill behind his desk.

"I'm listening."

"There's a gentleman waiting in the other room right now who stumbled across something you might be interested in. His name is Michael Robbins. I'd say he's about our age. On Friday night he was at a restaurant in Miami Beach—the same restaurant where the witness was reportedly spotted. Happens to be the guy she was spotted with."

"Go on."

"Miami-Dade Police referred him to me shortly after I talked to you this morning. Michael's wife Crystal is missing. Says MDPD gave him the runaround when he tried to file a missing persons report since she'd been missing less than twenty-four hours. Truthfully, I think they were just trying to figure out what to do after they saw the photo of her."

"The photo?"

AJ hesitated a moment, wondering how his friend would take the news. "Phillip, she looks identical to your witness. Mr. Robbins is sitting outside my office waiting for some word. The man is about to pull his hair out. I gotta believe his story."

"Which is…?"

"Michael is an attorney in Dallas. Crystal is an undercover cop who's on sabbatical to raise their son.

They've been here in Miami since Friday searching for Crystal's—get this—identical twin sister. Her sister's name is Karina Rubenski."

There was silence on the other end of the line.

Finally, Phillip took a deep breath. "How is it that Karina is a twin? She never said anything to us about that."

"Don't know all the details yet. Evidently, Crystal only recently found out. Karina apparently isn't aware of Crystal either."

"And you're sure of this?"

"It's hard not to be. Mr. Robbins is visibly shaken, and with the photographs he's shown me of his missing wife, it's as obvious as the nose on my face. No wonder my contact spotted her on Friday night. If that's not enough, I've had Mr. Robbins checked out. He's a member of the Texas Bar, practicing corporate law in Dallas. It appears he's well respected. Everything he says corresponds. I've no doubt. It's legit."

"What were the circumstances that led to her being missing? And do you think it's related?"

"It looks suspicious. Crystal drove to Karina's house on Saturday mid-morning, searching for her. Michael was back at the hotel taking care of some business. Crystal just left the subdivision and placed a call to him to fill him in with what she learned about Karina from the neighbors. While they were on the phone, she was rear-ended. But something spooked her because she panicked. She gave Michael her location and told him two men driving a black Cherokee hit her. He heard a struggle; then the phone went dead."

"That doesn't sound good. Are there fingerprints

on her car?"

"No. They must have had gloves on. It was definitely premeditated. We're doing traces now on all the black Cherokees we can come up with. But it's tough. This is Miami."

"What about Michael? He must be a basket case." Concern laced Phillip's words.

"In all fairness to him, I had to be up front with him. I explained the trial and suggested Crystal could've been mistaken for Karina. Maybe I said too much..." The responsibility that lay on AJ's shoulders was heavy, but it didn't hold a candle to the weight that was in Michael's eyes. What other choice did AJ have? Saying less wasn't fair to him either. AJ let out a weary sigh.

"What a mess. Why did it take them so long to come to you?"

"Red tape. Makes me sick. That Michael had to wait twenty-four hours is a disgrace to victims and family members everywhere. Even then, nothing happened until an alert member of the MDPD came to work Monday morning and contacted me."

"I'm sure there'll be an internal investigation."

"You'd better believe it," AJ agreed.

"For now, we need to put our heads together and come up with a plan. What have you done so far?"

"We're putting up photos everywhere. Problem is, we can't use Crystal's name. It'll raise a red flag to the whole case and get the public and everyone else in on it. Plus, what if word got back to Karina somehow? I'm certain she isn't aware she's a twin. It's complicated. She'd end up being the last to know."

"But yet you have to publicize it to find Crystal."

"Exactly."

"Plastering her photo is the right thing to do, but use Karina's name. If anyone spots her, they're bound to mistake her for Karina and call it in automatically since she's been listed as missing for so long. We can use that to our advantage. Plus, if Crystal is an undercover, she'll be able to take care of herself. That should account for something."

"That's seeing the cup half full."

"It is, but it's the truth. Is Michael aware that Karina is a protected witness?"

"Yeah. He suspected it as soon as I told him about the trial."

"Unfortunately, he's probably suspecting all sorts of things."

"Likely so," AJ agreed. "If anything jumps out at you, call me. Make sure Karina is being careful." His voice grew quiet. "I know Lowville is a long way away, but even so, she can't be too careful. Stick close to her. Play it safe."

"Not to worry. I'm watching her very closely."

"I'll keep you posted and call you tomorrow. Meanwhile…" AJ tapped the pencil nervously on his desk. He hated asking. He wasn't much of a religious guy.

"Meanwhile what?"

"Will you say a prayer for Michael and Crystal?" Phillip's faith was the central part of his life. Maybe Phillip could put in a good word for the couple.

Phillip was quick to agree, and AJ hoped it would work.

After a brief good-bye, AJ hung up the phone and pushed away from his desk. He hurried back out to the lobby where Michael sat with his eyes closed and head bowed low.

8

The early evening breeze prompted Leah to tug on the sleeves of her bright red sweatshirt as she started weeding a section of the flowerbed outside the front porch of the bungalow.

The first signs of spring were in the air. The thought excited her. She breathed in the scent of the rich soil—something she'd never taken time for in Miami. Like tiny veins of life that had grown under the ground before her, the small town began to grow on her as well, causing her to be more rooted each day.

The sound of a horn caught her attention as she yanked on the stubborn weeds with her fingers.

"Beautiful day, isn't it?" Mrs. Yancey called from her open car window as she backed out of her driveway.

Leah waved. The silver-haired neighbor introduced herself shortly after Leah arrived. She still paused to chat every now and then at the front porch, particularly since the weather was nicer. It seemed it wasn't difficult for the friendly woman to find an excuse to stop by and say hello.

"It's perfect out here," Leah answered.

"Need anything at the store?"

"I'm good for now. But thanks."

The woman nodded again before she backed out onto the street.

Leah warmed at the thought of some of her stories. According to Mrs. Yancey, the small town had a rich history in befriending underground slaves. Wealthy aristocrats housed slaves in the area while rebels scoured the land to eliminate them for good. Some of the wealthy land owners freed them by leading them into their basements which connected to underground tunnels, winding a path under State Street and on through the upstate New York region. Finally, they traveled underneath the border to the safety of Canada before they emerged a good distance away.

Leah looked out onto the street in front of her where numerous escapes allegedly took place. It *was* possible, she supposed. But Mrs. Yancey also told her she'd grown a twenty-pound tomato for last year's farmer's fair.

She picked up her garden tools and went back inside to get cleaned up. The phone rang right as she stepped out of the shower.

"Hello?" She snatched her robe from the hook on the door and pulled it around her as she held the phone in the crook of her neck.

"Hi. It's Richard."

"Hey, there." She was pleased to hear from him. Several days had gone by since they'd spoken.

"How are ya?"

"All right," she replied. "You?"

"Fine. What are you up to?"

"Just came in from outside. I was working in the front garden area."

"Oh, yeah? You enjoy gardening?"

"Now that I have the time, yes. I was always too busy before."

"I understand. A mixed blessing, right? So what are you growing?"

"I'm weeding a lavender and daffodil garden."

"Sounds beautiful."

"The blooms are teeny nubs. I can't wait to see them in all their glory. Flowers do wonders for moods, you know."

"They do. Each variety evokes a different mood. People can tell a lot about you by the landscaping around your home."

"Hmm. I never thought of it like that."

"How's everything else with you?"

"Not too bad. I'm adjusting more as each week passes." She hoped her words rang true.

"That's good."

"Any news on the case?"

His silence was a dead giveaway. Obviously, he knew something.

"You don't want to tell me, do you?"

"I want to tell you everything. But some things are better left unsaid."

"That doesn't sound too fair to me." She meant it in an upbeat kind of way. Yet deep inside, her curiosity was getting the best of her.

"Suffice it to say there's a lead that could potentially be a big break for us, but things would have to line up…strategically. But let me assure you that you are entirely safe here in New York."

"Any word on Patrick?"

"Not definitive."

"He's still being held?"

"He is. The cell phone lead is pretty much dead. If we can't find his source, he can be tried for conspiracy, kidnapping, and interfering with a federal case, even if it was short-lived."

Leah settled on the sofa and pulled her feet up as

she talked. "So, give me the 4-1-1 on Richard." She hoped she wasn't being too forward. They always spoke about her. She was clueless about him personally. She presumed there was no Mrs., since he usually called her at odd times—something he might not do if he had a wife at home. Besides, there was something in his tone. He almost seemed flirtatious at times.

"That's a loaded question. Like what?"

"I assume you're married, and your wife doesn't have a clue of your involvement in the WITSEC Program since it's so secretive. You know, classified, as they say." A little reverse psychology never hurt.

"Well, you assume wrong."

"Which part?"

"Both. I'm not attached, so I've no one to share my grueling experiences with regarding WITSEC, even if I were permitted to talk about it. What else is on your mind?"

"You're leaving yourself wide open," she warned. "How old are you?" Her own boldness surprised her.

"Thirty-eight."

"Nice age."

"Thank you, ma'am," he said teasingly. "I hope you'll think so when you get there."

His sense of humor reminded her of Phillip.

"I'm not that far away," she admitted. "How long have you been with WITSEC?"

"Thirteen years."

"Where were you born?"

"Arkansas. My, you ask a lot of questions. I'm glad my water's boiling for a cup of tea. At this rate, I think I'll need it."

"An avid tea drinker, are you?"

"I drink both coffee and tea."

She heard his teakettle whistle in the background. Richard must've walked closer to turn it off, because it got louder. In her mind's eye, she pictured what he might look like while the sound of clangs and dings reverberated through the phone. He was probably stirring his tea. Was there an app that could dissect a voice adapter and reverse it to its original tone?

"It can't hurt to learn a little about you for a change, so I can attach a personality to you, even if I can't put a face on you."

"And you have a specific need to do that?" His voice was gentle, inquiring.

"Actually, yes. You know everything about me, or I would assume so. And I have no clue what you look like." She tightened the belt at her waist. "You might have green hair for all I know."

Richard laughed. "I can assure you I don't have green hair."

"Will I ever get a chance to meet you in person, buy you a cup of coffee—or tea—and thank you for all you've done for me?" She hoped his answer was yes.

"Only if you are in imminent danger, which would necessitate my meeting you, or after the case is resolved."

The case. She was only a case to him. The thought hurt but she brushed it off.

"How's the job?"

"Good. I'm enjoying it even though I hit a few road blocks at times."

"How's that?"

"Oh, silly stuff. Like when people ask me about my personal life, that sort of thing. I'm never sure how to respond."

But it was more than that. Phillip asked her a question yesterday that threw her into turmoil. It shouldn't have surprised her, since anytime the aviator was nearby, he had a way of doing that. She cringed as she replayed the conversations she'd tried to avoid with him. If only she had a good friend to talk with about everything she was going through. But that wasn't an option. She had no one to confide in except Richard.

She stretched out on the sofa, got comfy, and soon her words began to flow.

9

Phillip carried his tea into the family room and placed it on the coffee table in front of him. He truly ached for Leah and what she must be working through. It was obviously difficult. If it were up to him, he'd walk down the street, knock on her door, and wrap his arms around her and make her forget everything. But that wasn't about to happen.

"I'm sorry for sounding out of sorts. I need an attitude adjustment." Leah's words brought his mind back to the present.

He laughed. "No, you're all right. I do feel badly for you. I wish there was something I could do."

"You're a good listener."

"Thanks. Try me out. What happened at work to ruffle your feathers?"

"Nothing in particular and everything in general. Do I appear confused? Sometimes people ask me where I'm from, and I tell them I'm from Toledo. I've never even been to Toledo. I've become a perpetual liar. That's not like me."

"Shall we get you a ticket to Toledo to force some honesty out of you?" He smiled at the thought. Maybe he'd scarf up the arrangements. He could fly her there himself…

"No," she answered with a light laugh. "That's not necessary. But I'm living so guarded. I have to think twice before I say a word. Yesterday, for example, my boss and I were talking about flavors for a cake for an open house that he recruited me to coordinate, and it led to a conversation that almost got me in trouble."

"Oh?" Phillip's ears perked up. He remembered the dialogue. She'd come into his office requesting his opinion. When he asked what flavor her favorite birthday cake was, she looked flustered. He regretted bringing up something that caused her discomfort. Yet inwardly he adored the spark of determination he sensed. Plus, he learned that she loved white chocolate with raspberries.

"He asked me when my birthday was."

"And this is a problem for you?"

"I didn't remember the new birthdate I'd been given on my identification."

He hoped his laugh would put her at ease. At least her attitude was playful, even though she was frustrated most of the time. The only way to help her now was to talk with her.

"I hope you found a way to get out of that one."

"It took me a minute, but, yes. I evaded the subject."

"Good move. Did he notice?"

"I'm not sure. If he did, he didn't bring it up again. He's pretty observant though."

"How so?" He shouldn't continue to press her, but he wanted her to keep talking.

"He's so in control of who he is and where he's going. Sometimes it's as if he can see straight through me."

Phillip dropped his forehead into his hands. Was he that obvious?

"Richard?"

"So, you think he sees through your façade?"

"At times, yes."

"I'm sure it's your imagination, especially given the situation. Do you get that impression from others?"

"No."

"What does he do to give you that idea?"

The other end of the line was silent except for a deep sigh. Finally, she spoke. "He's got the greatest eyes, and I think I'm vulnerable around him. I suppose that's part of what throws me off."

Phillip lifted his eyebrows with a guilty sense of satisfaction. He was on dangerous ground. He should stop. "And the other part?"

"The man is terribly handsome. And he's completely out of my league."

Phillip took another sip of tea. "How so?"

"He just is. Unbelievable...why am I telling you this?"

"Because I'm here, and I'm the only one you're free to talk with."

"Poor you. You're getting an earful. I'll try to spare you in the future."

He hoped she wouldn't. "That's quite all right. I'm glad you're able to confide in me. You definitely need to talk to someone, although, I must admit, I'm a little disappointed."

"Why?"

"Sounds like you're drawn to him more than you are to me."

Leah's quiet laugh warmed him. "You accuse me of that although I've never met you?"

"Maybe someday we can meet, after this is all over. But for now, you'd better take your chances with you-know-who while you can."

"Oh, no." This time Leah's laugh sounded self-conscious. "I'm making no moves in his direction. It is strictly professional. You caught me shy of my thirty-thousand words for the day. I'll shut my mouth now."

"I enjoy listening to you talk."

"You mean ramble?"

"I wouldn't say that, but if you'd call it that, it's kind of a cute ramble. If you're anything like this in person, I'll bet the guy has his eyes on you, too."

"I highly doubt that. From the teeny bit I've learned, he's Mr. Eligible, and most everyone knows only that much about him. I gather he stays to himself."

Phillip reached for his cup again. So that's what people thought of him? "If things don't work out between you two, and your case gets solved, don't forget about me."

"I'll keep that in mind."

"So, what kind of cake did you choose that hurled you into your big dilemma."

"White chocolate with macadamia nuts and raspberry filling."

"Wow. Going all out, are we?"

"He said to go for it."

"Sounds like a good choice." He couldn't wait to taste it.

"He's stuck with it now whether he likes it or not."

"He'd be a fool not to love you. I mean love it—he'd be a fool not to love it."

"Thanks for the clarification."

Hopefully, she didn't get the wrong idea. He almost blew it. He needed to end this exchange before he said something irreversible. "Sorry."

"You're incorrigible, Richard. I can say anything to you with no strings attached. I appreciate the times you call."

A heavy cloud settled over him.

If she were a perpetual liar, what did this turn of conversation make him?

"Thanks, Leah. It's always good to talk with you. But I need to let you go now. I'll call you again soon, OK?"

"I'll look forward to it."

Phillip breathed out a good-bye, hung up the phone, then tossed it onto the sofa. But the deceit still lingered in the air.

He stared at his ringless finger for a long time, while the tea in front of him turned cold.

~*~

Voices echoed from the other room as the heat sweltered around Crystal. The walls of the apartment she was being held in were thinner than they must have realized, or maybe her senses were on high alert. Her cheekbone ached, and when she touched it, the swelling magnified the pain. Her ears rang, but the noise did nothing to prevent her from hearing more than she cared to.

The one gentleman, the elderly one, was attractive—distinguished even. It never ceased to amaze her that criminals readily infiltrated any status of life. Low-lifers weren't the only ones who dabbled in crime. Crystal had no doubt that he would cover his tracks without blinking an eye. Panic rose in her throat, and with it, the taste of bile.

His sidekick was younger. Scordino was a yes-man whose mission in life was to please the elder. But the way he watched her was disturbing. She feared what he might do, and she sensed her margin of time narrowing. He deserved the scars she'd given him yesterday that earned her the confinement.

The two men came and went several times in the last few days. While they were gone, she was left in the hands of another guy they referred to as Sam. She tried talking with Sam, hoping to form a little camaraderie and maybe eventually attempt to negotiate with him. She sensed he was the weakest of the three. Yet all she got was a harrumph when she tried to ease into a conversation.

She brought her wrists to her teeth to pull on the tape that secured her. The more she heard from the other room, the more aggressively she tugged at the adhesive. She didn't catch what, but something was planned for later today. Her skin felt raw where her teeth had tried to slip under the tape. But the tape was tough. She must get the rip started. As soon as her hands were free, her feet would follow. She formulated a plan, but whether it was good or not, time would tell. It was her best attempt while being oblivious to her surroundings.

A door shut and it was clear to her the distinguished man and his sidekick left. Once again, she was alone with Sam, whose apartment she was apparently in. She continued to gnaw at the tape and determined it was time to ask for a restroom break. Perhaps she'd squeeze a sliver of trust out of him. He appeared to be her only hope.

Her options were quickly running out.

10

Leah returned from lunch on Friday to find a bright-eyed girl staring at her from the hangar lobby. The tip of her crayon held fast to the page she was coloring, yet her emerald eyes remained fixed on Leah's.

"Well, hello there." Leah smiled at her in surprise. The girl's dark hair framed her face with a few ringlets that touched her cheeks. Apart from the child and Marci, the office was vacant.

"Hello," the girl responded politely while she lowered her head in sudden shyness.

"So, who is this little one?" Leah asked Marci as she walked behind the counter.

"You haven't met Jessica? Sally and Joe left for an emergency. Dropped her off for the rest of the day."

"Who are Sally and Joe?" Leah slid her purse into the cabinet.

"The nanny and her husband."

Leah tilted her head and tried to process the information. "I don't understand."

"They take care of Phillip's daughter," Marci clarified. "You weren't aware he had a child?"

"No. No one ever mentioned it." She realized once again how little she knew of the man she'd reprimanded herself over on a daily basis. It disturbed her that she'd given him the slightest thought, since he was not only way out of her league but also had a daughter. Plus, he was probably tied up in a nasty divorce dispute, considering his bare ring finger.

"When Daria was killed, Phillip was devastated," Marci whispered even though Jess had already gone back to her coloring. "She looks like Daria, but she has her father's eyes. Isn't she a cutie?"

Leah bit her lip, moved by the child who sat quietly, intently coloring the pages before her. That explained a whole lot.

"I had no idea. How long has it been?"

"It happened when she was a baby."

"That must've been dreadful for her—and for Phillip of course."

"It was unimaginable."

"He's raising her alone?"

"Yes, with the help of Sally and Joe. They live in his guesthouse and are like family to him and Jess. They've been a godsend, especially with his parents gone. Phillip's father was killed in the line of duty, and his mother died shortly after. It happened a long time ago. His mother was never quite the same after his dad died."

"That's so sad."

"I know."

The child scooted off the sofa in the lobby and walked toward Marci. "May I have a drink, please?"

"Sure you can, Jess," Marci answered. "Be right back. Why don't you show Leah what you're coloring?"

Leah nearly melted when Jess looked up at her with excitement as she lifted a page to show her. Evidently, this was the icebreaker she needed. "It's an airplane!" Jess shrugged her shoulders and squealed. "My daddy flies this."

"How beautiful is that?" Leah's heart warmed as

she observed Jess. "Your daddy must be very proud of you if you can draw like that."

Jess raised her small fist to her mouth as if it were a best-kept secret. "He tells me that sometimes."

"How old are you?"

"Three," she blurted out, lifting three fingers. "And a half."

"You want to sit up here?"

"OK."

Leah scooped her up and set her on the countertop.

"You two are getting along good," Marci said as she returned with a sippy cup of juice. "Maybe I'll take my chances and head to lunch if it's OK with you."

"Go ahead. I'll be happy to watch her."

"Charles is down in the garage for a meeting with the mechanics. Tom will be back before long. He's out on the tarmac checking the mileage on a couple of the planes."

"Great. Enjoy your lunch. We'll be fine," Leah assured Marci.

She turned her attention to the child after Marci left. "So what are some things you enjoy doing?"

"You mean now or when I'm at home?" Jess asked as her feet dangled over the counter and bumped into the cabinet door.

"Either."

"I like Veggie Tales, and I like my tricycle. And Dora the Explorer. But Sally only lets me ride in back."

Leah gave her a questioning glance.

"She says she has to watch me so I don't have an axe-dint."

"Oh. Well, I'd say that's very wise of Sally, isn't it?"

"Uh-hum."

"What else do you like to do?"

"I like ballet. I go to school for that. And I like to color. Want me to color something?" Her eyes lit up.

"Sure." The child's enthusiasm caused a grin to stretch across Leah's face.

"I need some more paper."

Leah reached for a plain sheet of paper and picked up a crayon that lay on the floor. Within minutes, Jess handed her an indiscernible drawing.

"That is beautiful."

"You think so? Really?"

"Yes, it is. You're the best three-year-old artist I've met."

"Three and a half," Jess informed her.

"Three and a half," Leah corrected in a serious tone.

Jessica's eyes lit up as she focused on movement behind Leah's back. "Daddy! Daddy!"

Leah turned to see Phillip push himself from the doorframe he was leaning on. She wondered how long he'd been standing there. He straightened his tie at the neck of his pressed, lavender shirt.

"Hey, babe." He stretched his arms when he reached the counter and enveloped his daughter in a big hug. Leah stepped to the side, warmed by the obvious bond between them. A lump formed in her throat as Phillip winked a hello to her while Jess clung to his neck.

"You've met Leah." Phillip drew Jess back, his eyebrows raised in question.

"She's nice," the child answered.

"She's adorable." Leah forced herself to smile at her boss, although her discomfort was growing in his presence.

"Thank you." His gaze was fixed on Leah even as the energetic bundle waved a paper in front of him. The space between them was stifling, causing Leah to shift her attention to the bright eyes that danced before them.

"Daddy, look what I drew."

Leah relaxed now that his focus was back on the one who bore his resemblance.

"That's a lovely picture. What is it?" He glanced sidelong at Leah with his lips parted. It appeared the drawing was indiscernible to him as well.

Jess's lip scrunched. "Daddy...it's Leah."

His eyes went wide, and his grin turned into a playful smile as he glanced at Leah and compared her with the piece of art. "Why, of course it is. It's a perfect replica. Isn't it, Leah?"

"It sure is. Thank you, Jessica."

"Look at her shoes Daddy."

Phillip's eyes moved to the scribbles at the end of the abstract figure that Jess pointed out. "They look just like hers, don't they? 'Cept I didn't have that color."

Phillip's eyes dropped to the feet beside him and then back to his daughter. "I think they're perfect." He drew Jess into his arms for a hug as his gaze met Leah's. "It's time we let Leah alone, babe. We don't want her to grow weary of us."

To Leah it seemed an impossibility.

"Thanks for covering for me. I owe you." Phillip turned to leave.

"It was no trouble." Leah leaned back against the counter as they walked down the hall. A pleasure like that could never be considered a debt.

11

"Wow," Marci and Leah exclaimed in unison as they stepped from their dressing room stalls and glanced at one another. The open house was a week away, and they were determined to find the perfect dress at Salmon Run Mall. They laughed at their reaction to each another.

"That purple is fantastic on you," Leah announced.

"Think so?" Marci glanced sideways into the mirror for a better view.

"Absolutely. It's perfect. Really."

"Thanks. I like it, too."

"You should get it."

Marci turned to focus her attention on Leah. "Now that is great dress."

Leah examined herself in the mirror as she pulled, tucked, and smoothed the soft, black fabric at her fingertips.

"I'm not sure. Maybe it's a little too black."

"How can anything be too black? It's perfect."

She wrinkled her nose and did a three-sixty as she scrutinized herself from all angles. "Does it make my butt look fat?"

"You're kidding. I wish I'd be able to wear something like that. You'll turn Phillip's head for sure. Not that you haven't done so every day of the week since you started."

"What does Phillip have to do with this

conversation?" Leah turned her head to hide the heat from her face.

"Oh, please. It's obvious the way he looks at you. Even Tom and Charles have noticed it, and you know how dense they are at times."

"I hardly think so," Leah argued.

"You don't think they can be dense?"

"No, silly. I don't think there's anything to what you're saying."

"Where have you been?" Marci challenged. "Phillip's eyes haven't sparkled like that since before Daria was killed."

Leah slipped back to the safety of the dressing room.

"Why do you always avoid any conversation having to do with him?" Marci questioned through the thin walls that separated them while they changed clothes.

"Because he's so far out of my league. Goodness' sake, I'm a *peon* in his sight."

"If that's true, he must prefer peons. Jess loved you, too."

"She's an angel, isn't she?"

Leah finished dressing and joined Marci in the aisle. "So, are you getting it?"

"I will if you will," Leah dared, despite her reservations.

"Deal. Let's go before we change our minds."

They went to the counter together to make their purchases. For the next hour, they sauntered through the mall, the pressure of finding the dress off their plate. "Mind if I hit the bookstore?" Leah asked as Marci perused the shoes on a clearance rack.

"Not at all. I'll be there in about fifteen minutes."

"Good deal." Leah walked the other way and stepped into the familiar chain, not searching for anything in particular. She browsed the bargain tables and eventually ended up near the magazines and periodicals. A section of wall was shelved with newspapers from around the country. Most were already a week old.

A thought crossed Leah's mind as she scanned the shelves. Surfing her usual social media sites as herself was off limits, and she purposely tried to avoid specific Internet searches on her electronic devices. Besides, AJ had worked hard to shut the back door in cyberspace. Where was the harm in reading an old-fashioned newspaper? With no cookies to delete, she remained untraceable. A quick glance around her confirmed no one was nearby. She reached for the *Miami Herald* from the bottom rack and hurried to the checkout counter, paid for her purchase, and tucked the bag under her arm.

Minutes later, Marci caught up with her. The two headed to the parking lot and went their separate ways.

At home, Leah hung the black dress in her closet and put on a fresh pot of decaf. More importantly, she pulled the newspaper from the bag and felt an immediate connection. News from her hometown brought tears to her eyes. Advertisements for area restaurants she'd patronized flooded her with memories of times past. Her favorite housewares store boasted a coupon, urging consumers to check out their new selections. She ran her finger across the ad, hoping the small gesture would ease the intense longing inside. But it wouldn't be so. It only made her long for home even more.

The coffeemaker gurgled to announce the brew was ready. The sounds comforted her. She poured a cup, tossed in cream and a spoonful of honey, and sat back down to take in the news of her hometown.

She flipped to the local section where a photo and corresponding article suddenly pulled her in. Her heart began to race. Slowly, she put the cup down and glanced at the front door to be sure it was latched. The article was off limits. She knew it. Wrapping herself up in news of the past would do her no good. But wasn't the back door shut?

The forbidden read drew her in further, and soon, she was consumed.

~*~

Phillip tucked Jess into bed. She was worn out from the day's activities and was half asleep already. "Sleep tight, babe," he whispered to her. He brushed a kiss on her forehead and fingered her hair. What a princess. Despite the fact that she was without a mother, Jess adjusted. Yet he still grieved.

He slipped from the room as the phone vibrated at his belt and glanced at the display. Leah. He opened the voice adapter app and answered the call.

"This is Richard."

"I'm sorry to bother you. It's Leah. Got a minute?"

"Sure. What's up?"

"I'm so frustrated." She sounded shaken.

"Why's that?" He walked over to the window and peered out the blinds. The small brick home was a stone's throw away. Her blinds were closed, but the lights were on. Hers was the only car in the drive.

"Before you get angry with me, hear me out. I got

my hands on a *Miami Herald* at a bookstore in the mall. I couldn't resist. There was an article about the case and a picture of me."

Phillip tried to sound nonchalant, imagining what she must have read. "First of all, I'd never get angry with you. But you do know that it's better for you to stay away from things like that, right?"

"Yes. But it's pretty hard sometimes. It's been months since I've been on social media, and I need a little interaction. Some word from home."

He detected her conscious effort to hide the tears.

"I think I've made the biggest mistake of my life, Richard. I want my life back. If you talk to AJ, you can tell him that. I mean it. Tell him to come get me."

Phillip pitied her. What could he say to offer her the comfort she deserved? At times, she seemed so confident and poised. But other times, he suspected she was crying inside, alone and insecure about the decisions she'd made that affected the rest of her life. Her struggle was real. He longed to gather her in his arms, to tell her all would be well. If only he could assure her the agency was doing everything possible to locate the scoundrels that threatened her safety. How badly he wanted to tell her there was someone else searching for her, too. Unfortunately, Crystal was still missing. When he talked with AJ yesterday, things were at a standstill.

His shoulders drooped, realizing how complicated things had become.

He longed for her in many ways but forced the thoughts away.

"I'm sorry," Leah said, her voice shaky. "You have plenty to do without me complaining to you about things."

"I have nothing to do right now that is more pressing." Phillip pulled out his desk chair and propped his feet on the windowsill as he peered out again. His gaze was intent on the sliver of light that escaped her window. "It's easy to doubt, but let me assure you this is perfectly normal. Tell me, what did the article say?"

"It wasn't anything extraordinary. But it was such a vivid reminder of who I had been to who I am now. It appears that people from my church put out a missing persons report right after I left. I hate thinking I put them through all that."

"They'd certainly understand if they knew the reason behind it."

"I know. The article reiterated the case and showed my photo. Said if anyone had seen me or heard from me, they were to report it to the police."

"A reasonable request. Anything else?"

"A few people reported spotting me. The photo was captioned "Kari Sightings," but with no apparent validity since I'm still missing."

"People say all kinds of things, don't they?" Phillip tried to make light of it. "Elvis is seen at least once a week. He must've discovered the fountain of youth, since he apparently hasn't aged since the seventies." He detected a hint of a laugh. "But seriously, you can do something while you're waiting for things to come together."

"What?"

"Did you find a church yet?"

"I visited Community Fellowship a few times. I like it."

"Then get involved. Get plugged in. You need a good support group."

"But that's the problem. Put yourself in my shoes. How can I fit in at church, of all places, when the life I'm living is a lie? I'm the worst of all hypocrites. My foundation is a farce."

"I understand what you mean. This is not the life you've chosen, but you can choose to completely trust in the Lord to work all things together for your good even when things are in disarray. Remember, you're in a situation that's temporary. It's subject to change."

She remained quiet on the other end.

"Look at it like this. We live in a world where lawlessness runs rampant. Sometimes God uses people to expose and right the evil around us. Although you're finding yourself in the middle of this situation, consider it a privilege to be part of His solution to a very real problem. He has a plan and a purpose for you—as well as the entire network of people and circumstances that surround you—even now as Leah. It's clear you doubt your decision to be in the program, but no matter what choice you've made as Leah or as Karina—even if it was a wrong one, which it wasn't— you still remain in His hand of protection. There's a hope for your future. That's just fact."

He heard her stifle a sob. "I don't belong anymore. To anyone...not even myself."

"You're a vessel of honor, a special treasure, Leah, fit for the Master's purpose. Isn't that the main reason we're here, to be used by Him however possible? Right now, you're seeing through a glass darkly. Everything is muddled and obscure for you. But I'm confident that it won't be long before you find clarity in your life and see beyond the darkened glass."

He wished he was closer to her to wipe her tears away. He hated not being able to comfort her the way she needed to be comforted. The way she deserved to be comforted.

After a moment, she answered. "I read that this morning."

"You're also aware circumstances can change in a moment, right?"

"As long as I didn't mess things up too much."

"You did not. But let's say you did. You need to remember that God takes you right where you are, weaknesses and all, in whatever situation you find yourself. More importantly, He will turn it into something beautiful—something good."

"You think so, huh?"

"Without a doubt."

She sighed again and took a deep, raspy breath.

"You OK?"

"I'll be fine." Strength was returning to her voice. "Thank you, Richard. It means a lot to me."

"Get some rest."

"You, too."

After they said good-bye, Phillip laid the phone down, but he couldn't get his mind off her. He'd do almost anything to reach out to her in a more tangible way.

He peered through the blinds again. Her light was out. It wasn't what he wanted, but at least for now, she was safe.

12

The sounds of the night were all about her as Crystal trudged along the marshy terrain. Strands of hair were matted together around her face, held in place by the mud she awakened to this morning. Her hand tingled as she reached for her cheekbone. The pain in her face seared through her, and she wondered what happened to her in the days since they'd taken her away.

She squeezed her eyes shut and tried to remember. Some of it came easily; some of it was sketchy, and some memories did not come at all. What was she missing?

There was someone named Scordino. She remembered the look in his eyes. But who was he, and how had she met him? What setting had she seen him in?

Another face came to her memory. Someone they called Mary-something. What did they want with her? And who on earth were *they*? Nothing made sense. She looked down at her hands and a fight came to her recollection. In a bathroom. The diamond on her finger glistened in the moonlight. Evidently it wasn't a robbery. What did they want from her? And where was her gun? She always carried one with her when she was on duty. But why the street clothes if she was on duty? Or was she undercover?

Michael. She must reach Michael. He had to be terribly worried. Where was he?

And more importantly, where was she?

Mosquitoes swarmed as she willed her feet to take one step at a time toward the light in the distance. She needed to find a phone. What happened to her cell phone? Michael was surely trying to call her. She probably dropped it. A few more steps, and she would rest for the night.

Fog settled in, wrapping itself around her like a constricting blanket, stifling her with incredible loneliness. Something croaked afar off, beginning a chorus of mating calls that sent chills down her spine. It sounded like a series of alligator growls she'd read about once.

Oh, God, help me get through this place of death.

The fear was all-consuming and made her stomach churn. She wretched and only dry heaves came. How long had it been since she'd eaten?

The calls that echoed gave her the incentive she needed to keep moving into the darkness, one painful step at a time.

13

Phillip was pleased as the open house unfolded. A continual flow of guests signed in and mingled with the instructors and employees of the hangar. From a distance, he saw Leah, who appeared to be in conversation with a client. He tried countless times to cross the room, only to be detained as friends and clients were eager for a few words with him.

The hangar quickly took on the atmosphere of elegance as fresh bouquets of flowers and tall candles graced the linen-covered tables which were surrounded by a tempting array of delicacies. Silver platters boasted a spread fit for a king. There were definitely no pre-packaged-looking-smidgens around here. Soft music added to the mood, creating all the more desire for Phillip to approach Leah.

"Phillip, meet my daughter, Terri." One of Phillip's distinguished clients reached out to stop him as he narrowed the distance to where Leah stood. "Terri is my youngest—the flight attendant I told you about."

The leggy brunette offered her hand. Minding his manners, Phillip shook it but gave the top of her hand a gentle pat as he continued on his way. "Pleasure. And great to see you, Earl. Thanks for coming."

Phillip scanned the room. Leah's back was toward him as she stood near the beverage table. She was alone.

"Leah," he whispered as he approached her from

behind and touched her elbow. She did a quick turnabout.

"Hey. I was just catching my breath." Her warm eyes drew him in.

The rush to get to her was over, and the sound of the crowd fell into the background. "This is incredible. You've done a splendid job." He eased his fingers from her arm.

"Thank you."

"I've been trying to get over here and talk with you for the past forty minutes. I keep getting detained."

"Well, you are the reason everyone showed up, Mr. Z."

He grinned at her playful reprimand, taking in the black dress and her honey-blonde hair that was swept up in an elegant chignon. She was breathtaking and she exuded confidence that was undeniable. The woman was definitely in her element. He tried not to be too obvious with his reaction to her, but he was certain his attempt failed. From across the room she was exquisite, but to be this close to her was far more than that.

"Can I get you something to drink?" Leah asked.

"Sounds great." He didn't take his eyes off her as she moved closer to the beverage table and ladled out some Frappuccino cooler for each of them.

"It's decaf." A twinkle shone in her eyes as she offered him a cup.

"Perfect." He gazed about the room. "You thought of everything, didn't you?"

"I hope so. If not, everyone is being really polite by not mentioning it. Did you get something to eat yet?"

"I was waiting for Jess. Sally and Joe will be

coming with her shortly. I did sneak some pistachio shrimp. It was wonderful."

"I'm glad you like it." Leah took a sip of her drink. A wisp of hair pulled loose and brushed her face. "Tom, Charles, and the mechanics did a great job on the exhibits. Have you checked them out?"

"I haven't." Phillip tilted his head in her direction. "Care to give me a tour?"

"I'd love to."

They moved through the lobby and weaved in and out as they greeted people en route. The breeze was refreshing as they stepped outside.

The mechanic's exhibit showed a small-scale, three-dimensional diagram of a private plane as well as an internal illustration of the mechanical components. Technical information was displayed on easels. Two mechanics were there, engaged in conversation with what he guessed was a mechanic wannabe.

Several airplanes were on the tarmac to view. Display boards explained a bit of their history. An instructor sat at a table passing out brochures, chatting with a couple of young men. Clients, beckoned by a teaser sign at the table, dropped their names in glittered boxes hoping to win a free hour of flight time.

After checking out the displays, they moved further onto the tarmac. Phillip was thrilled to get away from the activity of the hangar. "Did you get a chance to see the new Piper?"

"No. Which one is it?"

"It's right over there." He lifted a finger from his cup to point it out. He pushed his other hand into the pocket of his trousers, and they walked toward it.

"Sweet!" Leah exclaimed when they got to the airplane.

"It flies great. It's very comfortable inside, too." He opened the door.

"Looks like it." She peered in to get a glimpse of the interior.

"Go on in. Sit down."

Leah's gaze fell to her dress and shoes. "I don't know that I can...in this."

"Sure you can." He took her cup and set it on the wing with his. "Nice choice, by the way. You...are...breathtaking."

Her eyes met his for a moment. "Thank you."

"I'll help you up." Giving her no chance to debate, he lifted her to where she could easily climb inside. "That wasn't so difficult, was it?" He hoisted himself up on the pilot's side.

"I suppose not. You're right. This is very nice. Smells like a new plane."

"It's only a year old. The previous owner defaulted, so I got a pretty sweet deal."

Leah scanned the instrument panel.

"You're still due for a ride, aren't you?"

"That's not necessary."

"We'll have to remedy that one of these days." He ignored her response. "Where would you like to go?"

Leah tugged at the hem of her fitted dress. "Really, you don't have to take me anywhere."

"I know that, silly girl," he said. "But I want to." He turned to her and his thoughts took a turn. He felt the professional barrier shift as her dark eyes captured a ray of the lowering sunset that escaped the cover of a cloud. "Besides, it's one way I can thank you for all you did to make tonight a success."

She glanced at him with a pleased expression and focused her attention to a commuter jet that thundered off in the distance. His eyes held her profile.

"Either that jet really intrigues you, or I've made you uncomfortable," he whispered the words he was thinking before he realized it.

Her lips twisted, but she said nothing.

Before he could stop himself, he reached up and touched her cheek with the back of his forefinger, following it from her ear to her chin. He urged her to face him.

Her confidence, evident earlier, dwindled as her eyes finally met his.

He cupped her cheek lightly as a stray wisp of her hair brushed against his finger. She was so delicate, like a precious petal of life that bruised easily with mishandling. She smelled like flowers, rain, and spices, all pooled into one exotic scent. Reluctantly, he withdrew his hand.

He clenched his jaw. He'd stepped over the line. She made it nearly impossible not to. Silently, he reprimanded himself. "We should go."

"Yes." Leah's voice was barely audible. "People will be expecting to see you. You are the guest of honor, you know." How tactfully she steered the subject to the occasion at hand.

Phillip stepped down from his side of the plane and walked to the passenger side. He reached up and guided her down, lowering her gently until her feet touched the tarmac. Her dress felt soft and smooth under his fingers.

"I'm sorry if I offended you." He forced himself to release her. "You…make things difficult for me," he whispered.

He breathed in her scent while the battle raged inside.

"You didn't offend me."

Quietly he nodded and extended his hand toward the light of the hangar.

The battle was his and his alone. Somehow in the course of the night he'd inched his way to the front lines.

His professional barrier had slipped. It would only be a matter of time before it crumbled, completely out of his control.

And when it did, would his heart survive beneath all the rubble?

14

The early morning sun crept through the blinds in Leah's room, splashing narrow strips of brightness on the wall. Her hand instinctively went to her forehead as the memory of last night lingered.

The open house was a success in every way. She could still feel the warmth of his hand as he held her chin. She closed her eyes as the memories washed over her including the reserve he couldn't hide. He'd apologized to her before they made it back to the safety of the hangar.

She was drawn to him. Way too drawn to him.

They returned to the party, careful to mingle with others as though nothing happened.

But it did happen. The attraction wasn't just a figment of her imagination like she'd been telling herself for nearly two months. He'd made an advance toward her and his touch had been far better than she even dreamed. There must be someone to talk to about her feelings. But who? Definitely not anyone at work or at church. The WITSEC Program made things impossible for her. The only one to confide in was Richard. And she didn't dare talk to him about this. She must resolve it herself.

It shouldn't be this hard. How many times had she dealt with people who fought life threatening situations? She could perform a tracheotomy, remove bullets from within the body, and restart a heart. But working out this relational dilemma didn't compare.

Nurse's training hadn't taught her a thing about concealing her emotions and suppressing her growing love for the one she was in the process of deceiving.

No, she wasn't dealing with anything physical at all. Instead, she was tampering with a man's heart—a man who'd already gone through more pain than was reasonable to bear in a lifetime. Every single day he dealt with the agony of his loss. His advance was an act of courage after everything he'd been through. It was probably his first attempt toward anyone since the death of his wife.

For Phillip to give her the slightest thought was a compliment beyond Leah's comprehension. And her attraction to him was as real as the sun that rose each morning.

But Phillip was clueless that he'd made a courageous advance to a façade.

She wasn't being fair to him. Nor to herself.

How on earth would she ever repair all the damage?

15

AJ walked into his office Monday morning, leaving the door slightly ajar as he carried a fresh cup of coffee in his hand. Mondays were usually a zoo, and today was no exception. He had left a voicemail for Phillip and eagerly awaited the return call as the shadow of fellow agents came and went through the crack in the door. The moment the phone rang, he grabbed the receiver, enthusiasm difficult to hide.

"I've got new information. We may be nearing the bottom of this."

"Great. How so?" Phillip asked.

"Crystal's been found. She's been admitted to a small, private hospital."

"That's wonderful."

"Michael is breathing a sigh of relief, but there are still a lot of complications. The word is that yesterday she wandered into a gas station halfway between Ft. Lauderdale and Miami, east of the Everglades. She has a form of amnesia and can only remember bits and pieces. Her long-term memory is intact, though. It's like a three-dimensional puzzle to try and put the clues together. Things are pretty vague right now, but the prognosis is good according to the specialist. They're hoping she'll regain full memory within the next week or two. Maybe sooner. When she does, I'm confident the information will be beneficial."

"Was she hurt badly?"

"Nothing she can't heal from. She's got a swollen

face and a black eye. She also has a concussion among a few other things, and it appears she was drugged. It doesn't look like she was raped, but she's still being checked out, so we'll see. She got some nasty scrapes trampling through the Everglades. They're doing a series of tests on her."

"It must be terribly hard on Michael, but I'm sure he's ecstatic she's alive."

"Most definitely. He laughed for the first time today. He's a really great guy. You can tell he loves his wife deeply."

"So what are the facts?"

"She was picked up by two men. The names that keep coming up are Mary-something, which she refers to in the masculine sense, and someone named Scordino. She's lost all recollection of where she was kept or what happened from there, so it's very sketchy. We can't figure out her method of escape, but it's obvious she wasn't released voluntarily. There are still so many blanks to fill in. It might be a while, but it's a good start."

"What have you told Michael about Karina?"

"Nothing more than what we first disclosed to him. He has no idea where your witness is hiding. But I assured him you were taking good care of her."

Phillip's agreement was barely audible.

AJ was puzzled at his hesitation. "You are watching her closely, aren't you?" There'd never been any reason to doubt Phillip. He wasn't sure why he detected something now.

"I am. She's fine."

"Great. How is she taking to her new life?"

"She's adjusting."

"What's she doing for work?"

"Probably a question you shouldn't ask," Phillip warned.

AJ's brow furrowed. "What's going on, man?"

AJ heard the sigh.

Finally, Phillip spoke. "When I gave her a list of job options, well, I sort of threw in something at the hangar."

"The hangar, as in *your* hangar?"

"Yeah."

"And that's the very job she chose?"

"Affirmative."

"So, you see her daily?"

"Daily."

"And she doesn't have a clue?"

"Not the slightest."

AJ chuckled. "You've gotten yourself in a little deep there, haven't you, bud? You're protecting someone who thinks you're someone else, while at the same time she's pretending to be someone she's not. You're playing the role of two people. What a tangled web we weave."

"Not an easy thing to do."

After all the years AJ had known Phillip as co-worker and friend, he was convinced there was something Phillip wasn't saying. "Are you all right with that? We can take you off the case if you're in too deep."

"I'm fine with it."

"If you say so. Keep me posted if you change your mind." AJ wasn't about to push. "Once Crystal's out of the woods and her memory is restored, we'll debrief her fully. They can return to Dallas. Michael assured me they'll lay low with future attempts to locate Kari until they're cleared to do so. He has no desire to hamper our investigation. He's obviously well aware of the danger involved and wants to keep Crystal protected. She's quite eager to make contact with her twin and will do whatever is needed after she's back in shape."

"And what about her mother?" Phillip asked.

"We've agreed to her knowledge as long as she agrees to the same terms as Crystal and Michael. These are uncharted waters. It's an odd case."

A tap on the door announced the arrival of a messenger needing a signature.

"It sure is," Phillip agreed. "But one thing is certain. This is a good out-of-the-way place for her to be. At least for now. You should come and visit when this is over."

AJ scanned the document and scrawled his name and returned it to the messenger. "It's been a while since I've been to Lowville. That might be nice."

"I'd love if you'd visit."

AJ considered the offer as the door latched shut. He took a swallow of the now lukewarm coffee in front of him. He was eager for Crystal to regain her memory. If only there was some way to push her so time wouldn't slip away from them too quickly. The doctor's prognosis was good. Perhaps the God that Phillip prayed to really did hear his request.

Maybe God could speed up Crystal's recollection as well.

~*~

Days had passed since the spunky witness disappeared from their clutches. Scordino knew all along she'd be a difficult one, but especially when she deposited her manicured nail into his face.

But finally, their luck changed with a clue from inside. She certainly moved fast.

He ran his hand along the dark stubble of his chin. Its growth seemed to accelerate with stress. He touched his finger to the two-inch scab beginning to form.

The search program loaded on the screen in front of him. He kept clicking the mouse, growing more frustrated by the moment. He never claimed to be a computer whiz. But orders were orders.

Mariucci gave him one sketchy word to go on that passed through the ears of an informer to Canali, to Mariucci, and now to his own.

Lawville: No word in database.

Louville: Suggestion? Yes. He selected the box. Calixa Lavellee, a Canadian songwriter? No clues there.

Lavelli: Dante Lavelli? Cleveland Browns 1946-1956. Not hardly.

Lively: She was. Had the scratch to prove it.

Lovely: Definitely, but not in the correct context.

Lowville: Lowville, New York.

Hmmm. He lifted his eyebrows in thought. It was the only geographical location so far. Not a lot of information, but it would be a start.

16

Phillip sat in his office trying to go through the audit report Marci gave to him earlier. Concentration eluded him. His office door was shut as it had been for the past hour.

The information about Crystal was a game changer. What if her memory returned before it was too late to make a difference? Cases like hers could take a while from what he understood with limited knowledge of amnesia. Yet the doctor's prognosis was good.

But Leah, well, she was a different story altogether. The open house Saturday night had nearly been too much for him.

He'd actually made an advance toward her.

What was I thinking?

All day today he avoided her, speaking to her only when necessary. Determined he would not let himself slip so easily going forward.

For the most part, Leah seemed pretty laid back about things. But he wasn't ignorant. Confidence and determination were hidden inside, unable to surface because of her circumstances. She would feel devastated, hurt, and betrayed, if or when she discovered who he really was.

He was in over his head.

Glancing out the window he caught the brilliant colors of the sunset. Was it that late already? Tomorrow was another day. He picked up his desk phone to make a quick call to Sally to let her know he was on the way.

~*~

Leah was at the hangar much later than usual on Monday night. What a busy day.

The occasional chatter from the air traffic controllers echoed through the overhead speakers. There were still a few loose ends to clean up. She boxed up the punch fountain and stacked the silver trays nearby. The unused party plates were in a bag, ready to be taken to the car. Marci and Tom both left at five after offering to help finish up, but she declined. She hoped for a chance to talk to Phillip in private. Not that she had the slightest clue what to say.

He'd made himself scarce today. The fact that she was bothered by it puzzled her even more. It was something she should be grateful for, considering her decision to distance herself from him going forward.

A few minutes later, Phillip came out of his office, startling her.

"I didn't expect you to be here so late tonight." His surprise look faded, and his voice was quiet and controlled. He stopped near the counter where she was stacking the last of the party goods. His jacket was on his arm, and his briefcase was in his hand.

"I'll be out of here soon."

"All this needs to get returned, I presume?"

"It does. I'll drop the rental things off in the morning before I come in."

"Can I give you a hand with that?" He reached around her and dropped his jacket and briefcase on the chair beside her.

"Sure, thank you." She was instantly challenged by his close proximity.

She grabbed her keys and a stack of trays while he picked up the large box and followed her out the door. Soon everything was loaded into her car.

When they came in to gather their personal things several minutes later, Phillip reached out and lightly touched her elbow, prompting her to turn around and face him.

"You did a wonderful job Saturday night, Leah." If his proximity challenged her before, his nearness to her now was fatal.

"Thank you."

"Everything about you—what you did—was perfect...is perfect." His eyes never left hers, even as she inwardly questioned his faltering words.

She must talk to him. But where would she begin?

Her ears were drawn to an anxious-sounding voice that crackled through the speakers, interrupting her train of thought. "Did you hear that?"

Phillip's brow furrowed, and he answered her with a silent, affirmative nod. She slipped away from his touch and hurried to the window. Phillip followed her. A commercial airliner careened toward the runway that stretched out before them.

"Large passenger planes never land here unless they've been re-routed in an emergency." Phillip raced back to the counter and snatched a portable radio from its charger. "No landing gears." Phillip repeated the tower jargon as he moved to the door in one fluid motion, holding it open in an unspoken invitation for her to follow.

As they rushed outside, Leah cringed at the view that dominated the skies above the north runway. The

DC-10 approached in obvious distress as the air traffic controller guided it, yet it was clear it was losing control. The static dialogue indicated there were bigger issues than the landing gear.

Within seconds, sparks like off-course firecrackers erupted as it contacted the ground then skidded across the runway on its belly. The thundering reverberation shattered the evening air. A wavy vapor hovered as if it would ignite at any moment. It twisted as it slid, snapping a wing as if it were a brittle twig that it had grown weary of supporting. As if separating the rich from the poor, the plane split in two, dividing first class from coach. The separated fuselage slid to a stop with the noise of the impact blending together in anticipation of an ominous boom.

Popping noises went off in a series of explosions as flames licked the cabins. An exit door opened, and the screams of panicked passengers added to the sound of chaos as they tried to escape the cylinder of death. Leah and Phillip watched from a safe distance nearly one hundred yards away as the airport fire department surrounded the plane, and two rescue ambulances raced to the scene.

The next moments were a blur as mothers who were separated from their children screamed in agony, calling names of those they loved. A person near the back of the plane jumped from a broken window, landing on top of pieces of sizzling twisted metal that had once been part of a wing. An elderly man, unable to jump on his own cried out for the merciful ear of someone to help.

Leah turned to Phillip. "We have to do something. By the time more help arrives, it may be too late."

With that, Leah took off and Phillip bolted at the

same time.

The temperature increased with each step as they ran to the wreckage. Cries of panic intensified as they reached the scene. Phillip steered to one side, and Leah moved to the other. Rescue workers scoured the plane all around them.

A pregnant mother was pinned in her seat. The woman cried out to a toddler who'd been tossed into the aisle like a used toy. Leah's heart melted.

"Brandon!" The woman screamed hysterically. "Brandon—somebody, save him. Please help!" The panic in her eyes sent chills down Leah's spine.

Leah unbuckled the woman's seatbelt and pulled away another loose seat from on top of her. "Do you think you can walk?" Leah shouted to her as confusion surrounded them.

"I don't know," she cried, holding her own swollen belly.

Leah reached down to the limp form and placed him in the arms of the woman. "Hold him." Leah embraced the woman from behind, wrapping her arms underneath her upper torso and dragged her through the aisle and out an exit door with a strength that wasn't her own.

In tandem, she pulled the twosome away from the plane, step-by-step, while she took in the scene around her. One by one, bodies were carried out. Some looked dead, some were alive, and some hung by a thread, halfway between life and death. Smoke hovered in a dark cloud as flames were extinguished. Sirens roared in the background, growing louder as they grew closer to the crash site. The air smelled of bodies, electric energy, and jet fuel, all mixed into one sooty rain that fell onto those who lay along a nearby bank. A news chopper hung low in the sky, and a van came to an abrupt halt a short distance away. A reporter and camera man jumped out, obviously eager to catch the unfolding story.

"Let me have him now," Leah said as she touched the woman's arm when they were far enough away from the wreck. The woman agreed and gave up the limp form. Leah detected the faintest bit of breath. She laid the boy down and ran to a vacant ambulance whose medics worked nearly thirty feet away to lift someone onto a gurney. She searched the van until she found what she needed, stumbled through the rubble unnoticed, and began checking the vitals of the small toddler. She worked diligently, positioning an oxygen mask on his face and administering an IV to his near-lifeless body. The mist and smoke covered her in blackness as the woman waited in silence.

Leah pulled her jacket off and wrapped it around the toddler. Ashes and soot clung to her satin tank as she tried to force life into the child that now lay in her arms. He squirmed, his first sign of movement apart from the shallow breaths he took. Leah breathed a sigh of relief. The child's hand reached for her, and he cried out for comfort. Tiny fingers latched onto the gold chain around her neck that glistened from the smoky embers. The young mother lay back, giving way to shock and exhaustion.

Leah brushed the toddler's cheeks with a kiss and watched the commotion continue to unfold while dusk turned into darkness. Flashes of light danced all around as anxious photographers tried to capture the chaos.

What seemed a lifetime later, Phillip walked toward her. With his necktie pulled loose, his weariness was apparent. The remains of his shirt suffered from trauma as well. He dropped to the ground next to her.

Neighboring emergency crews arrived to pool their efforts. They began to transport the wounded. Leah gave up the child to the medics who'd taken his mother moments before.

"There's nothing more we can do," Phillip finally said as he touched her shoulder. Leah was silent, unmoving, until he stood and offered a hand to help her up. Mechanically, she took it and followed him back to the hangar.

"Wait here. I need to lock up," he told her when they got to the main entrance.

"I left my purse…"

"I'll bring it down."

Leah waited, numb, as she leaned against a cool pillar. The commotion continued in the distance. She didn't even hear Phillip approach when he returned moments later with her purse in hand.

"C'mon." Phillip led her to the parking lot. She walked beside him, saying nothing as the knot in her stomach grew larger with each step.

Was this what her parents had suffered before they took their last breath? Horrible chaos and confusion? Or did they die instantly? She hoped it was the latter. Tonight's reminder was vivid. Their death had only been the start of the events that shaped her life today.

Pain crowded her mind, and tears continued to build. Phillip reached for her and gathered her into his arms. Her shoulders shook with sobs. He drew her into the crook of his neck, and his fingers caressed her smoke-filled hair.

After a few minutes, she relaxed.

"I'm sorry." Her voice was weak, and she realized just how tightly she was clutching the back of his torn shirt. She withdrew and heard a sigh escape his lips.

Their eyes locked as he held onto her forearms. Was a battle going on in his mind, too? Phillip was no doubt thinking about his wife and the pain she suffered during her last moments. Yet he pushed his own grief aside to comfort her. He was an amazing man. Despite her earlier resolve, Leah sensed herself being drawn to him even more.

"C'mon, Leah. It's time to go home."

17

The morning breeze chilled his back as Phillip walked to the edge of the driveway, shirtless in his runabout sweatpants. Mornings were always cool. But his daily routine to get the newspaper invigorated him. It made him long for the bold brew that was almost finished, even though it wasn't as good as hers.

He pulled the *Watertown Daily Times* from the plastic wrapper, grateful that the neighboring town still valued the printed word. He still loved a real newspaper, contrary to the digital world in which he lived. There was something about peeling through the thin crisp sheets that helped him relax before his day was underway.

He glanced at the bungalow, still void of early morning lights and wondered how Leah fared despite the difficulties of the night before.

When he gave in and spilled his tug-of-war to Joe late last evening, he'd gotten a sense of relief. He could confide in Joe, for more reasons than one.

His nanny's husband knew too well about losing someone at a young age. Joe's personal experience made him a comrade when dealing with frustrations of learning to love again while holding tight to the memories of the past.

Phillip told him all about Leah.

Joe listened and understood.

Today was a new day.

When he stepped inside, the warmth of the house

greeted Phillip. He poured a cup of coffee, sat at the breakfast bar, and then unrolled the paper to read the headlines. Last night's crash dominated the front page, and rightly so. Sadly tragic, nothing quite this big had graced Watertown's landscape in a long time. Like a magnet to metal, Phillip's eyes were drawn to a full-color photograph on the bottom half of the page. The candid shot captured Leah holding the young child she'd rescued. Tiny fingers gripped the gold chain at her neck as if it were his last hope in life. The purple jacket she'd wrapped him in stood out against the child's pale skin, and an IV bag lay in the palm of her hand. The photo showed her staring into the distance.

Phillip then saw himself, slightly faded in the background, the photographer's talent capturing the moment. He appeared tired and worn, a true depiction, as his eyes were on Leah. He'd no idea they'd been photographed.

Together.

It was a good shot, one of the best, he reasoned. It accurately reflected the mood of the night. However, the timing was wrong. He must warn her. The last thing Leah needed right now was her face on the front page of a newspaper issue that lay on countless driveways throughout the town, throughout the country, and all over the Internet and social media.

Phillip downed the last of the coffee and then hurried upstairs, the thought of speaking to her again drawing an unexpected catch inside. For weeks, he'd tried to convince himself that his concern for her was purely professional. But deep down, he knew it was more than that.

He couldn't hide his feelings much longer. He'd do his best, but now there were no more guarantees.

18

Leah bit her lip nervously as she anticipated what to say. She hated being put on the spot. The photo of her on the tarmac with Phillip at her side prompted an early morning call from Richard. Although she remembered flashes in the distance, too much chaos had erupted in the darkness around her, so she'd been oblivious to the fact that the photographer had focused his lens on her.

But Richard was right. The candid proof of her presence could easily jeopardize the case should the wrong set of eyes recognize her. She wondered how many people might question the IV bag in her hand. Thinking twice about offering help to the child in need didn't occur to her, nor did she regret doing so even now.

Richard warned her of the persistence of the media. They'd stop at nothing to get an interview with survivors or eyewitnesses eager to share their side of the story. Anything to boost their ratings. If she showed up at work today, she most certainly would be cornered. She didn't need that.

Reluctantly, she phoned the hangar. Since it was still early, she got Phillip's voicemail. The message was ambiguous. There was a personal situation that required her attention. She left her call-back number out of habit, fearful he would use it.

With little to do except stay out of the limelight, she spent the morning cleaning the house. That accomplished, she reached for a cherished cookbook her mother had given her, hoping to find something sweet to tempt her palette. Her fingers rested on a well-worn page where a jute marker was nestled into the spine of the book. Paper beads dangled from both ends, and stirred memories of the past as she thought about the Haitian women and children she'd grown to love who had carefully hand-rolled the colorful beads from recycled magazines.

Leah and her mother had taught them how to craft and market the beads the last time she'd traveled to the poverty-stricken country.

The legacy her parents had left still lived on. She smiled at the thought.

As she focused back on the pages in front of her, a recipe for a blueberry braid seemed tempting. She had already rolled out the soft dough and was spreading the fillings onto it when Phillip returned her call.

"Good morning. Thanks for calling me back."

"Not a problem. Is this a convenient time?"

Leah cradled the phone at her neck as she pushed aside the baking sheet and tried to wash the remaining flour from her hands all at the same time.

"Sure. I'm cleaning up a doughy mess," she admitted as she finished, turned the water off, and dried her hands. "I'm sorry I put you in such a bind today." She covered the braid with a thin towel and carried it to the table to let it rise.

"It's not a problem." Phillip assured her. "I hope you're all right—after last night. It was a stressful thing to go through."

"It certainly was," Leah agreed as she sat down. "But yes, I'm fine. I've… kind of a personal emergency to attend to."

"I understand. No explanation needed. Take it as a JB Day."

"What's that?"

"It's a *Just Because* Day. You get three hooky days per year. No questions asked. You didn't know that?"

"No."

"Well then, we're going to need to step up our orientation game around here."

She laughed.

"Actually, you chose a great day to be away from here," Phillip continued. "It's a circus. The media is relentless."

"That bad, huh?" Leah was thankful she was nowhere near.

"It is. The ruckus is mostly outside though, except for some reporters who call or stop by hoping to catch an interview. Your face greeted me from the paper this morning. We were photographed last night without knowing."

"Oh, you're kidding." She feigned a surprise.

"You didn't see it?"

"No."

"I'll save a copy for you. You're quite photogenic." His voice tapered.

"Thank you." She was glad he couldn't see the flush on her face as she toyed with the edge of the towel covering the braid.

"What is it you're baking?"

"How did you know I was baking?"

"You told me you were cleaning up a doughy mess. That typically indicates baking."

"Oh, yes, of course." She shook herself into reality. "I'm making a blueberry braid with a ricotta cream filling and lavender-infused lemon sauce. But to clear the record, this is not the reason I stayed home today."

"Sure it's not," he teased. "Never mess with a woman who has a craving for sweets. I won't say a word about it—if you'll save a piece for me."

Before she responded, a noise in his background distracted her.

"Will you hold on a second?" he asked.

"Sure." Leah moved to the living room and curled onto the sofa.

She heard what she thought was Marci's voice, followed by a door shutting. That she was in the privacy of her own home while speaking with Phillip—who was behind his closed office door—made her uneasy. This was a level to avoid at all costs.

"So, where were we? Oh, that's right. You were inviting me to come by later and try a few slices of your blueberry braid."

"So now it's plural?" Her wit was beginning to match his. She ignored his blatant invitation.

"If it's as good as I expect it to be, plural won't be a problem."

"You are smooth." She was finding that fact to be more accurate by the moment.

"Thank you. Seven o'clock, then?"

She tensed at his assumption.

"Unless you have other plans, or prefer to decline, crushing my psyche."

"Of course not."

"Of course not as in you don't have other plans?" he asked.

"No, I mean…I don't have other plans, I don't prefer to decline, and I don't wish to crush your psyche." She couldn't believe she agreed.

"Great. It's settled."

"And you already know where I live."

"Sure do."

"You're welcome to bring Jessica." She hoped he would. She needed a diversion, a buffer.

"I'd love to, but she's leaving this afternoon to spend a week with her grandparents. I appreciate you asking though. This'll give me something to do this first night without her."

"Sounds good."

"Until tonight then, Leah."

They said good-bye, and Leah closed her eyes and clenched her lips together. There wasn't a worse idea on the face of the earth than for Phillip to come to her home tonight. She wondered how her decision to distance herself from him diminished so rapidly with the sound of his voice.

The tender dough wasn't the only thing rising, she thought to herself as nervous anticipation rose in her. She pulled the afghan over her head and wondered how she'd make it through this time.

19

Mariucci walked up the porch steps of Addington's Attic Bed & Breakfast with Scordino right on his heels. He rang the buzzer.

"You think there's room for us?" Scordino asked.

"No clue. I didn't even get voicemail when I called earlier."

The front door opened and a woman greeted them. "Good day to you. Something I can help you with?"

"Yes, ma'am. Your ad was on the placemat over at Gary's Restaurant, and we wondered if you might be able to rent us a room."

"I usually require a day's notice. I like to freshen up the sheets, and what have you."

"My apologies, ma'am."

The woman peered over the rim of her glasses. "Where are y'all from?"

"Boston," Mariucci was quick to respond before Scordino piped in.

"I suppose I can get a couple of rooms ready for you. You need two, right? They rent for one hundred thirty-five dollars a night. How long do you plan to stay?"

"Yes, two rooms are good. Not sure yet how long we'll be here. Do you have anyone else scheduled this week?"

"Not yet. Come on in, and I'll show you what I have."

Mariucci and Scordino followed the woman inside where she pulled the keys from a rack and led them up a mahogany staircase.

"Cherubim's Peak is on the right, and Addy's Alcove is on the left. I usually like to refresh the rooms with a little lavender spray. I need to pick up some more. They sell it at the lavender farm just outside of town. You came in that way, no? The fields are about to burst with color."

"I don't recall passing it. But this is fine as it is."

"Well, that's good. Breakfast will be between eight and nine in the morning. Anything you men are allergic to? I always like to ask that 'cause you never can tell nowadays. People eat low carb, gluten free, no sugar, paleo. We don't eat much like that around here unless someone asks special for it."

"No. We're fine. Whatever you prepare is good."

"Go right on and make yourselves at home." She pulled up the lace shade in Cherubim's Peak and, with it, a cool breeze rushed through the raised window.

"Thank you."

"There are a few sheets of stationery with matching envelopes on the dresser in case you wanna write home. Clothes hangers are in the closet, and there are towels and some complimentary toiletries on the bathroom counter. We serve dessert in the family room around eight o'clock if you're interested. Fresh lemon bars tonight. Come help yourselves. It'll be on the buffet."

"Sounds good," Scordino answered.

"That was some awful crash last night, wasn't it?" The woman handed them the room keys.

"Yes, it sure was."

"You two reporters?"

Mariucci's stomach lurched. "We are."

"You tell me if you need anything t'all. I hope you enjoy your stay in Lowville." She gave them a polite nod and walked out of the room.

"Let's bring our stuff in," Mariucci barked at Scordino. "We've got work to do."

20

The lamp atop the wrought iron post flickered as it made the transition from daylight to darkness, providing the only light on the brick patio except for the amber cast that spilled from the back window and door. The empty dessert plates sat beside each other on the small table as Phillip and Leah spoke comfortably while darkness settled about them.

All day, Phillip had caught himself glancing at the time, counting the hours until evening. An hour slipped by, and he didn't want to think of how slowly the next one might pass. The air was pleasant. A perfect night to be outside, depending on the company one shared it with.

There were a thousand questions he wanted to ask.

"It's a given that you're a wonderful cook. That was amazing. What was in it?"

"Oh, a little of this and a little of that. Throw in some sweet cream cheese and fresh blueberries, and soon you have yourself a little treat."

"Just like that?"

"Yeah, just like that." Leah smiled.

"Tell me, what other surprises are hidden up that sleeve of yours?" He picked up the cup of decaf from the table.

She seemed relaxed and reached for her coffee. "That would ruin the surprise, wouldn't it?"

Good answer. "A tactful way to encourage me to

mind my own business?"

"Don't be so hard on yourself."

"Me? You invite me over to sample your culinary delights then shy away from my questions?" Phillip laughed.

"Oh, *I* invited you? Is that how this came about?"

"Color me ignorant, but I am here, right? Must be true."

"Fire away. But I maintain my right to plead the fifth at any point."

"Fair enough." He tilted his head toward her. "For starters, how are you liking it in the upstate."

"It's OK. Takes some getting used to though."

"Probably a lot different from Toledo," he said, intently focused on her.

She shrugged her shoulders but said nothing.

"What do you do in your spare time?"

"That's new to me. This is such a slower pace. I suppose I like to do the typical things: shop, read, garden, jog. I love tennis."

"Are you any good?"

"I'd like to think so."

He sat forward with his palms on the knees of his jeans. "So even though you work at a hangar, flying didn't make it to your list of favorites."

"True statement. Not that I mind it. I fly when necessary, and I understand how you find it enjoyable. But it has its risks." Her voice grew quieter with each word.

"Why? Were you in a close one?" His eyes stayed fixed on hers. Her faraway look revealed there was something he wasn't aware of, as her CM or as a friend.

"Someone...well, a couple actually...who were

very close to me were killed in a plane crash."

"I'm so sorry." Phillip reached out his hand to her, regretting that he'd brought up something that troubled her. He, of all people, related to that kind of pain.

"I've worked through it for the most part, or so I thought. But it tends to touch every area, even years later. A trickle-down effect."

"Believe me. I understand."

"Oh, Phillip, I'm sorry. Of course you do. I'm so sorry about your wife."

"Daria…" he said with reverence.

"A beautiful name."

"Yes. As she was," he added.

"What a difficult thing to endure."

"It has been. Still is. Flying has been therapeutic, despite the irony."

She said nothing.

"I admit there's a lot I don't understand, but whatever trickle-down effect you spoke of—God can sustain you in the midst of it."

"True. But things get complicated," Leah said.

He sat back, searching for a response as he fought the urge to expose the truth. He locked his jaw with forced determination. Finally, he spoke. "I'm still a work in progress. For a long time, I lived in a state of regret, in constant defeat over what happened. I won't bore you with the details, but suffice it to say, I blamed myself for encouraging her to fly, which ended up in her death. Maybe it was my fault. I can't change that now. But recently someone reminded me that when we walk around in defeat, questioning God and blaming Him for what's on our platter, we undermine His authority. We second-guess Him and His ability to help us overcome and essentially call Him unworthy as we elevate our thoughts and ideals above Him, which is ultimately pride."

"But what if we're the ones who put the stuff on our platter, even purposely?"

"That's the beauty of it. It makes no difference. He takes everything—our achievements and failures both, and works with them just the same. Have faith. It's impossible to please Him without active faith. This is what carries you through when you can't see the outcome from the middle of the battle. If you can see it, then the battle is already over and believing is no longer necessary. I think about that when I'm flying a lot. When I'm maneuvering through a storm, I'm solely dependent upon the instrument panel. If I keep looking out the windshield for reassurance, I'll fail, guaranteed, because I will have leaned on my own understanding. The instrument panel is the only tool I can trust in, even when everything around me is bleak."

"Good analogy."

"People always say seeing is believing. But that's a farce. No, believing is what will ultimately bring you to a place where you can see clearly. It's through faith and patience that we inherit the promise."

"I wish maintaining faith in my current circumstances was as easy as you say it should be."

"It's simple, but it's not easy. Just take the first step, then another. Believe. Even when you think you blew it, intentionally, accidently, or ignorantly, trust that He is a restoring God, no matter what you did to contribute to your dilemma. I'm working on this myself, too, so you're not alone."

Leah sat in silence for a long while. Finally, she

turned to him and nodded. "You've given me a lot to think about."

"By the way, for whatever personal reasons you needed off today, if you need another couple of days, I can work with that."

"That's awfully nice of you. Thanks for being so accommodating."

"So, was it completely forward of me to invite myself over to see you—I mean to come over and try your delicious pastry tonight?"

She pushed a wisp of hair from her face and her eyes met his. "I'm sure if Tom baked a tray of pastries, you'd visit him as well." She brushed it off playfully as a flush crept up her face.

He tapped his cheek with his forefinger. "You really don't know me, do you?" Phillip asked as he stood and extended his hands to help her up. She took them, and he clasped his own around hers.

Her gaze dropped. "Maybe not."

"But I'll admit, if Tom were to bake a tray of pastries, it might warrant a visit from all of us if only to appease our curiosity. Tom is someone I can't quite picture in the kitchen, let alone imagine that his concoctions would be edible."

Her laugh warmed him from head to toe.

"Have you any idea how long I was subjected to his coffee before you came along to rescue me?"

The smile played at the corners of her mouth. He gave her hands a gentle squeeze before releasing. "I need to go." Better to leave now while he could reason than for him to stay and know he'd failed. He reached to gather the plates and opened the patio sliders. Leah slipped past him with the empty cups and napkins in her hand.

Phillip deposited the dishes on the countertop. "Thank you for having me and for the wonderful dessert. May I help you wash these?"

"Thanks, but I'll take care of them."

"This was well worth my wait today," he said as they walked toward the front door.

She turned on the porch light. "I enjoyed it, too."

He pursed his lips as he faced her. "Seriously, does it bother you that I invited myself over to see you?"

He watched her toy with the words before she spoke them. "I thought you came for the dessert."

"You're avoiding my question. But perhaps we should talk about it another time. It's getting late. I only hope I haven't offended you, since I'm—considering our—"

"—our working relationship?"

He exhaled, grateful for her tactfulness.

"I'm flattered," she admitted, her voice guarded. "It's just that—"

His eyes held hers. "What?"

"Well, there's a lot you don't know."

Phillip struggled with his emotions. Listening to her betray herself was not an option. He needed the upper hand. "Trust me. Nothing you say could dissuade me from you, Leah, unless of course you've no interest in me. I'd reluctantly take my intentions and attempt to move on in order to respect your wishes."

He watched the struggle in her eyes and regretted the pain he'd caused in the proverbial corner they'd found themselves in. But before she spoke, he took her hand in his and brushed her knuckles gently with his thumb. "Let's discuss this later. Forgive me if I've put you on the spot. But for now, at least consider what

I've said?"

She told him she would, yet the battle was still evident on her face.

He really needed to leave. He lifted her hand toward his lips to brush it with a kiss but paused midstream. He had no right. Things were complicated enough without adding more to the equation. And there was much to talk about. He patted it instead.

One day.

"I'll talk to you tomorrow. But if you're not in by eight thirty, I'll assume you took me up on my offer for another JB Day."

"Thank you." Her reply was faint.

"Good night, Leah." Phillip forced himself to release her hand. Then he walked out into the stillness of the quiet night before he changed his mind.

21

Cords, wires, and makeshift news stations lined the tall chain link fence around the airport, prompting a sense of panic as Leah drove into the parking lot Thursday morning. She'd been off for two days and thought by now things would have settled.

Ever since DeFresnio's trial, she cringed when she spotted a news crew, for fear someone was in search of her. Methodically, she lowered her sunglasses and hurried inside. Her instinct was clearly wrong about things quieting down, but it was too late. She was already here.

Tom and Charles greeted her as she entered the safety of the hangar. "Welcome back."

"Good morning, Tom and Charles."

"Zoo out there, isn't it?" Charles rolled his eyes as he spoke.

"I'd say so."

"Great photo, Miss Photogenic," Tom said. "You and Phillip earned a front-page slot."

"The photo is quite becoming," Charles added.

She frowned at the two of them.

"Hey, don't like being in the spotlight?" Tom put his arm around her teasingly.

"Not especially." She slid her purse into a cabinet.

"That was a terrible crash, wasn't it?" Charles asked.

"Too horrible for words."

"Eighteen dead, forty-seven survivors. It could've

been worse. The plane could've been full."

"True." Leah nodded, relieved when both lines rang at once, forcing the conversation to a natural close.

For the next half hour, Leah answered phones and scheduled appointments. Three calls were from news crews, requesting interviews from anyone who saw the accident. Playing ignorant, Leah took the messages and addressed them directly to Phillip. She wanted nothing to do with speaking to the media.

When Phillip walked in, he greeted everyone as he passed by the front counter. He seemed surprised to see her.

She gave him a cautious wave, careful to blend in with the others. She tried to avoid thoughts of his visit to her home, but it was difficult. Their eyes met briefly before he disappeared around the corner.

"Leah, line two," Tom announced to her a few minutes later.

"Who is it?" Her hand hesitated on top of the phone. If it turned out to be a reporter, now was her time to make a quick exit.

"Some guy by the name of Richard. Didn't give his last name. But he sounds like he's in a tunnel."

Richard? He never calls me at work.

She hoped he wouldn't be upset that she'd returned already. She took the line off hold and greeted him as quietly as possible while she reached for the cell phone in her purse.

Three missed calls.

"Sorry. I forgot to turn my ringer on this morning. Is everything OK?"

"Yes, but I was starting to wonder. I've been trying to reach you. Are you sure it's wise to return to work so soon? That photo, although good, is not your friend."

With Tom and Charles so close within earshot, she didn't know how to respond.

Fortunately, Richard jumped back in. "I don't mean to scare you, but we need to give it some time. It'll blow over eventually. How crazy is it there?"

She shielded her mouth with her hand and whispered into the phone. "A few reporters are trying to get interviews. But I'm deferring all the calls to Phillip."

"Aah…the aviator you spoke of. Good thing. Doesn't appear he was aware that he was photographed either. Hopefully, he'll ignore the media, too, so you won't be dragged into a forced interview or anything. He could make it hard on you. Milk it to get publicity for the hangar."

"True, but I don't think he'd do something like that." Leah glanced around. She didn't need Phillip walking in, making her lose all concentration.

"Can't you use your leverage and ask for more time off?"

"What leverage? What on earth are you talking about?"

"You know what I mean. For all practical purposes, it's too late to ask for the day off, but do your best to stay behind the scenes. Remember, no matter what, I'm with you. I'm only a touch of a button away. Is your transmitter on?"

"Yes," Leah answered quietly as her hands grasped the gold chain at her neck. It was a comfort that Richard was this accessible.

"Great. Cell phone?"

"I turned it on."

"Good. You're covered. Do what you can."

"I'll try."

"But whatever you do, don't let yourself be talked into an interview. We can't afford to take any chances."

She thanked him and hung up the phone a moment later, wondering how on earth she would find a way out of this one.

She should've known better than to come back to work so soon.

22

Phillip hung up the phone satisfied. At least he'd made contact with her—as Richard. She was well aware of the dangers, but he wasn't certain if she'd muster up the courage to ask for the day off now that she was here. He wouldn't give her much time before he'd intervene and get her busy doing something else.

He walked out to the break room and filled his empty mug with coffee, trying to appear as casual as possible when he walked to the front desk. He was certain she didn't suspect a thing.

"How's it going, Mr. Z?" Tom asked in passing as he walked toward Marci's office.

"All right, I guess. Be glad when this rat race is over." He stirred a half packet of sugar into his cup then turned to Leah who was now alone at the counter. "Get a chance to recoup?"

"I did," she answered with a slight nod.

He sensed her uneasiness as he took in the view through the panoramic windows and pushed his free hand into the pocket of his pants. He was concerned about the ever-growing crowd of media who'd set up camp on a portion of the tarmac. "Reporters still making their rounds?"

"Yes, quite thoroughly." She reached for a few phone messages. "These came in a few minutes ago."

"Thanks." His eyes met hers as he took them and scanned the contents. He shook his head at the offers for interviews.

"Not into the interview thing, are you?" Her voice held a laugh in it despite the complexities that were clearly on her mind.

"Not in the least," he admitted. "You?"

"Fat chance."

"You know, today would be a great day for me to take you on that ride I promised you."

Relief flooded her face. Then uncertainty crept in as quickly. Before she responded, the door buzzer sounded announcing someone's arrival. Tom walked back into the room as a man entered. The guy carried himself like a typical journalist.

Leah must've warned Tom that she wanted nothing to do with the media, because he quickly intercepted the visitor and pointed him in a different direction. Phillip hoped it would be enough to convince her to go away with him.

"All right," Leah said. "I'm game."

"I'll put a quick flight plan together and come get you in a few."

Gratitude laced her eyes.

Phillip headed to the pre-flight room, relieved that she agreed. He could hardly wait to lift off with her at his side.

23

Something about the hum of the plane mesmerized Leah as they lifted off nearly thirty minutes later. Every part of her was conscious of Phillip as he sat next to her, handling the aircraft with the ease of a professional. Of course, he was one. She scanned the horizon, now at an angle, and forced her thoughts elsewhere.

"Relax. You're safe," he said to her after he leveled off.

His words surprised her. It was as if he could see right through her. Was she that obvious? Or maybe he thought she was only fearful of being in a small plane. She hoped it was the latter.

"It's beautiful up here, isn't it?" he asked.

"It is."

"No hustle and bustle." He gave her a playful wink.

"No argument from me." A nervous laugh escaped as she adjusted her headset. She was safe up here. She may as well learn to relax. But was it possible to do so and still maintain her guard with this man? So far, she'd failed miserably. And after his visit to her home, she'd spiraled further. Was she foolish to accept his offer this morning? He'd offered her the opportunity to get away that she didn't dare refuse. Besides, maybe today would be the day to clarify a few things, although she was still at a loss with what to say. That they desperately needed to talk was no exaggeration.

"I've never been one for much hoopla," he offered.

She was reminded of his lack of enthusiasm in planning the open house, even though he seemed right at home when it came down to it, despite his personal preference. That someone with his charisma and charm was that understated puzzled her.

"You're not the easiest to figure out at times." She blurted out her thoughts.

"Oh?" His eyebrows lifted in question, and the noise of the engines almost drowned out his answer.

"You're not into the hoopla, yet when you're in the midst of it, you pull it off pretty well."

"The open house?"

"Exactly."

"I do what's necessary, although I prefer low key," he admitted. "But that's like the pot calling the kettle black."

"Oh?"

"You're the same way. You attracted your own following at the event. But for a woman who handles herself with such poise and confidence, you seem to shy away from the ruckus of the reporters who are eager for an interview. Tom handed me several more messages clearly intended for you, not me. I'll bet the ones you passed off to me were meant for you as well. You were only trying to spare my feelings."

"Yeah, right." She made light of it. If he only knew.

He reached forward to make an adjustment. His hands moved with ease over the instrument panel, reminding her of the warmth and security she'd felt in his arms the night of the crash. His breath against her hair made her feel alive again.

She forced her mind to switch gears. "Where are we headed?"

"We? As in our relationship or geographically?" he said as he looked straight ahead.

"Nice." His quick wit caught her off guard, and she turned away. "I meant geographically."

"The Thousand Islands. Ever been there?"

"As in geographically?"

His glance was apologetic. "I deserved that, didn't I?"

"A little." His expression was priceless. She was beginning to relax, despite her personal apprehensions.

"Seriously, it's early in the day, and it's perfect outside. The Thousand Islands are beautiful. We can even take a ferry to Boldt Castle if you're interested."

"Is it worth seeing?"

"Absolutely. You've heard the story behind it?" he asked.

"No."

"In the late 1800s, Mr. Boldt, a wealthy hotelier, purchased one of the Thousand Islands and had it shaped into the form of a heart. His plan was to build a dream castle for his wife, to display his love for her. It's really a tragic story. They stayed on the island for four summers during the construction, but then his wife died. Broken and in despair, he sent all three hundred workmen away and never returned to the island. He left it as is, as a monument of his love for her."

"Goodness, that's sad." Although tragic, maybe a little tour was the very thing she needed to take her mind off things. A day of leisure with no reporters, no one peering over her shoulder...If she could just get past the company she was with.

At least Richard would be proud of her. He was

still accessible at the touch of a button. There was nothing to fear and nothing to prevent her from having a good time. She fingered the vintage timepiece at her neck, savoring the comfort it brought her.

For now, she'd concentrate on the day that stretched out ahead of her and deal with her concerns of the case later. Being with Phillip would be enough to keep her mind occupied for the next couple of hours anyway.

Everything about him seemed to guarantee it.

24

The sky was a pleasant shade of blue as the Uncle Sam's Tour Boat scooted across the channel near the Canadian-American border. The St. Lawrence Seaway alongside Alexandria Bay was dotted with islands as far as the eye could see. A few were large, but most were modest in size and strikingly beautiful as springtime was well under way.

Phillip was pleased to hear Leah laugh at the tour guide's announcement of the smallest of the islands that barely held enough earth around it to support a tree. He was certain the day would be profitable, if for no other reason than to distract her mind from the complexities of her life.

He smiled at her expression when she took in the first glimpse of the turn-of-the-century castle.

The guide gave a brief history of the extravagant structure and urged those who were stopping for the castle tour to make their exit. Phillip led her through the crowd to exit the double-decker boat.

"Breathtaking, isn't it?" Phillip slipped their ticket stubs into the pocket of his trousers as they walked toward the gate. They strolled down the walk that wound around toward the main entrance. Flowers bloomed inside stone borders that were arranged in the shape of a heart on the sloped grounds.

"This is amazing." Leah exclaimed, absorbing the beauty around her.

"The castle was modeled after a medieval

sixteenth-century Rhineland Castle. The exterior walls are layers of hand-picked stones. Imagine all the building materials that were shipped here."

"What an expense that must've been. I'd never even heard of this place before."

"Shall I pull out my handy-dandy smelling salts?" he teased.

"Might not be a bad idea," she laughed.

"I reacted the same way the first time I came here. It still amazes me."

"Amazing."

"This place is constantly changing as the Thousand Islands Bridge Authority continues the multi-million-dollar renovation project. Call me a romantic, but I never get tired of it," Phillip admitted as they walked up the steps to the entrance of the castle. "This is a self-guided tour, so I will be your official guide at no extra charge."

"Wow. This is like stepping back in time into a fairytale dream," Leah announced as she scanned her surroundings.

"This ground floor interior is the only floor that was nearly complete before the project came to an abrupt halt. Check out the height of the ceilings. The stone pillars were hand carved in the replica of Mr. Boldt's wife. Notice the intricate rose castings that border the room."

"He spared no expense."

"Very true." When a man loved a woman, wasn't that the case? Phillip forced his eyes and thoughts back to the flier in front of him. "There are one hundred and twenty rooms in the main castle." He held the brochure between them, showing her the layout of the complex that stood nearly six stories tall at some points. "The swimming pool is in the basement, surrounded by a medieval maze of sorts. It's easy to get lost down there. It's pretty cool. We can check that out in the end. There's also an underground passageway that the servants used to transport supplies. The ground floor we're on now has the billiard room, the ballroom, the library, and some other private rooms, including Mr. Boldt's spacious office."

It took nearly thirty minutes to make their way into the hallway surrounding the grand staircase that led to the upper levels. There was so much to see, and so many people to dodge. It wasn't long before they decided to climb to the top story and work downward in an effort to avoid the crowd of visitors that began the tour from the ground level moving upward. Gridlock was what Leah called it. He'd never seen her more relaxed.

They stood at an upper story window and surveyed the lush grounds. Phillip pointed to another large stone structure. "That's the Alster Tower Playhouse."

"And what is that exactly?" she asked.

"During construction, Mr. Boldt and his family lived there. It was actually intended to be a kid's playhouse. There's even a two-lane bowling alley in it."

"For real?"

"It's pretty extravagant. You'll love it. Jess'd go nuts in there, too."

"I'm sure she would. Goodness, I'd be content to live in the playhouse as an adult, at least from this vantage point. Compared to most people's homes, it's huge."

"It is indeed."

For the next two hours, they strolled through the maze of the Castle's multi levels, working downward. On the way down the grand staircase, they met several large groups that were climbing upward. They glanced at each other knowingly, pleased with their choice to avoid the crowds. They laughed and talked about everything from medieval horsemen to modern day avionics and New York State apples. Phillip learned a lot during their walk along the castle floor. She liked Jonathon and Winesap for cooking, much better than Rome or Granny Smith. And Yellow Delicious was her favorite eating apple, especially with caramel dip. He couldn't agree more.

"Mrs. Boldt's chamber, and bath," Phillip announced as they walked through the private entrance on the second floor. The spacious, intricately furnished room lay before them with windows along the perimeter that overlooked the grounds. They spoke quietly as they compared the printed layout of the couple's private quarters to the rooms that were before them. As they moved around the room, Phillip pointed out the various wardrobes. "This is a serious amount of closet space."

"True. Hard to imagine the need for so many closets under one roof. But think about the elaborate clothing of the early 1900s. It probably took up a lot more space than the type of clothing we wear today."

"You're right." How culture had changed.

As Phillip stood next to Mr. Boldt's adjacent chamber, Leah walked to a nearby window and looked out onto the grounds. Her sudden quietness puzzled him, and he wondered what she was thinking. So far, the day had been a therapeutic success. Her mood was light. She appeared unguarded at times considering how she looked at him and interacted with him. He recalled their conversation the other night, fully aware he'd left her an open-ended question. Their need to talk was no doubt on her mind as much as it was on his. Yet their hands were both tied.

His eyes took in her form as she stood with her back to him. Her demeanor definitely turned reflective. The weight of the world seemed to burden her shoulders.

Her linen jacket was rolled up at the sleeves and matched the natural highlights of her hair. Her jeans fit her perfectly. Too perfectly. When she turned to face him, he tried to redeem himself, but it was too late. His eyes searched hers, but she turned away as if to avoid his gaze.

Their time to talk was beckoning.

He'd frightened her, and rightly so. But his feelings were unavoidable. She interacted with him as the CEO of the company she worked for. A CEO who'd made advances toward her. He should have practiced caution. The last thing he wanted was for Leah to experience harassment. Men who preyed on innocent women in the workplace had their own place in hades in his opinion. Of course, anyone in Phillip's inner circle knew that he wasn't that kind of corporate mogul at all.

His attention to Leah didn't seem to offend her. In fact, she said she was actually flattered. But that was before. Perhaps something changed to make her feel differently now.

Things were too complicated. He must change the way she perceived him. Yet he couldn't expose the truth to justify his reputation. His was a harassment case waiting to happen.

He walked over and stood behind her. He wanted to reach for her elbow to encourage her to face him, but that would only make matters worse.

"I'm sorry if I offended you, Leah."

She was silent, unmoving. Finally, she lowered her head and shook it back and forth. Dare he invite her to turn about? To stand behind her and try to converse alone was pointless. He touched her elbow and urged her to face him. When she did, he saw that she'd been crying.

He closed his eyes in an effort to force his mind to think of something to say. As if on cue, to ease the tension, a text tone sounded from his phone. He opened his eyes and reached for it from underneath his flight jacket. It was AJ with three short words. *Call me now!*

"I need to go make a quick call."

"OK."

"You'll wait for me here?"

"Sure."

Phillip headed for the privacy of the ground floor veranda, eager to find out what AJ wanted. Perhaps it wasn't as urgent as AJ made it out to be. But at least the fresh air would do wonders for him.

One thing was certain—he needed a good, cool breeze.

25

Leah sat down Indian-style and leaned against the cold, stone wall beneath the window opening. She was relieved when Phillip was interrupted with a text. She needed time to get her thoughts together. She had no idea that being with him for an all-day event would be so difficult. She should've known better. It was barely afternoon with the rest of the day to go.

Although the case itself wasn't exactly the focus of her mind right now, the way it permeated every other area of her life was. Her desire for Phillip grew stronger. Her resistance toward him faded.

Until a few moments ago, she was fine. She didn't remember when she felt as relaxed as she was with Phillip at her side today. Perhaps the romantic mood of the island was the cause. The tragic but compelling love story between George Boldt and his wife Louise captivated her. Their story evoked an emotion deep inside, mesmerizing her as she and Phillip wandered through the medieval maze.

All day they laughed together.

All day he made her forget.

She forgot everything, like the reason she was here in New York in the first place, trying to stay out of sight from someone who wanted her killed. The fact that Phillip was not just a nice guy, but rather he was her boss, was a detail that vanished from her mind as her guard fell at her feet.

But the charisma between them was real, and their

need to talk so great. Where should she begin? Today, she purposely forced herself to relax with him in order to enjoy their time. And now, in her attempt to do so, she completely dropped her guard until they ended up in the couple's private chambers.

Then she remembered everything.

How dismal sounding, when she analyzed it.

She should be up front with him, spilling her story to free herself from the façade. But doing so guaranteed a breach to her security…to the program. It would jeopardize the situation even more. Perhaps her best option was an act of integrity by forfeiting his advances since she was prohibited from being fully truthful to him. That was really her only choice. She must forfeit her feelings as well.

Oh, how much this case had cost her.

Leah recalled a conversation with Richard not long ago. He reminded her that she was privileged to be the one God chose to use in this situation. He called her a vessel of honor. But was that still the case if, at times, she cried out to be something else? Would her attitude negate her position in God's eyes?

Deep inside she wanted to be all that God wanted her to be. If participating in the program was her lot in life, she must proceed with joy and willingness. She didn't want to fail God, no matter how much she wanted to quit. Her calling was to be honorable in her commitment and to be fair to Phillip by forfeiting her growing feelings for him. Living a lie in front of him was not fair to him. He deserved far better.

She needed strength now more than ever. Tears welled in her eyes.

I'm so weak, Lord. I fail at each turn…and there are so many turns these days. Forgive my shortcomings. I want to take the high road so I can truly become the vessel of honor that You want me to be.

I don't want to ride the fence, trying to mold myself to my own agenda. I do want Your will, despite my failures. Keep me tried and true. Search me and know my heart. Try me and know my thoughts. Perfect what concerns me, and keep me within Your hand of protection.

Her face was wet with tears. But peace poured over her spirit. Being in the presence of God exceeded all else that life offered.

Although the circumstances remained the same, she had peace. Somehow, God's wisdom and strength to manage every task at hand would suffice. For now, she'd rest in that security.

~*~

Phillip punched in AJ's number and waited for the connection. The sudden sense of dread that tried to dissuade him was hard to shake.

"What's up, AJ?" Phillip leaned against the wall of the open veranda.

"Good news bad news. Are you at your computer?"

"No." Phillip answered. AJ had no idea he was spending the day with his witness at Boldt Castle.

"Crystal improved a great deal over the last few days. Most of her memory is back. In fact, she's been able to tell us enough to allow us to come up with composite sketches of her abductors. I sent you an e-mail a minute ago with an attachment of the sketches. You'll want to check them out as soon as possible."

"That's great news." Phillip was encouraged.

"We've done a trace on the two guys. The older

guy is Frank Mariucci. He's a rather distinguished Italian with silvery hair, probably around fifty-five. The other one's name is Anthony Scordino. He's short and stocky, guessed to be in his early forties. The guy carries himself like he's all that. You'll notice a fresh scar down his face in the sketches. You can thank Crystal for that."

Phillip listened intently but didn't interrupt.

"They're definitely linked to DeFresnio," AJ continued. "It seems as though DeFresnio's cohorts are working on their own behalf. With Karina as their only witness, it's clear they want her dead. She's their one loose end. With her out of the way, they're free for life. It's amazing that Crystal was able to escape. She's been instrumental in helping us out."

"I'm sure she has," Phillip agreed, sensing the bad news would be next.

"When we ran a check on the two men, we uncovered a small glitch."

"Go on."

"They left the Miami area. We traced them in Syracuse, and a short time ago they made the mistake of using an ATM on James Street in Alexandria Bay, New York. I'm sure they've no clue we're on to them. Do you have any idea where that is?"

Alexandria Bay? James Street?

It was as if someone gut-punched Phillip. Had he heard correctly? James Street was near the Uncle Sam's Boat Tour launch. They were tipped off. Was Leah's photo the cause of it? But even if it was, what prompted them to come here—to Alexandria Bay? They were still a good forty-five minutes away from the hangar.

"An internal investigation is in progress, but it's

pretty certain the leak was somewhere under our noses. It goes deeper than Patrick, although we're certain he played a substantial role. Security tapes are being reviewed. We're questioning a messenger who spent excessive time in the department the other day. We think he eavesdropped on a conversation I had with you and then tipped someone off."

"I can't believe it..." Phillip ached for Leah. His mind raced. He had to view the sketches so he was aware of the enemy. But first, he had to return to Leah to be sure she was OK. He padded through the corridor as fast as possible, the phone to his ear, avoiding groups of relaxed tourists.

"Be on alert and watch your back," AJ warned. "These guys are equipped, and they have an agenda. Do what's necessary, if you know what I mean. Bring them in alive if possible, but more importantly, keep her alive. Don't be afraid to call for back up. No chances."

"I'll do whatever's needed," Phillip confirmed as he approached the entrance to the private chamber where he'd left Leah. "I'll be in touch."

"Check out those sketches. I'll call you when I learn more."

Phillip pursed his lips as he ended the call. He glanced around to be sure he was alone and reached for the 357 he kept concealed at his belt to verify the number of shots. He hoped there would be no need to use it, but he must be ready to act. He slid it back in place and tucked it carefully underneath his jacket.

He scrolled through his e-mail and opened the attachment, memorizing the details of the men who wanted to take Leah's life, determined he would never let that happen.

He gained his composure, and found Leah sitting on the floor, safe and sound. He prayed for a double dose of wisdom, considering he had the oddest sense the day was only beginning.

26

Mariucci waited with Scordino at the docks for a sign of Karina and the aviator, even though it would likely be a while. Her picture on the front page of the local section of the *Watertown Daily Times* was like finding a pot of gold at the end of the rainbow. The IV bag in her hand—well, that was just the break they needed to confirm her identity.

Their nurse was in their radius. Her face was unmistakable, the same way it had been that day in the Connor Tower. He and his partner spent hours hanging out near the airport earlier, but tracking her from the hangar to the Thousand Islands was downright good investigative skills. He had to hand it to Scordino, although the self-centered man irritated him at times. His alias as a reporter put them over the edge.

While Mariucci and Canali spoke on the phone earlier, Scordino caught a glimpse of the witness boarding the Leer Jet that was waiting on the tarmac. The voice of the air traffic controller echoing through the speakers confirmed their destination—Alexandria Bay.

When their inside contact shared the Lowville location with Sam Canali a few short days ago, they'd moved on it quickly. It wouldn't be long until the leak was discovered. There were lots of tracks to cover before the inevitable happened. In reality, they were buying time. But perhaps today was a day that would change all that. If only they could catch her alone.

In the meantime, Sam Canali was good about keeping them abreast of the developments. Still in Miami, he worked diligently to provide them with any leads that might be helpful. That was the name of the game. Mariucci only hoped Mrs. Addington wouldn't prove to be trouble. The proprietor at the quaint little B & B seemed a bit too meddlesome for his taste. Hopefully, things would pan out quickly to allow them to vacate their rooms and get out of this godforsaken place.

Mariucci peered at Scordino as he rubbed the cat scratch on his face. In all honesty, he was surprised at the scar that was now imbedded on his partner's face. That woman was tougher than she looked. How Canali managed to let her out of his sight, he'd never understand. Something to work on in the future. He supposed everyone learned by their mistakes, even in a game with such high stakes as this. The important thing was that they found her again. He looked forward to seeing the surprise in her eyes the moment they were once again face-to-face.

"I'm going to get us some coffee while we wait." Mariucci opened the door of the black sedan. "Keep your eyes peeled."

"Will do." Scordino's voice was husky.

"As much as I'd love to jump on the next ferry and take care of things now, there are far too many people around. Let's stick with the original plan and wait 'til dark. The ferry returns on the hour. Black or cream?"

"Black. Can you make it a double?"

"I will." A double sounded good to Mariucci, too.

This day was going to be a long one.

27

Phillip stepped toward Leah.

She looked up. "Are you all right, Phillip?" There was concern on Leah's face, but as he thought about it, it was probably a reflection of what she observed in his. He needed to be careful. She stood and walked toward him, her gait slow and guarded.

"I'm OK. Sorry. That was an urgent call—a little complication on a project I'm working on." *God help me...*

"Shall we head back? If you need to, it's OK with me. Do whatever is necessary."

"Thanks, but I'm good for now." He scanned the hall, hoping his attempt to be thorough but not obvious would go undetected.

"More airplane crashes?" she asked as they walked into the hall and down the steps toward the ground floor. "Not that I mean to pry."

"No, nothing like that. I didn't intend to frighten you."

Oh, God, no! The airplane...

The thought was another sucker punch.

Would they have? Could they have?

Before he and Leah returned to the Leer Jet, it must be checked thoroughly from top to bottom, and then searched again with a fine-tooth comb. Better yet, he'd make other arrangements. They'd leave the plane here. He had to reach Sally and Joe before they left to go out of town.

"I have a bit more business to tend to." Phillip formulated a plan as he reached for his phone. There weren't many options, but he sure hoped to find one that would work.

"OK. How about I use the ladies' room while you make your calls?" She pointed to a sign up ahead off the main corridor.

Phillip agreed. Was she safe to go into the restroom alone? There wasn't a lot of choice. Plus, his privacy was critical. As they approached, an elderly woman walked out and brushed past them with no sign of distress on her face, so it had to be safe in there. Phillip drew in a deep breath and held it. Maybe this would give him enough time to throw together a plan. He wondered if Leah concocted the excuse, perceiving he was in need of a few minutes to himself. Either way, he didn't complain.

"I'll wait right here."

"Thanks. I won't be long."

He dialed the number as she walked through the door. Sally picked up on the first ring. His eye remained on the door of the restroom as he spoke to Sally in hushed tones. He gave her the list of instructions he'd played out in his mind, relieved beyond words that she understood every detail. He was never so grateful for her sharp organizational skills as he was today. Everything should be in place within a few hours. But first there was time to kill.

"All taken care of?" Leah asked as they walked back outside.

"For right now."

But for how long, he didn't know.

~*~

Leah was glad Phillip was able to remedy his emergency with a phone call or two. For a time, she wondered if something happened to Jessica. It was obvious how much he loved her. His eyes lit up whenever he spoke of her. She admired the bond between them.

According to Phillip, Jess had been with Daria's parents since Tuesday to give Sally and Joe a little downtime before they left to go out of town. Phillip's in-laws lived an hour or so away, and from the sound of it, he took Jess there every couple of months for doting purposes. Grandparents were like that, he told her. They needed interaction with their grandkids. Jess was their last link to Daria. Reason enough to dote.

They toured the playhouse and the rest of the grounds and picked up a couple of souvenir mugs from the gift shop. "Are you hungry yet?" Phillip asked several hours later as they sat on a park bench near the water's edge.

"I'm OK for now. That ice cream cone is holding me over." Phillip gave her hand a gentle squeeze. A reminder that the time to talk with him was drawing near.

"Up for a little adventure?"

"I could be. It depends," she answered, her skepticism rising to the surface.

He said nothing more as a cool breeze rustled his neatly cropped hair. Leah watched as he scanned the waters in front of them. Various boats and even a freighter or two passed by. He appeared to be deep in thought. She pushed thoughts of him aside, but it was difficult not to think of him when he was sitting so close. The breeze flaunted his masculine scent her way, mocking the battle she was facing.

His world seemed so ordered, even though something was clearly troubling him. What was going through his mind? What private affairs did someone like Phillip Zellmer of PRZ Aviation face? She wondered what the R stood for.

From out of nowhere, a bright red Scarab rounded the shoreline in front of them. Phillip stood and extended his hand.

"Our ride is here." His voice was light, and there was a twinkle in his eyes.

"What are you talking about?"

"I arranged it when you were in the restroom." He lifted his hand to the small of her back to guide her. His light touch sparked an emotion she tried to ignore. Perhaps God's timing had accelerated, and she should talk to him now. Leading him on like this was not fair. Not that telling him would make it any easier for her. Being in the same room with him was difficult enough.

There was no opportunity to question him. The driver of the boat greeted Phillip, but she had no idea what they were saying. Phillip helped her in and got aboard himself. In under a minute, they were racing on the open water.

The ride was exhilarating, and Leah might've enjoyed it under different circumstances. Instead, she was helpless and uninformed.

Within moments they approached a small seaside village, and the driver docked the Scarab near a fishing ramp.

Leah read the inscription on the pier. "Sacket's Harbor?"

"We're taking a little detour. I hope you don't mind."

"No, of course not."

Phillip and the driver spoke again, and again Leah did not hear the words that passed between them. The understated charm and charisma of her boss were overpowering at times. Why was this becoming more difficult for her, now that she finally agreed to forfeit his advances as soon as she sensed the time was right?

Phillip led her to his black sport utility vehicle, and Leah wondered how it had gotten to this quaint little fishing village. She wanted to ask but decided against it. Instead, she kept her thoughts and questions to herself.

She would ask him on the way.

The way to where, she didn't know.

28

Phillip was relieved that his SUV was parked near the dock at Sacket's Harbor. Thank God he was able to reach Sally and Joe before they left. He hoped he and Leah wouldn't arrive at the cottage too early and catch them before they had a chance to make their exit.

They made the drive in silence, but he wondered what thoughts played out in Leah's mind. Forty minutes passed as they drove away from the harbor and through the small farm towns that dotted the way. Finally, they rounded the corner that led to a private lake.

The crunch of stones under the tires reminded Phillip of the last time he and Jess visited the vacation cottage at Pleasant Lake a few weeks prior. She'd asked him about the noise, and he'd explained the process of crushing something.

"Like when you crush a aspurn for me?"

"That's exactly what I mean," he told her, not bothering to correct her pronunciation of "an aspirin." She'd learn soon enough. She was growing up too fast.

Dim lights were on in the stilted lake house when they arrived. The timing was perfect. Sally and Joe were already gone. They were dependable, as always. If anyone understood the situation he was in, Sally and Joe would be at the top of his list.

It wasn't that long ago that Sally was a protected witness under his care, even though her case was different altogether. She worked for a federal firm for a number of years as a company accountant when she discovered a huge coverup by one of the corporate officers. An elderly chairman whom she cared about dearly was being taken advantage of. She tried to warn him, and bow out gracefully, but it was too late. The corporate officer who stood to lose millions of stolen dollars discovered how much Sally knew. When the chairman was murdered and the corporate officer went missing, the feds suspected she'd be next, and she was forced to join the WITSEC program.

Years later, the officer was located and incarcerated, and Sally was free to go. But she'd become so accustomed to her new life as Sally Fisher that to go back to her previous life was difficult. Besides, she'd already met Joe.

"Tell me something," Leah said as he brought the vehicle to a stop under the cottage carport.

"Sure. What?" He pulled the key from the ignition and turned toward her.

"I mean tell me something...anything. I don't have a clue what's going on. It's like you're hiding things from me."

"You'll see." He lifted his door latch, exited, and circled to her side of the vehicle and opened her door.

Even in the dimness of the cab light, her face was flushed, and her soft, pink lips were forcefully shut—like she wanted to say more but held her tongue. She took the hand he offered and stepped down, but quickly pulled her hand away. He sensed her confusion toward him. But what else was he to do? He had no choice.

A good run along the shore might help. He suspected Leah would be furious if she discovered what was happening behind the scenes. He needed to brainstorm, but there wasn't much time. Nightfall would be here before he knew it. Yes, he owed her an explanation. He understood that. He might even be forced to tell her everything. God help him find a way to do that without getting himself killed.

By her.

They walked up the open steps of the cottage, and Phillip unlocked the door. Her expression was guarded as he held it for her to go inside. It felt good to bring someone here again. Apart from Jess, and Sally and Joe, no one visited the cottage with him in years.

He wished tonight was under different circumstances.

The table was set, and the smell of something scrumptious filled the air. A mellow radio station played in the background. Leah stood in the center of the large room, taking it all in. A soft expression crept across her face, and a twist formed on her lips.

"Now are you hungry?"

She was still guarded, but offered a trace of a smile.

"Have a seat?" he suggested. "Or if you prefer to freshen up a bit, the restroom is down the hall to the right."

She turned toward the hallway.

What was she thinking? He almost said the words aloud as he took off his flight jacket and hung it on the back of the chair.

What do you expect her to think?

He reached for the gun at his belt and slipped it into a nearby drawer where it would be within easy reach if he needed it. He dropped his keys, wallet, and cell phone on the counter and washed his hands at the kitchen sink.

He opened the oven door and brought out two stoneware plates wrapped in foil and carried them to the table just as Leah returned. The smile on her face surprised him. She appeared refreshed.

"The rest of dinner will be ready shortly. I'll be back in a minute." Phillip excused himself.

When he returned from the restroom a few minutes later, she was standing near the picture window that boasted a perfect view of Pleasant Lake and the lowering sunset.

"It's beautiful here."

"It is. I always enjoy coming to the lake, although it's not as often as I'd like." He poured a sparkling beverage into the tall, crystal goblets, lit the candles, and flipped off the light in the kitchen. "Dinner's ready."

She turned around and walked back to the table, thanking him as he pulled out her chair. "You've really outdone yourself," she said as she lowered herself into it. The candles played with her soft highlights, and he wondered how it would feel to brush his face against her hair.

"I worked hard all day for this." He grinned and sat down across from her.

"Yeah, right."

Phillip blessed the food and dinner began.

~*~

The eggplant parmesan was splendid. The French bread melted in her mouth, and with it, Leah melted as well. Phillip obviously planned a beautiful evening for them, down to the cherry cheesecake for dessert. Surely, God wouldn't ask her to talk to him tonight.

Not after all the effort he'd made.

For now, she'd enjoy every moment. Plus, she was still doing her part to keep out of sight of any pesky reporters. She was following Richard's advice. That was honorable, wasn't it? She made a mental note to text Richard later.

At Phillip's beckoning, they carried the dinner plates into the kitchen and moved into the cozy living room with cups of hot tea in hand. "Do you trust me, Leah?" The question came as a complete surprise to her.

Leah tried to hide the catch in her throat as she placed her cup and saucer onto the coffee table. Phillip settled onto the sofa and urged her to sit next to him. She lowered herself onto the overstuffed cushions, calculating the space between them.

"Why do you ask?"

He sat forward, and she noticed the determination in his eyes.

"Because I want to know. I need to know."

The candles were burning much too low. The mood was even more mesmerizing than it had been earlier. She could use some fresh air. She also needed to be honest. Neither was plausible right now.

"Yes, I do trust you," she finally admitted. She probably trusted Phillip more than anyone at this juncture, apart from Richard or AJ.

He pressed his fingers to his temples. "I wouldn't ask you to do this if it wasn't important to me..." She wondered about the anxiety in his voice. He reached for her hands and held them tightly. "You've come to mean far too much to me, and now I have no idea how to begin—"

"Phillip," Leah broke in. It was time. She couldn't

bear to hear the intent of his heart, only to refuse him. It was cruel to lead him on. But he spoke again before she was able to continue.

"You'll probably think I've been in one nosedive too many, but I need to ask you if you'll stay the night."

"Phillip...I..." she interrupted again, not fully grasping what he said. She was too busy formulating the words she rehearsed earlier. "I haven't been up front with you."

~*~

Phillip stopped her. "It's OK." He didn't want her to betray herself. If she would do it for him, she'd do the same for others if pressed, and it could cost her.

"No, it's not OK. For me to continue to lead you on, and accept your advances is not fair to you if I can't be completely honest with you." She withdrew her hands and stared at them.

Phillip was silent as she continued.

"You've always been the perfect gentleman and as much as I enjoy your company, it's not going to work out between us. I may regret it later, but for whatever it's worth, I'm truly sorry."

She was making this difficult for him. On one hand, she was turning him down. On the other hand, she cared enough about him to spare him from hurt. The struggle in her eyes all day long was real. Even then, she chose to respond out of integrity and put a stop to things. And now he was completely stuck between a rock and a hard place.

In most instances, the acceptable thing to do would be to bow out gracefully, to leave now and take her home, making her decision easier for both of them. But that wasn't an option. He dare not leave her side, nor could he drop her off at her home that was no doubt staked out. Returning to the hangar, let alone flying in a plane that was likely sabotaged, was not going to happen on his watch either. He must convince her to stay here tonight—not a completely ethical thing to do. But what choice was there? She'd take the bedroom, and he'd take cover on the sofa within earshot of the door just in case.

As if to break the silence that was growing uncomfortable, Phillip's cell phone rang.

"Will you excuse me for a minute?" He walked into the kitchen and snatched it from the kitchen counter. The digital clock on the oven read eight fifteen.

A call from Marci at work at this time of the night surprised Phillip. But far greater was his element of shock as he listened to the purpose of her call. He spoke in hushed tones and hung up a few minutes later. After scrolling through his missed calls, he laid the phone on the counter and braced against the edge as he contemplated what to say to Leah. There were no easy solutions after what he'd learned.

He forced himself to move back to the living room and prayed he'd find a way to tell her. He owed Leah an explanation. "That was Marci."

"She sure is working late."

"Yes, she is. She asked me to check up on you. Keep my eyes on you."

"Why?"

He was hoping she wouldn't ask but knew she would. The uneasiness weighed him down. "Before she left the hangar, a reporter phoned, claiming he scheduled an interview with you tonight about the plane crash. Does that ring a bell?"

"No."

"She was pretty sure that was the case. He seemed nervous and kind of odd to her."

"That's strange," Leah answered.

"Her biggest concern is that he asked for your home address."

29

Leah's mouth went dry as panic flooded her, followed by a sinking sense of dread.

"Did she tell them?" Her voice was barely a whisper, even to herself, and her throat constricted, making it difficult to breath.

"No, she didn't." Phillip's face showed genuine concern. But there was nothing he could do to help her now.

"Excuse me." She rose and moved to the kitchen, leaving him standing alone. Out of his view, she leaned into a corner cabinet and cried silently. Had it all come to this? She thought she was safe. Clearly a misnomer.

It was time to alert Richard.

She reached for her phone, fumbling with her password as she struggled to concentrate. Maybe it was time to use the panic button instead, but she didn't want to worry him needlessly. It wasn't like she had a gun to her head. Yet.

She'd text him, and then slip outside to talk in private when he called her back.

"Leah?" She gulped back a sob and turned around.

Phillip stood at the kitchen entrance. How long had he been there?

"I'm sorry." Her voice was shaky as she paused from her texting. "I'll be with you shortly. I need to text a friend."

"Leah," he repeated, reaching for her just as she

hit the send button. Compassion was in his eyes as he drew her into his arms. The warmth of him was difficult for her to ignore. But she must.

"Phillip, I can't." Leah pushed him back at the same time an alert sounded from his phone.

He reached for the case at his belt and she noticed the look in his eyes as he came up empty-handed. He'd left the phone on the kitchen counter. Apart from the soft music that played in the background and the occasional notification from his phone, the silence between them was growing uncomfortable.

"You're not curious as to who that is?" Her gaze fell naturally to the unattended device. At that moment, the screen lit up, then faded.

Stunned, she stepped back.

Was that her imagination? Like the aperture of a lens that narrowed to focus on its subject, she focused on his phone—common courtesy aside—willing it to come to life one more time to be certain. The screen lit up again, and she read the sender's name clearly. There was no need to read the message. She knew every word of it.

Leah's body went cold and a nervous shudder escaped. Phillip reached for her again and cupped the back of her head with his hands, drawing her toward him as he kissed her forehead then gently brushed his lips against her fists that shielded her face.

"I couldn't tell you," he whispered.

His breath was warm as he drew her closer, urging her hands away from her face.

"I'm sorry, Leah. You understand that I couldn't tell you."

Embarrassment flooded her as she recalled her conversations with Richard, particularly when she admitted her attraction to the aviator who was out of her league. A spectrum of emotions overwhelmed her. The knife of betrayal cut deeply.

"You're not talking." He drew back and urged her to look at him.

"How could you not tell me? Have you no thought for my feelings? I feel like a complete fool—worse than a fool, actually." Her eyes closed in shame as she wrestled with the reality of her situation.

"You've no reason to feel that way." He took her hands and held them between his own, lifting them close to his chest. "I wanted to tell you. But please understand that it was not possible. Every case is different. We are forced to customize our procedures to each one individually. This has been enormously hard for you. I do understand."

"Have you sympathized with me professionally? Is that what this is? Am I just a case?" She wanted the truth. Needed the truth. All this time she worried about him, concerned for his feelings since she was the one who lied to him from the moment they met. She opened her eyes and glared at him.

"No." His voice was gentle, but firm. "This is not a matter of me sympathizing with you professionally at all. And you are not just a case to me."

His gaze penetrated hers until she wondered if he'd see right through her. But he'd never understand how betrayed he had made her feel at this moment. The firm squeeze of his hands only caused her to sense numbness, like the life was being sucked from her very being.

"Leah, from the very beginning you've challenged me in many ways—professionally as your CM, professionally as your employer, and personally as..."

His breath against her was warm as he stepped closer. "Personally, you've completely dominated my thoughts and intentions, challenging me to the core. These worlds of mine were never meant to cross, let alone collide and intertwine so forcefully."

"Well, my apologies to you if your orderly little world has become so disrupted." The edge in her voice was clear. She didn't care. "I'm sorry for your inconvenience, Phillip, or Richard, or whoever you are."

"I've no regrets except that you completely misunderstand my position."

Leah's emotions swayed. How was it possible he'd hidden his true identity from her for so long? Of course, it was his job. She meant no more to him than the last case, or the next one. Still, she needed to ask. "So what exactly is your position?"

His shoulders slumped as he drew a labored breath.

"Oh, never mind." Leah stepped out of his reach and spun around to go down the hallway. "I don't need to know," she called out to him. "Just show me which room I've been assigned to."

30

Phillip sat at the edge of Pleasant Lake. The sky awakened around him. Swirls rippled on the surface of the water as hungry fish chased after their prey for breakfast. He should've brought a heavier jacket. He didn't expect the breeze to be as brisk.

But it wasn't as cool as Leah's response. Phillip had never seen her so angry. Their words were few as he showed her to her room.

After a restless night on the sofa, he got up, showered, and poured a fresh cup of coffee, carrying it outside to wait. He needed to give her space.

Lots of space.

He understood her anger, whether she believed him or not. But what was he to do? She didn't have a clue how much he loved her. Of course, it wasn't as if he could entertain the thought of telling her—at least not now. She wouldn't accept it. She was angry, and rightly so. There needed to be a whole lot more calming down before he'd try to convince her otherwise. From the expression on her face when she abruptly closed the door on him before going to bed, it would be a long time before the ice melted between them.

It was the opposite of what he'd sensed at dinner.

He called AJ after the sound of her crying quieted. An APB was issued for the two men that scoured the area in search of Leah. He hoped something broke this morning. He couldn't endure much more of this cold treatment, and only a few hours had passed.

At this rate, he'd have frostbite before the sun was fully up.

~*~

Leah awoke with a banging headache. She pushed the comforter back and wondered if it was safe to come out.

The clock on the nightstand read six thirty seven. The diffused sunrise slowly brightened the room that she'd spent a restless night in. If she weren't still so angry, she'd have enjoyed the idea of being in a quaint little lake-house cottage like this. The bedroom was tastefully decorated with white, cobalt, and a splash of yellow, both comfortable and elegant all at the same time. It might've been cheery under different circumstances.

A guest basket sat atop the maple dresser that was filled with toiletry items, along with a thick white towel and washcloth that smelled of fresh detergent. An oversized, white oxford was folded neatly for her. At least Phillip's accomplice intended to make her as comfortable as possible—whoever his accomplice was. No doubt, someone she was acquainted with as well. The thought irritated her.

She slipped into her jeans and found the house quiet as she moved into the bathroom. After a hot shower, she felt better, at least on the outside. She towel-dried her hair, ignoring the blow dryer on the large open shelf that lined the far wall of the bath. What did it matter anyway? There was no need to impress anyone. Her hair could fly in a hundred different directions for all it mattered to her.

When she wandered into the kitchen, Phillip was nowhere to be found. All of last night's dinner dishes were cleaned and put away. Fresh coffee was waiting in the pot and a clean mug sat on the counter with a honey bear beside it. He left a note. He was outside by the lake.

New tears came to her eyes. She thought she'd cried enough during the night to last her a long while. But when she read his scrawl, even his handwriting evoked her emotions again.

What did he expect of her anyway? She had trusted him. And he deceived her.

She opened a drawer in search of a spoon.

There was no one for her to talk to. The only person she confided in was Richard.

Richard.

What a farce.

She slammed the drawer shut and yanked another open until she found the silverware. Never in her life had she experienced such isolation, such humiliation.

Here she was in the midst of forfeiting his advances to find out the only interest Phillip had in her was professional empathy.

The program asked too much of her. She wanted out. Instead, here she was in a safe house, and without a clue as to why. What was really happening with the case to warrant the sudden move?

Will you give him a chance to explain?

He could've explained if he'd wanted to. Why had she fallen for him? He was a man of deception. A man of betrayal.

But you deceived him, too.

She had no choice. That was different.

Leah sloshed the morning brew into the cup,

doused it with cream and honey, then stirred it with more force than was necessary. She threw the spoon onto the counter and marched back into her room, kicking the door shut with her foot, hoping it would shield her from anyone who might further wound her broken spirit.

31

AJ peered out the window of his Miami office. Dark clouds approached from the west, a prerequisite to the typical front that was forecasted for the late afternoon.

He needed to get home, but still, he waited.

Crystal and Michael had returned to Dallas. He'd spoken with them yesterday. Crystal was recovering nicely. Michael said she was eager to move forward, and help, but how?

Their leads on Scordino and Mariucci had all but dried up in the past couple of weeks. It was suggested they might be back in Miami laying low, getting lost in the crowd. AJ wasn't sure. He was grateful Phillip was at the safe house with Leah, although Phillip said it posed a few problems for him.

Thoughts of the case plagued AJ. Things had gone so wrong. The leak in the system weighed heavily on his mind. Both Patrick and the messenger betrayed their positions. They were working on additional safeguards, yet it was still tough for his division.

AJ talked with Phillip yesterday and noticed regret in his voice. He sounded like that a lot lately. AJ didn't understand all that transpired between him and his witness, but clearly, Phillip was not himself. It grieved him to think of Leah and what she'd gone through. Pulled away once more from her community, she waited on the sidelines for any word of progress on the case.

AJ grabbed his jacket from the back of his chair and turned to go, but the photo on the wall caught his eye. He and another special operations buddy posed for a friendly bear hug. He hadn't seen Kevin for nearly five years. It seemed like too long, especially considering all they'd been through together in their earlier military days. Kevin was the best SEAL on their team before being transferred to a base in San Diego.

The photo caused an idea to formulate in AJ's mind. Crystal and Michael did say they'd help in any way possible. Maybe it was worth a try, at least if Michael gave his approval.

He walked out of his office, wondering why he hadn't thought of it earlier. It may take a little time and planning, but it might just prove to pay off.

32

It was Thursday evening, exactly two weeks since Phillip and Leah arrived at the cottage. The forecast called for rain, but so far only a light drizzle fell to the ground.

The weather hadn't been too bad, but to Phillip, it was still cooler inside the small cottage most of the time than it was outside. At times, he wondered if he wouldn't need an ice scraper to clear the frost that grew between them. But he supposed it was better this way. Better than if there had been warmth, considering their close quarters and his growing adoration for Leah. Had things been different, the last two weeks might have been diametrically opposite. Torturous even. He should count his blessings.

"I'll need toothpaste when you go out tomorrow." Leah's voice brought his mind to the present as she walked into the kitchen. Phillip glanced up from the report Marci sent him. He tried to read it at the table for the past hour, yet his efforts were unsuccessful. Concentration eluded him.

Leah's back was toward him as she reached to open a cabinet door. Her bright red t-shirt was rolled up at the sleeves, and the white jeans he'd purchased for her in town last week accentuated her curves. Her hair was pushed back behind her ears. She poured equal parts of grapefruit and orange juice into a glass, and combined it by twirling it with the rhythmic motion of her hand. She reached for a few ice cubes.

At least she wasn't snapping at him.

He forced his gaze from her.

"Is there anything else you'd like me to get from town?" he asked, fixing his gaze on the report in front of him.

"No. That'll be it."

"OK. I'll take care of it." He jotted a note to himself. She was still in the kitchen, now pulling out the ice cream from the freezer. When would the cold front dissipate? "You do realize you can tell me if there's anything…personal… you need." He bit his lip as soon as he said it.

She turned and her eyes met his sharply. If looks could kill, he would be six feet under.

"That's not what I meant," Phillip attempted a retraction.

"I appreciate your concern." Her tone didn't reflect the sentiment.

There was so much he wanted to express, but he held the words inside. Deep down, he thought she cared for him. That's what he wanted to believe. How long could he go on like this? He wasn't getting a whole lot of sleep, and the little he got was restless. He prayed for her incessantly and thought about her every moment in between.

He missed Jess terribly. He'd spoken to her before she'd gone to bed. At least his daughter loved him and missed him. She was enjoying her time with Daria's parents. Staying with them a little longer wasn't an issue. Sally and Joe were still out of town, so things were less complicated on the home front.

The muscles in his neck tightened as he tried to stifle his frustration. It was no use. He needed a cool breeze. A breeze that wouldn't hurt him. "I'll be outside if you need me."

He picked up his jacket and walked out the door, pretending he didn't have a care in the world. But he slumped his shoulders in defeat.

~*~

Leah stared at the ice cream in front of her. Her appetite dwindled even more after Phillip's exit. The last few days she forced herself to eat, and ice cream seemed a viable option. A familiar lump formed in her throat as she thought about him. For days, his eyes appeared less bright. There was a deep crease on his forehead that she hadn't noticed before. And when he smiled, it looked strained.

For two weeks, she had argued with herself—and with God. She'd been hurt, confused, and utterly humiliated. She'd worn her heart on her sleeve. Where had it gotten her?

But what have you done to him in the process?

The quiet words in her spirit startled her amidst the absence of peace. She sensed only dread for the future. Where was the joy in her life anymore? With every beat of her heart, hope distanced itself further.

You've allowed strife in your life.

How could she have avoided it, considering the roller coaster of emotions she'd experienced? She was only human.

As is he. Give him a chance. You don't have a clue the issues he's dealing with. You've allowed him no leeway.

"But look what I've been through," she voiced to the empty kitchen.

His core hurts and bleeds like yours. In fact, his response has been nothing less than considerate toward you.

But it's his job.

He's willing to put his life on the line for you, the same way I have. And you won't even give him the time of day.

The heaviness inside was unbearable. As the words filtered through her spirit, reality began to seep in. Soon tears welled in her eyes, and with it, her shoulders shook with sobs. The tightness in her chest made it difficult to catch her breath.

"Oh, God. Help me."

Her body weakened and she sunk into a kitchen chair. She thought about the past two weeks—two weeks that were irreparable. What had she done? She was a complete failure. How was it possible for one person to mess up this much and still be alive to reflect on it?

Leah dropped her head into her arms and grieved as if she'd lost something precious. She had. She'd lost her peace with God, along with Phillip's trust and respect, no doubt. Her face was wet with tears and her throat was raw with emotion.

Was it possible to ever return to a place in life where she might live in peace again?

The words came in a rush, as did her tears. "What a broken, clay pot I've become. I'm in need of repair and reshaping. Please don't give up on me. Start over if You must. But please don't toss me out forever. What a fool I've been. If there's even a chance that You can use me, then forgive me, dear Lord Jesus."

It is finished, My child.

This time it was almost as if the words were audible. She looked up, tears still streaming down her face.

Talk to Phillip. He needs you.

She closed her eyes and dropped her head in her

arms on the table, lamenting what she'd done. She didn't know how much time had passed, but when she came to, the ice cream had melted into a pool and her concoction of juice turned warm.

She knew what she needed to do.

God forgave her, but would Phillip be as merciful?

And could she ever forgive herself?

33

Phillip sat on the damp grass that sloped along the shoreline and pulled his knees to his chest. A light mist was in the air, and the heavy rain threatened to begin at any moment. For a long time, he stared at the waters as they broke gently before him.

Many waters cannot quench love.

He finally understood Solomon's song. Now *there* was a man full of passion, love, and unfathomable wisdom. What would he have done?

The forecast called for buckets more to be dropped down on him as evening approached. He wasn't certain whether he was thinking literally or figuratively at this point.

Phillip wished for a chance to talk with his own father, if only he were still here.

He yearned for Leah. That must be what the wise king meant when he spoke of being sick with love. Well then, Phillip was terminal—completely incurable. And what would happen when the case was over? Leah would go home and resume her life in Miami. The thought tormented him. It had been years since a woman affected him this way.

"Phillip..." The voice behind him was strained as a trembling hand touched his shoulder. She circled around in front of him.

He lifted his face, and his eyes followed hers as she dropped down and knelt before him on the grass. The war he'd been fighting must have been a walk in the park compared to the battle scars that were evident on her face. She looked remorseful, broken. Her shoulders bent with sobs of grief. He reached up instinctively and touched the back of her lowered head in comfort. The mist fell harder now, as she wept uncontrollably.

"I'm so, so sorry," she sobbed.

He pulled her close and cradled her tightly. Her body shook, but he didn't let go. A few moments passed before her weeping subsided. When she lifted her eyes to meet his again, agony was on her face. Yet she was beautiful.

"I've been such a fool."

"No, that's not true," he reassured her tenderly as he caressed her damp hair and brought her closer again. The nape of her neck was warm at his fingertips.

New tears fell as she spoke. "What have I become? Self-reliance has always been one of my best attributes. Or so I imagined." Her voice was barely above a whisper. "Be the right person, do the right thing, and everything will work out no matter what. I've been proud of my positive attitude. But I see now that self-motivation gets me nowhere on my own. What a hypocrite I've become."

Her voice was saturated with regret.

"Please don't say that," Phillip answered. "You're so precious." He cradled her in the crook of his neck.

"I'm no better than those members of the church of Laodicea," she continued as she wept. "They thought they were rich, but they were poor. They thought they had it all together, but they were wretched and miserable. For two weeks, God's been nudging me, and I was too stubborn to listen."

He kissed her hair, holding her tightly against him

with the palm of his hand. Even though the rain moved in, she seemed in no hurry to go inside.

"Will you ever forgive me?" she whispered as she raised her face to his.

The tenderness in her eyes made his heart do strange things. She'd never been more beautiful—or more vulnerable—to him. He could look at her forever and not grow weary. Her hands were wet with rain when he took them into his own.

"Leah, I forgive you. How could I not?"

He stood and helped her up, drawing her back into the circle of his arms. That the wind was picking up and the rain was falling harder now didn't matter. All else faded at this moment, but this fragile, beautiful woman, and what she was becoming to him.

"There's so much to talk about," Phillip whispered.

She gripped him tighter. "There is."

"Maybe it's time we go inside and get started."

34

By the time they walked up the steps of the cottage, Phillip and Leah were dripping with rain, but Phillip had never been happier or more content in his life. It didn't matter that they were being hunted or that the wind turned cool and angry all around them. The ice between them melted, and that was the only thing that mattered to him now. The walls were down. Anything else, he could handle.

He started a fire in the small, stone fireplace to take the evening chill off the room while Leah changed into dry clothes. Even the sound of the hair dryer in the other room seemed too close to him all of a sudden. He was already being tortured, and they'd only been on speaking terms for a few minutes.

When she returned, he went to dry off as well. That would buy him some time to reason. He changed and towel dried his hair in the spacious bath. As he glanced into the mirror, the dark stubble on his face was visible and he realized that in his frustration this morning, he hadn't shaved. He rubbed his hand along his jaw, giving thought to the razor in the medicine cabinet but decided against it. It would take too long, and he was eager to get back to her.

"I made some hot tea." Leah was in the kitchen, refreshed in an oversized white oxford and a pair of jeans. Her hair was dry, and it effortlessly framed her face. She pushed a stray wisp behind her ear. "Sugar?"

"Yes, a half teaspoon." He walked up behind her,

tempted to reach for her but thought better of it. Now that they were in the confines of the house, any physical gesture between them was dangerous in ways he forced himself to push from his mind. Plus, the sound of the rain was intoxicating, and he feared his ability to reason might grow impaired.

"A half teaspoon is hardly enough to bother with," she said.

"For some things, no. But if you're a cup of coffee or tea, it's plenty." The smile on her face was warm as she stirred the tea and handed the mug to him, reaching for her own in the process.

They walked into the living room where Leah settled herself onto the sofa. Phillip deposited his mug beside hers on the coffee table then stepped over to poke the fire.

He returned to the sofa, careful to leave space between them. He picked up his tea and blew into it…stalling.

He'd no idea where to start.

She finally broke the silence. "How can I ever make it up to you?" Her voice was quiet and controlled as she pulled one leg underneath herself.

He leaned forward to put the tea back on the table, tilting his head to face her. She looked so right for him as she waited for his answer. Her eyes were fixed on his and she was poised to listen, completely unguarded. The oxford Sally had left at the house before their arrival was sizes too big for her.

Realization forced him to take his eyes from her. "You're wearing my shirt," he said as he stared into the fire.

"It was on top of the dresser the night we arrived."

He stayed forward. "It looks good on you. A little

large, but good."

"Thank you." Her laugh was lighthearted, almost playful. Soon she turned quiet and serious. "You still didn't answer my question. You've been wonderful to me, and I've been terribly rotten these last two weeks. How can I ever make it up to you?"

Marry me. He bit his lip to catch himself from saying the first thought that entered his mind. "You don't owe me anything except to promise that you won't take off and leave…in the midst of this case," he added.

"I wouldn't do that." She reached forward and touched his arm in a tender gesture.

He said nothing as he pinched the bridge of his nose in an effort to stay focused. Her touch was warm as she gently massaged his shoulder, making it difficult for him to breathe, let alone concentrate.

"Phillip?"

He turned toward her and his chin brushed against her hand. It was all he could do not to press his lips to her fingertips. "Yes?"

"I want you to know how much I appreciate you, in spite of how rotten I've been." The reflection of the fire danced in her eyes.

A lump formed in his throat. He couldn't stop wondering what would happen to him when the case was over and she was free to go. She said she wouldn't leave in the midst of it, but how would he tell her he wanted her to stay forever?

~*~

Tires kicked up the stones along the winding road. Mariucci and Scordino had been observing the cantaloupe-colored house at a distance for days. Between it, and the brick house down the street, there had been no hint of the aviator and the witness. Even the swing set in the back yard showed a lack of activity. The Leer Jet that was parked at a private hangar in Alexandria Bay hadn't moved since the day they'd almost overtaken them. Their brief visit to PRZ Aviation turned up nothing, and Mariucci was certain he and Scordino would raise suspicion if they returned to inquire.

They'd all but given up when Canali phoned them with a new lead earlier this afternoon. At least their contact in Miami was still able to pass along information. Any help was better than nothing.

If it weren't for the rain tonight, they'd have arrived sooner. Now that it was dark, it was difficult to make sense of the road. But either way he thought about it, Mariucci reasoned, the night was theirs to wait.

35

Maybe it was the chamomile. Maybe it was the dimming fire. Maybe it was the rain overhead that mesmerized him, but Phillip finally relaxed.

The tea had long since disappeared. The emotionally taxing day that weighed on both of them was coming to an end. Phillip caught Leah nodding off, and soon she nuzzled into him. His hand cupped her head and she relaxed on his chest as he held her close. Within moments, she was sound asleep.

He rubbed her hair between his fingertips. The strands were a perfect combination of soft and silk. There was so much he wanted to share with her, but so little he was permitted to say. She knew nothing of Crystal, Michael, and her birth mother. Nor was she aware of the plans that AJ was formulating. Phillip wanted her to know how much she meant to him. He lowered his face, gently brushing her hair with the stubble of his cheek as he took in the scent of her.

All in good time, Phillip. All in good time.

Before long, he found himself dozing off. It wasn't until Leah stirred at nearly ten o'clock that he woke up enough to encourage her to go to bed. Leah bade him good night and padded out of the room, leaving him alone on the sofa. He was asleep in short order.

When his cell phone rang from the top of the kitchen counter sometime during the night, his restful slumber was overruled. He glanced at the time, wondering who would call at such a late hour.

Phillip lifted his hand to his head in agony as the panicked voice of Daria's mother didn't even pause to greet him. Emotion flooded him as anguish rose from deep within in the form of an uncontrollable groan.

Jessica was gone.

~*~

Leah jolted in her sleep. At first, she thought it was a dream that roused her, and she laid in silence willing it to pass. Within moments, she knew it wasn't the case. She bolted to her feet and found Phillip slumped at the table, crying and uttering indiscernible words for help from above.

Her arms instinctively wrapped around him. "Are you all right? What happened?"

She pressed herself in toward him, rubbing his back to try and calm him. Finally, he lifted his head and turned to her. His eyes were pools of anguish, his face wet with tears.

Phillip's voice was barely above a whisper. "It's Jessica. Someone took her. She disappeared from my in-laws' home."

"No!" Leah's hands flew to her mouth as she slumped down on the floor beside him. Tears pooled in her eyes and panic threatened to choke the life out of her. She leaned on the legs of his chair, and her thoughts traveled a mile a minute as she spoke.

"When? How? Where? This can't be happening."

Phillip was obviously making a conscious effort to keep his cool.

"Nadia and Bill went in to check on her before they went to bed. Her covers were thrown back...and she was gone. There was a note."

Reality hit her square on and stole her breath.

"It's because of me, isn't it? It's them…" Fresh tears fell down her face as she shook her head in sorrow.

He reached for her, embracing her in comfort—for himself or for her, she didn't know. Suddenly, she snapped into action. There was no time to stop, no time to look back, and no time to grieve. They must get moving. They couldn't just sit here.

Realization dawned on Phillip as well. "We need to pray."

Leah agreed. Nothing was more critical now. He clung to her as words poured from his mouth in a cry for help.

"Father, we desperately ask for Your help and protection of Jess right now. Please don't let the enemy harm her in any way. Let Your bloodline be a shield about her. Guide us with Your wisdom and make it clear to us how to handle this situation. We thank You in advance because we believe in You and in Your word that prevails in all situations. We make a conscious choice to not consider the circumstances, but we place our hope in You. Thank You for being faithful, even now. Show Yourself strong on our behalf when we are otherwise weak. We ask these things in Your holy name."

Leah squeezed his hand, whispering words of agreement. God would be faithful. His word was true, and His faithfulness was altogether complete despite the storm around them.

"The police are on their way, so I need to get over there quickly. I can't leave you alone, but it's probably not the best to take you with me."

"I'm going with you."

"You'll be in danger."

"And you won't? And what about Jess? There's no way I'm bowing out now. You're leaving, I'm coming, and somehow, we're going to get Jess back."

36

Phillip and Leah arrived in Southwick Beach on Lake Ontario's easternmost side at two-thirty in the morning. Nadia and Bill Clepole's home was a flurry of activity as investigators scoured it for fingerprints and evidence. The FBI joined forces with the local district, pooling their efforts to make sense of the case. Phillip was on the phone with AJ.

To Leah, everything seemed intertwined as the pieces started coming together. The strain on Nadia and Bill's faces spoke volumes of love for their bright-eyed granddaughter. But the look on Phillip's face nearly made her cry.

The night wore on as the four now sat at the dining room table with the lead investigator while a timeline was formed. Jessica was tucked in at nine twenty, and Nadia and Bill went to bed at ten. At one in the morning, Nadia woke up to use the restroom and went to check on Jess to be sure she was adequately covered. Jessica was gone, but the bed was still warm. She couldn't be far.

An Amber Alert was issued. Roadblocks were set up in every direction. They hoped she hadn't been taken by boat, for if they took her across the waters of Lake Ontario and into Canadian jurisdiction, it would add complications to the already twisted equation.

Leah realized she was clearly responsible, and she agonized over the thought. The short note from the abductors lay face up in a plastic bag in the center of the table. They would call at nine this morning. There was little information they'd gleaned from the scratching, apart from the fact that it was written on a cream-colored piece of linen paper with the initial *A* embossed on top. It was the kind of stationery one might purchase at any gift shop from here to Miami.

"Leah, why don't you get some rest?" Phillip's voice brought her mind to the present as he gently rubbed her arm.

She shook her head in protest, considering the sense of responsibility that was hers. Why should she rest when she was the cause of what they faced?

"I think you all need to go to bed," Tom Riley, the lead investigator, addressed each of them. "We have the area covered. When nine o'clock arrives, you'll be needed. There's nothing more you can do until that time, so you need to save your strength."

The lines on Phillip's face told Leah that Riley was correct, even if it was difficult to admit. He was worn and weary, and his voice was raspy when he spoke to her.

"I suppose you're right," Phillip agreed with a decided slump to his shoulders.

"He is right." Bill's eyes met Phillip's for a moment. Nadia nodded her head in agreement and reached for Bill's hand. "It's so hard to think about getting some shut-eye, but we need to be alert tomorrow for whatever action is necessary after we take their call."

"I'll ready the beds for the two of you," Nadia announced as she stood. Leah followed. She was certain she wouldn't be able to sleep, although her eyes felt heavier than they had in years. She also didn't know how comfortable she'd be staying in a room by herself under the circumstances. She'd do better to sleep in the living room on the sofa where she had the comfort of the authorities within earshot. Nonetheless, she complied.

Ten minutes later, Phillip met her in the upstairs hallway. "Thanks for being here, Leah. It means the world to me."

Tears threatened as she bit her lip in an attempt to stifle her emotions. She must be strong for him, but it was difficult. She said nothing as he pulled her close, fearing she would collapse under pressure. Even in Phillip's weakness, he exuded strength that far surpassed hers. Yet the strain in his eyes was gut-wrenching when he drew back from her.

"It's going to be OK." He spoke with conviction although it was clear to her that his response was more faith than feeling. "We must trust. Like never before."

"I know," Leah agreed, wishing her faith were as strong as his. She sensed a new understanding of what Paul meant when he referred to the woman as the weaker one. Not that it gave her an excuse to be a wimp, but most men were able to remove their emotions from a situation long enough to get the job done. Phillip was no different. He exuded strength beyond her comprehension. If it were left up to her, she'd sulk and brood under the weight of their circumstances, wasting valuable time in the process. Great intentions were a good start, but Leah admittedly was a slow finisher.

"I'm praying they won't do anything to harm her. I doubt they would," Phillip said.

"Why not?"

"Apart from the fact that we prayed about it, it wouldn't make sense to hurt Jess. They're obviously negotiating. To get it, Jess has to be in perfect shape. They've got to hold up their end of the bargain."

Leah nodded, her lips quivering in the process. It was clear they wanted her in place of Jess. Phillip must have read the look on her face.

He traced her cheek with his finger. "Don't worry about a thing. Our team of experts is on the case, and they understand how to handle these types of situations. For now, get some rest. I promise we'll come wake you as soon as we learn something."

"But what about you?" she asked. "You need your rest, too."

"I'll be in the study. There's a pull-out sofa in there."

"How can you be so strong at a time like this?"

He shook his head as if to negate her observation. "I'm not, in my own strength anyway. Usually, I'm on the outside of a case peering in. It's pretty tough being on the inside, especially as a father. I love Jessica more than life itself."

His eyes were moist with tears, and she reached up to touch his cheek.

"She depends on me for everything. I can't stop thinking that she must be wondering why I let her down—why I didn't come for her. I want to get out there myself and head things up, go find her on my own. But that's not the way it works, no matter what I think about it. My confidence has to be in the Lord, and in the system. AJ will be here tomorrow with Kevin, a friend of his who's a former Navy SEAL. AJ, Kevin, and Riley are the best in the field. All that's left to do is trust. I cannot allow myself to be overcome with fear. If so, I'm guaranteed to lose focus completely. That can't happen."

To exude just a sliver of the strength Phillip conveyed, she'd do well. Perhaps a rest would do her good. Phillip squeezed her shoulders and pivoted her toward the guest room.

Thoughts of Jessica and her bright, emerald eyes played in Leah's mind as she struggled to sleep. Phillip was on her mind, too. He was a good father who ached for his only daughter. That fact alone brought fresh tears to her eyes that formed a pool on her pillow. By the time she finally settled, it was nearly sunrise, and she drifted off to a fitful sleep.

37

AJ raked his fingers through his sandy-colored hair as he checked the overhead monitor for the incoming flights at Miami International. The flight from Dallas/Fort Worth was due to arrive in ten minutes.

He'd gotten their cooperation for the plan, but that was before things changed so drastically during the night. With Jess missing, everything was different. Their weeks of planning didn't apply anymore. A new game plan was needed. Whether they'd be as quick to cooperate was yet to be seen.

His plan to save time and have Crystal and Michael re-route to Atlanta to meet him and Kevin was unsuccessful, as their flight was already en route. He glanced at the monitors once more as he paced the floor near the gate and waited.

~*~

Crystal peered out the window as the lights of the runway grew larger and brighter upon descent. Through the reflection, she saw Michael lean his head back and take a deep breath. He was anxious about the plan. Yet there was little choice in the matter. She reached over and squeezed his hand.

"Relax, honey. It'll be all right."

He drew out a labored breath. "You seem so certain."

"AJ has it under control. It's a good plan. You have to trust him and me, too."

"Easy for you to say. You won't be the one sitting on the sidelines waiting for word."

She laughed at his comment and winked playfully. "I've got the easy part, right?"

Michael tilted his head toward her and a grin played on his lips. At least she'd gotten a smile out of him. "I want to be sure you'll be OK. I can't afford for something to happen to you."

"I'll be fine. Nothing will happen to me. The plan is a good one, and as soon as we meet with AJ and re-hash the details, you'll be convinced as well."

"It's the variables that are nerve-wracking. Things can change in the blink of an eye."

"Yes, but remember we're working with professionals. AJ's a US Marshal himself. And his ex-SEAL friend knows what he's doing. We've covered every possibility. On top of that, we prayed for an opportunity to help. God's got this."

Michael wasn't convinced.

"And if that's not enough, it won't be long 'til I meet her. It'll be worth it all. And you'll have a sister-in-law."

The plane landed smoothly, and within minutes they exited the aircraft and walked through the jet-walk to the concourse. AJ was at the front of the line to greet them.

"Great to see you." AJ shook Michael's hand and reached for Crystal's.

"You as well," Michael replied.

Crystal read through her husband's enthusiasm, assured it was mere politeness. Although the men shared a bond in Miami, Michael was on edge. After six years of marriage, there was no hiding that fact from her.

"Did you check any luggage?" AJ asked as they walked onto the main concourse. He reached for Crystal's bag.

"No. We only brought carry-ons," Michael answered.

"Great. That'll save time."

Crystal detected a slight hesitation from AJ, and suspected Michael noticed it, too. "We've had a little change of plans."

38

Leah sat in the living room, trying to formulate her thoughts for the day. She wasn't hungry but forced herself to eat a bowl of cereal anyway. Phillip was already outside going over the timeline once again with the investigators, now that it was daylight and the footprints and tire marks were more visible.

Nadia walked in with two glasses of juice and handed one to Leah.

"Thanks." Leah smiled at the older woman.

In the light of day, even Nadia and Bill seemed hopeful. Perhaps the message they'd received earlier helped. Jessica was unharmed but scared when she'd spoken a few brief words to Phillip. The intent of her abductors was clear—they wanted the witness for the daughter. If Leah had any idea where they'd taken Jess, she'd leave now and present herself for the exchange.

Nadia sat next to her and laid a hand on her arm. "Did you get some sleep?"

"A little. You?"

"The caffeine kept both of us up. We finally got up and prayed."

Leah traced the edge of the sofa with her finger.

"Phillip has always been a winner," Nadia said after a while.

"He's holding up pretty well." Fresh tears formed in Leah's eyes.

"He's been through some tough things, as we all

have, you included. But he keeps his focus despite everything that's come against him."

Leah reached for her juice, letting the cool of it sooth the lump in her throat.

"He loves you. You know that, right?" Nadia asked.

Leah's eyes met Phillip's mother-in-law's, wishing it were true, yet understanding there were far too many complications for that. Jess was first in Phillip's life, as expected. And with photographs of Daria on the wall, Leah's emotions were on edge. She was a fifth wheel, a clunky one at that, and the cause of the trauma they now faced. She wanted to curl up in a ball and roll away.

"Phillip deserves far better," she whispered the words. "Besides, I'll never come close to what your daughter meant to him."

Nadia smiled as tears formed in her eyes. "Losing Daria has been hard for all of us, but we want Phillip to be happy again. He deserves nothing less. Bill and I couldn't have chosen a better son-in-law. Phillip is a remarkable man."

"He certainly is," she agreed as Phillip walked past the living room entrance.

He poked his head in the doorway. "Good morning."

He looked good, considering.

"Morning." Leah smiled weakly at him.

"Come on in. We were just talking. I'll get you a glass of juice." Nadia stepped out into the kitchen and returned with a glass for him.

"Anything new?" Leah asked Phillip as he took a seat across from her.

"We followed the tire tracks to the main road

before the tracks turned south. It was definitely a four-wheel drive. How did you sleep?"

"Between nightmares, not too well. But I slept a little."

"Same here. Probably twenty minutes total."

She let out a labored sigh. "I'm anxious for this to be over with. What can I do to help? I don't care about the case anymore. All that matters is getting Jessica back."

He moved over next to her. "Don't sound so defeated."

"I hate that you're going through this."

"I appreciate the sentiment. But we're making progress." Phillip tried to offer encouragement. He must be aching inside if he'd stop long enough to reason it out. But no, this man wouldn't give up. He was focused, as Nadia said.

"What kind of progress are you making?" Leah asked, wiping her eyes with the limp napkin in her hand.

"The stationery for starters. Tom is checking out every Bed & Breakfast within a three-hour radius."

"Why a B & B? They could have purchased it anywhere."

"But the scent. Did you smell it?"

"No."

"It passed us up last night, too. It was thrown into the evidence bag so quickly we didn't stop to take notice of it. It's faint, but it's clearly lavender, as if it was sprayed on deliberately. Tom discovered it this morning. From what we understand of the two men, they don't seem the type to exude that kind of femininity. That's an amenity only a B & B would provide."

Leah tried desperately to grab hold of this small ray of hope.

"Don't be distressed," Phillip said.

"How can I not be? All of this is my fault. I can't believe what you're going through on account of me." She leaned her head back on the sofa as fresh tears fell down her face. She'd never been so helpless, so destitute.

"It's not your fault, Leah. If it was, where do I fit in? I can say that if I weren't a case manager, it wouldn't have happened either. Am I wrong for being a member of the marshals?"

"That's different."

"How?" he pressed.

"It just is."

He ignored her comment as he reached for her, drawing her to him for a warm embrace. "You are exactly where you need to be at this moment, and don't you forget it. AJ will be here in a few hours. Remember, they won't harm Jess. We're OK for now. It's actually buying us time until AJ arrives."

"You sound so sure."

"I haven't always been that way, but I am now, without a shadow of a doubt. Remember, faith is the substance of what is hoped for, the evidence of what is not seen. Without it, it's impossible to please Him."

Fresh tears fell again as his words poured over her. How could she ever be the person she was supposed to be when she was lacking that kind of active faith to sustain her? She was a failure in every sense of the word.

Her only conclusion was that she was absent the day the prized mustard seeds were passed out.

39

Phillip hated to leave Leah at the house while he and Captain Riley went to the airport, but he had little choice in the matter. A few minutes of privacy were needed to verify the hastily made plan between the key players.

He pulled up to the terminal loading zone and got out of the vehicle when he spotted AJ and another man walking toward him.

"Phillip. Hey, man." AJ bear-hugged him.

"Thanks for coming. It's good to see you."

"You too, buddy. This is Kevin Douglas, an old friend from San Diego. He and I were SEALS together before we joined the marshals."

"It's a pleasure to finally meet you, Kevin." Phillip shook his hand. "Gentlemen, this is Special Agent Tom Riley, the lead FBI investigator in the case."

Pleasantries were exchanged, and Phillip became keenly aware of the couple behind AJ. When his eyes met Crystal's, he did a double take. AJ was right. She was the mirror image of Leah. It was unbelievable.

"This is Michael Robbins and his wife, Officer Crystal Robbins," AJ announced.

"I'm honored to meet you both." Phillip extended his hand to each of them. It was difficult to shake the overwhelming emotion of the moment. "I feel as if I know you both already."

"We've heard so much about you." Michael's smile was warm, but Phillip sensed his apprehension.

"I'm so glad to make your acquaintance, Phillip," Crystal said, pushing her hair behind her ear. Her movement matched her sister's.

"We're sorry to learn about Jessica's abduction. How is Karina taking it?" Michael asked.

Phillip stiffened at the mention of Leah's real name as he opened the trunk, prompting the group to toss their bags onto a pile. "She's having a difficult time. She's placing a lot of blame on herself."

"Understandable," AJ said. "But this is something she has no control over. These men are ruthless. If they didn't do it this way, they'd have done it another. Fortunately, we may be able to use the situation to our advantage."

"I hope so. I need to get Jess out of this mess as soon as possible."

"Were you able to speak with her?" Crystal asked as they started down the main highway.

"This morning. She sounded good. Afraid, but otherwise OK. They plan to call tonight and state their demands."

AJ gave Phillip the address of the hotel where he'd reserved rooms for Kevin, Crystal, and Michael. When they arrived, they spent the next hour and a half going over the plan with several backups in place in case one or more were needed. Notes were taken, scratched through, and revised.

Phillip's enthusiasm grew as he, Riley, and AJ left the hotel, leaving the others to get some rest. The plans were solid.

He only hoped they would fit in well with the ransom demands. The lives of those he loved the most were irrevocably on the line.

~*~

The clock on the mantel struck eight times, reverberating through the house as if a reminder were necessary. Phillip, Leah, Bill and Nadia, AJ, and Special Agent Riley sat around the table and waited. Two additional members of the FBI were in the living room. One was on the computer, the other on his cell phone speaking to someone in the field.

Leah tensed with anticipation. She rubbed her temples with her fingertips, hoping to calm her mind. She was weary and her guard was down. Perhaps if she'd been better rested, her thoughts might be more rational. There'd been little opportunity to speak to Phillip in private today since AJ's arrival. A part of her wanted to draw strength from him, but he needed all he could muster without her distraction.

Come unto Me all you who labor and are heavy laden, and I will give you rest.

The verse tugged at her. She needed to get alone with God, but how was that possible? Especially when her thoughts were so muddled.

She was torn and completely gutted. Everything in her life seemed to be coming together for one gigantic boom. She was ill-prepared for the repercussions. Neither Phillip nor AJ had given her any information yet as to her duties during the exchange. She assumed she'd go it alone, but she was in the dark. Perhaps the details weren't fully drawn together. Still, it added to her insecurity. She was useless, apart from the fact that she was needed solely for the purpose of giving her life for Jessica's. Maybe that's why she was alive. Born to die.

The phone rang at the center of the table, and she

jumped. AJ hit the button on the recording device and gave Phillip a questioning glance. At Phillip and Riley's confirming nod, AJ placed the call on speaker.

"Hello, this is Mr. Zellmer." Phillip's face was solemn and his voice tight.

"A pleasure, Mr. Zellmer. We assume you're in agreement to our demands." Their speech was distorted.

Phillip clenched and unclenched his fists.

"We are."

Leah cringed. Even though it was necessary, the abrupt agreement reminded her of her worthlessness—her dispensability.

"Seven o'clock in the morning at Alex Bay. There's a private boat dock. Karina must meet us alone. Anything less, the deal is off the table."

"But someone has to be nearby to pick up Jessica," Phillip countered.

"Jessica will be seated at a park bench at the nearby boat rentals. You'll find her soon enough. Come for her at seven thirty. Not before."

"She's only three. She can't be left alone like that."

"Do you wish to see your daughter alive?"

"Of course I do!"

"Then do as we say, and you'll meet her at seven thirty."

"Let me talk with Jessica to be sure she's all right."

"Jessica is unable to come to the phone right now."

"I need to speak with my daughter!" Phillip demanded.

"You have our word. She's OK. We'll call you at five o'clock in the morning to confirm. You can speak to her at that time."

"Tell her I—" A dial tone sounded abruptly.

Leah closed her eyes, and her shoulders shook with sobs. She pushed her chair back and hurried out the patio door.

When she told God she wanted to be a vessel of honor, she meant it with everything that was in her. But she wasn't prepared to be challenged so quickly.

She needed a few moments alone to absorb the news.

40

Phillip sank at the abrupt hang up. He wanted to talk to Jessica so badly, he ached.

Questions assailed his mind. How were they treating her? Did she get enough to eat? Was she able to sleep without her dolly if she even slept at all? What was she dreaming about? She no doubt thought he'd abandoned her by not charging in and rescuing her. But at three and a half, she could not possibly comprehend the complications. All she would understand was that she needed her daddy, and he wasn't there for her. Let alone the fact she didn't even have a mother.

Phillip's heart was broken.

Yet he must believe that somehow, somewhere, a light waited at the end of this long, dark tunnel.

When he lifted his head, Leah was walking out the back door. He inhaled, reigning in his emotions, and followed her. But what would he say? He was sworn to secrecy. She didn't realize she'd be safe and sound tomorrow, under guard by Riley. She had no idea what the plan entailed, although it was clear she expected the worst. She had to be under the impression that her life didn't matter anymore.

But she did matter. More than she realized. Someday he hoped to show her how much.

Leah was sitting on a bench near the backyard fence. A light wind ushered her soft cry in his direction. He hated to intrude on her privacy. Perhaps it was needed above his words of comfort. But to stand by idly and allow her to face this on her own was cruel. He must say something to offer comfort.

He moved toward her. "Leah?"

She didn't respond. He sat down next to her and wrapped his arm around her shoulder. "I promise you everything's going to be all right."

"No, it won't." Her answer was muffled.

"Don't say that. You've got to be strong."

"How can I help but say that? Everything is falling apart." Her gaze met his, her face moist with tears. Even in the approaching moonlight, her warm brown eyes were pools of liquid.

He drew her closer and caressed her. "You mean so much to me, Leah. I promise you'll be perfectly safe. Please trust me in this."

"Yeah, right. I wish it were that simple."

Phillip pursed his lips tightly together in an effort to remain silent. He wanted to tell her, but he must not. The advice of the Special Agent resonated in his mind. Leah could not be told about Crystal until after the fact. If something went awry in the morning, Leah's ignorance of her twin's existence and participation would be beneficial. Leah would be broken at losing a sister she'd just met.

No, the introduction must wait until after the fact.

But first, Jessica must be rescued. His thoughts were mingled with pain and hope all mixed into one. At times, it seemed his strength failed him. He reminded himself on a moment-by-moment basis that God promised to meet his every need.

"OK, you're not required to trust me," he said after a moment. "I'd love it if you did, but it's more important to put your trust in God. He's the only one who will never fail you. I'll do whatever possible, but we men tend to miss the mark at times. Will you do it for Him?"

She was silent for a long time as she pondered his words. "I'm trying. But I'm only human."

"I understand. He's aware, too. He'll meet you as you make an effort."

"What if something goes drastically wrong?"

"God is aware of the outcome." He brushed her face with his fingers, wiping a pool of tears from under her eyes. "Besides, He's given me peace about it. Confidence in Him and in His word is essential."

She didn't respond. It was clear she was growing weary. She needed a good night of rest. He did, too, for that matter.

"The plan is to be up early. AJ and the team are going over the final details now. In the morning, we'll talk again. And then all you'll need to do is do exactly as I say, OK?"

The temptation to divulge more to her in an effort to ease her mind played loud in his ears. Even his role was reduced to an observer from now on. He was too closely involved. AJ warned him, telling him as much on the drive back today. No point taking a chance when he was so close to the situation. The mood would be tense, and he might do something regrettable, trying to remedy the situation on impulse. No matter his training, he was only human when it came to those he loved. Sitting back and waiting was difficult. But that was his required role.

"You ready to come in?" he asked after a while.

"Not quite. You go on. You have plans to make. I'll be inside in a bit."

"Don't stay too late," Phillip answered, brushing

the top of her head with a reassuring kiss. "I'll see you in a few minutes."

He rose to leave, sensing a loose end. Was there something more he should've said? His desire to express his love for her must wait. The moment must be right, not overshadowed by the trauma that engulfed them. No, he would need to declare his feelings another time.

He wanted to wait until everything was perfect.

~*~

Leah sat outside for another forty-five minutes. A glance at her phone told her it was pushing ten o'clock. She needed to go inside and get to bed. It would be a short night with little sleep.

She stood and walked toward the light of the open kitchen window. The air outside was crisp, refreshing. She'd have enjoyed it on any other occasion. She stopped abruptly when she heard the words spoken in low tones that spilled from the window.

"You haven't told Leah about Officer Robbins, have you?" AJ's voice was clear.

"No. I took your advice. Besides, how could I in light of all this other stuff?"

"You're in a tight spot, I know. It's best that Leah won't find out 'til afterward. Tomorrow morning will be tough enough without anything more added to the equation."

"She's amazing, isn't she?" The voice was Phillip's.

Leah froze.

"She certainly is."

"She's so perfect for this. It was all I could do to

stay focused when I saw her today. I hope Leah accepts this. It may be difficult on her, you know. Sometimes I wish I'd told her sooner. But there was never an appropriate time to do so."

"But tomorrow is a new day. A lot is at stake…"

"That's an understatement. I'll be so relieved when I get Jess back. And after I break the news to Leah and the case is resolved, I'll be a free man."

"Not being truthful to Leah about her has really gotten to you, hasn't it?"

"Absolutely."

"You love her, don't you?"

"More than you know."

The knot in Leah's chest threatened to stop her heart beating. She forced herself to take a breath, bracing against the back wall of the house. Why had he led her on? Phillip clearly was in love with another woman, an officer with whom he shared a common bond. His interest in her had been purely professional, not personal as Phillip made her to believe. His plan was to hold Leah's hand, to take her through this change of identity. All the comfort he offered fell from her shoulders. A useless garment. That's all it was. She shook herself to remove the memory of his warm embrace a mere hour before.

*How could I have fallen prey so easily?*Her thoughts raced. She forced herself to move away from the wall. Perhaps she might slip through the hall by the kitchen without being noticed. Each step played out as if in slow motion as she lifted one foot in front of the other, heavy as lead. She was relieved when she passed by without being observed. Phillip's back was turned, and AJ was walking toward the refrigerator. Quietly, she stole to the guest room, slumped on the bed, and wept.

41

Phillip tossed and turned in the study across the hall from Leah's room. He sensed uneasiness, and wondered why, apart from the obvious reasons. His daughter was being held hostage and the life of the woman he loved hung in the balance.

Crystal and Michael were on board with the plan and seemed confident in the process. He was grateful for that. He recognized Michael's nervousness when meeting him, and for good reason. He'd be nervous, too, if it were Leah going into the front line of battle. He prayed for strength. Michael needed it, too—as did Crystal. He prayed for the entire team, but most of all, he cried out for Jess.

Phillip had to get some sleep. He finally dozed. He woke up intermittently though the night, and when he did, desperate words of prayer escaped his lips again.

The clock ticked on.

He didn't see her come in after their conversation in the backyard. When he went to check on her at ten fifteen, she was nowhere to be found. He'd gone upstairs to find the light on in her room. She was exhausted, of course, and probably sleeping. He'd almost knocked on her door but stopped midstream before tapping on the wooden barrier that separated them. At that point, making contact with her in his state of weakness wasn't prudent. Instead, he'd forced his hand deep into the pocket of his jeans and went to bed, tossing and praying ever since.

A noise startled him just as the digital display turned to two o'clock. It was probably someone walking down the hall toward the bathroom, but he needed to be sure. He slipped out of bed and peered down the hall. Leah's door was cracked, and light spilled from under the bathroom door. No doubt she couldn't sleep either. With his emotions still on high alert, it was best not to run into her at this time of the night. He pulled his door shut and went back to bed.

At four o'clock, the alarm woke him from a dismal sleep. When he stepped into the hall, Leah's door was still cracked but the bathroom door was wide open, vacant. Inside, he glanced at his reflection in the mirror. Nothing a hot shower wouldn't fix.

Ten minutes later, he donned a white polo shirt and a pair of Dockers, ignoring the obvious need to shave.

"Morning." Phillip greeted Nadia, Bill, Riley, and AJ who were already assembled at the kitchen table. He walked to the coffeepot and reached for a mug.

A series of greetings were exchanged as the group talked in hushed tones.

"Is Leah up yet?" He pulled out a chair and sat down.

"I don't think so," AJ replied.

"I'll go wake her," Nadia offered. "She's been exhausted."

"She has been. Thanks," Phillip glanced at the clock on the wall. It was four twenty-three. The call was scheduled in thirty-seven minutes. To hear Jess's voice would be a relief. He breathed in a sense of hope with an underlying prayer that all would go well.

Nadia's dark eyes were troubled when she walked into the kitchen a few minutes later. There was a note in her hand.

Phillip's brow furrowed. "What's wrong?"

"It's Leah."

"What about her?"

"She's gone."

"Gone? She can't be!" He pushed himself to his feet and knocked his chair over in one abrupt move.

Nadia handed the paper to him.

He quickly scanned the note and read it again, absorbing every scrawl. His breath came in short gasps as sorrow permeated his being. His hands shook, and the note fell to the floor. Nadia bent over him, encircling him with her arms.

AJ picked it up and read it aloud, telling them it was addressed to the team. "After much thought, I've come to realize it's best for me to leave. I regret what I've put everyone through, especially Jessica, and for that I'm truly sorry. She, most of all, doesn't deserve to be in the midst of such a mess. I've chosen to give myself up at the designated time in exchange for her, but I'm going on my own. It's not worth risking anyone else's safety. Please do not come for me. Trust me in this. Karina Rubenski."

Phillip's heart throbbed in his ears as the words tore at his emotions. The pain was evident in her handwriting, but when read aloud by AJ, they crushed him all the more.

And she hadn't even addressed him personally.

AJ was the first to break the sudden chill of the room. "We need to do something."

"You're right," Riley said as he glanced at the time. "We've got a half hour to come up with an alternative."

"That's not a lot of time, but let's do it. We'll get to

her." AJ reached for Phillip's clenched fist on the table.

Nadia released Phillip and went to the counter to get the pot of coffee. Phillip willed himself to his senses. It was true—there was precious little time to plot out a new strategy, and a safe one at that. But why the sudden change in Leah to warrant such drastic measures on her part?

And she'd signed it *Karina*...

That, in itself, was significant. It was her way of saying she'd chosen to step out of the program completely. She'd discarded Leah altogether, breaching the program due to the current problems with Jessica. Might this have been the uneasiness he'd experienced earlier? Was she contemplating this while he held her close last night? In hindsight, why hadn't he said more to her—reassured her to remove any inkling of doubt?

Phillip took another swallow of coffee, but it tasted bitter in his mouth. The activity around him became background noise. Calls were exchanged on cell phones in order to keep the main line clear for the expected five o'clock call. The kitchen was a hubbub of activity. To Phillip the words melded together like a conglomerate of languages that he didn't understand.

He was in a world of his own that consisted of the two people who meant the most to him—the two people on earth who were suddenly so far out of his natural ability to reach. He wanted to go immediately and search for Leah, but it was critical for him to be available for the scheduled call.

And the clock on the kitchen wall was ticking much too loudly.

42

It had been months since Leah experienced such a long run. The cold of the cinder blocks crept right through the oxford she wore as she huddled against the back wall of the bait shop, catching her breath. The shirt made her feel close to him, something she hadn't planned on. Sadness wrapped around her like a heavy cloak.

She blew into the Styrofoam cup to cool the breakfast blend she'd purchased at the bait shop and found herself annoyed at the warning. *Caution, Hot!*

Of course it was hot. What else would one expect when buying a cup of coffee? It was coffee, for goodness' sake. If only other things came with a clear-cut warning.

She should have known better.

There were still several hours to go until the exchange. Perched away from the view of the dock, she'd be out of sight in the event Phillip or the others came searching for her. Shortly before seven o'clock, she'd move into position. But now was not the time to take a chance of being discovered.

Sorrow stirred as she glanced down at the timepiece that dangled from the chain on her neck. The panic button attached to it was her last connection to Phillip. But there was no need to be connected with him anymore. Any reminder would only be more painful. She pulled it over her head and laid it on the sidewalk.

So much was at stake with a future so uncertain. Her life in Miami was a distant memory. Leah Merrins was the name on her New York driver's license, and with it, a new onset of pain flooded her. Who was she really? If she did, in fact, survive the day, what name would she carry? Truth be told, after this morning it might not matter, except for the purpose of her headstone.

She wanted to write a letter to Phillip. But for what purpose? It would only further showcase her vulnerability.

Tears stung her face as she downed the remains of the hot coffee. A fresh breeze moved in from the bay.

She closed her eyes…and waited.

~*~

God, help me get it together, Phillip prayed as he gazed out into the pre-dawn sky from the quietness of his vehicle. Alone, he waited as detachment and isolation held him captive. AJ, Riley, and the rest of the team took charge. Nadia, Bill, and Michael were out of sight at a location several blocks away.

His nerves were raw, as was his throat. They'd upheld their word so far, and he was amazed at how accommodating they appeared to be. That in itself was a miracle. He hoped they would continue in that vein until Jess was safe in his arms.

But what about Leah?

He already loved and lost once. To love and lose again would be unbearable.

Trust in Me, Phillip. Don't lean on your own understanding, but acknowledge Me, and believe that I can and will direct all of your pathways and make them clear to you.

The words gave him pause. He was trying. Why must it be so hard? The enemy pursued him at every angle, holding the reins tight. Was there no rest for the battle-weary?

Remember, My power in you is greater than the evil one who is in the world.

The words were true, yet holding onto them without being swept away was a challenge greater than he imagined. But now was not the time to falter, regardless of how defeated he felt.

Lord, I'm at Your mercy. I'm at the end of my rope. There's nothing more I can do, except fall down at Your feet and cry for help. You're my deliverer. I put my trust and my hope in You. Protect Crystal and Jess and everyone involved. And please, please help me find Leah. At least long enough to tell her I love her…I ask You to convince her to love me back, no matter what I've done that has turned her so far from me…

Phillip glanced at the clock on his phone, glad they moved the exchange time up an hour. It was five fifty-eight. He was a safe distance away, but through his binoculars, he could see a boat approach the dock. Crystal was moving slowly in place. Even the cool morning air suddenly felt thick with tension. Phillip's very breath was an unending prayer.

He gripped the steering wheel when he recognized the small form of Jess as she stepped from the boat. He turned up the volume on his transmitter. The two forms neared each other on the pier. As they passed, Crystal told Jessica to sit on the bench straight ahead near the shore and wait. Tears fell down Phillip's face at the sound of his daughter's response, frail and shaken. Crystal told her to move forward and to not stop for anything.

So far so good.

Keep walking, Jess. Keep walking. You're almost home...

43

Something was wrong. Crystal sensed it. AJ's rhythmic voice counted down through the wire, but where was Kevin's confirmation? Had she failed to hear it? She needed precisely sixty seconds from the moment she stepped onto the dock until Kevin would surface from underneath the water and overtake the kidnappers, ending her terrifying role. Years had passed since she'd participated in an undercover operation. Her heart raced, reminding her of that fact.

Standing near the hull was a tall, distinguished man. She recognized him immediately, even in the early dawn. Frank Mariucci.

Scordino, his short and stocky sidekick, stood at attention at the wheel, ready to accelerate as soon as she stepped onto the boat. Everything in her wanted to claw the man to pieces. Her adrenaline surged.

"Fifteen...fourteen...thirteen..."

God, no!

"AJ, Kevin's not answering," Crystal spoke into her mouthpiece, trying not to move her lips. She hoped her years of ventriloquism paid off at this moment. If these men suspected she was communicating with anyone, she would quickly become a piece of Alex Bay's history.

"Ten. Roger that," AJ responded. "Nine. Kevin, are you there?" AJ's countdown continued. "Eight. Crystal, I'll shoot if necessary. Hang in there. Confirm, Kevin! Do you copy?"

Crystal never intended to get into the boat, and now she was only steps away. Kevin hadn't confirmed, and time was running out. If he didn't surface, she'd be forced onto the deck.

"Well, well, Karina. Gotta hand it to you." Mariucci grabbed her arm and pulled her to him.

The diameter of steel above the neck of her oversized sweatshirt was cold. Not a lot of good the bulletproof vest would do her. She stiffened in his grip.

"You tried to break apart our corporate livelihood, didn't you? DeFresnio is trying to appeal, despite the evidence against him. And you certainly won't get anywhere with us. Your day is drawing to a close, once and for all, Miss Rubenski."

An unseen force knocked her from her feet and into the icy depths. *A bullet!*

Nothing prepared Crystal for the impact that threw her body from the edge of the boat. Her thoughts tumbled as the water drew her under, immersing her into its cold clutches. What on earth had gone wrong? The bulletproof vest under her sweatshirt was heavy. It appeared the weight of the intended lifesaver would sink her to her death. The irony. Her head was fuzzy, her body weak and limp. Suddenly, the water she prized as a kid became her enemy. She thought of Michael, on the sidelines waiting, praying. Then there was Trevor. Had it been wrong of her to take chances when she had a husband and son to care for?

Michael was always supportive, albeit nervous, but he'd agreed because of how much it meant to her to do whatever was necessary in order to locate her sister. And her mother would be thrilled when Karina was found…that is, if Phillip was able to do so.

Like a flash, the thoughts raced in her mind. The water was freezing, removing the life from her legs. She tried to swim, but it was difficult to orient herself with the weight of the vest pulling her under. She must return to the dock. What direction was it? She fought the unconsciousness as long as possible. Where had she been shot?

Suddenly someone —or something—gripped her. A cold shudder ran through her, and that was the last thing she remembered.

~*~

AJ panicked when Crystal plunged overboard.

Don't let her come up yet! He breathed a silent prayer of desperation. If she emerged before he was ready, they might take her out. She must stay under, although her natural instinct would be to fight for the surface. The motor revved, and Scordino gunned it.

"Patience, man," he warned himself in a whisper. The crosshairs were on its intended target, even as the boat raced away.

Three, two, one ...

An eruption of flames bolted upward from the engine with a deafening noise.

"Yes!" AJ pumped his fist. The Evinrude was history, and the rest of the boat would be as well. The fiery blaze raced its way toward the hull while the passengers scrambled. He grabbed the two-way at his belt. "Target ready for pick up. Be prepared for a wet fight."

"Ten-four. Defender five three zero en route."

Within moments, the noise of the chopper sounded overhead and an envoy followed. To bring in the soggy twosome alive to stand trial was AJ's utmost goal at this moment. He pushed himself up from the floor of the roof he'd been perched on, and swung over the edge of the building in one fluid movement. AJ hoped Crystal was more forgiving than her desperate voice sounded before his silent shot removed her from harm's way.

As his brisk run narrowed the distance to the lake, he cringed at the thought of being at the brunt of Michael's anger for what he'd done. Would he understand he'd been without recourse?

Either way, AJ was certain there'd be a whole lot of explaining to do.

44

Phillip smothered Jessica with kisses nearly four minutes later despite AJ's warning to not come prematurely. When the scene unfolded before him and the boat sped off, how could he not race at lightning speed to get there? He grabbed her and carried her to safety, away from the commotion.

He wondered about Crystal. She'd been so brave. A part of him wanted to jump in and help. But his first responsibility was Jess. She'd been through enough.

He tousled Jessica's dark hair and she grinned. Joy filled him to the brim. His only child was such a delight to him. "I'm so glad you're OK, babe." He held her close as her small body shook, her arms tight around his neck.

"I was so scared, Daddy. They were so mean. Where were you?" Her emerald eyes glistened with tears. But there was a smile on her face just the same.

"I'm sorry they were mean, honey. It wasn't safe for me to come get you until now. We didn't want them to hurt you, and the only way to keep that from happening, was to come and rescue you their way."

"What was their way?"

"They wanted...to speak with Leah." His voice was sorrowful.

"You mean they didn't want me? They only wanted Leah?"

"That's right, babe."

"Well then, why didn't they come get her? Why

did they get me if they didn't want me? That was pretty silly."

Phillip threw back his head and laughed. The simplicity of his daughter's thinking process made perfect sense, at least for someone her age.

"They couldn't find Leah because I was protecting her."

"But you protect me, too, Daddy."

"Yes, I do, but in a little different way. They used you so they could find Leah."

Jessica peered up at him with a worried expression. "Is Leah going to be OK?"

Phillip pinched the bridge of his nose. "I really hope so, honey."

"Do you love her, Daddy?"

The question came as a complete surprise. What did a three-and-a-half-year-old know about love? He pursed his lips in thought and then responded. "Yes, Jess. I do. Is that OK with you?"

"You don't love her more 'n me, do you?"

"I love her in a different way."

"It's OK then if you do. I think I kind of love her, too."

Phillip smiled at her chatter. She was smarter with each day that passed.

Nadia and Bill arrived shortly and bombarded Jess with even more wet kisses. Phillip breathed a bittersweet sigh of relief. At least she was OK. He hoped the medical checkup would prove it as well.

"Crystal's OK," Bill informed him. "We passed Special Agent Riley on his way to the dock. He heard from AJ that Kevin pulled her to safety. Michael should be here shortly."

"Thank God. What happened?"

"Kevin's transmitter failed. He was getting ready to chance it when AJ took the shot. They were only seconds apart in their manual calculation. But the clock was ticking, and AJ couldn't wait any longer. In his crosshairs, it was clear to him that Crystal was about to be taken out by them."

Phillip believed AJ's assessment of the situation was accurate. Mariucci's ultimatum sounded through his transmitter, too. The thought made him cringe, yet with it was an overwhelming sense of relief that everything turned out, despite the technical glitch.

Jessica tugged at Phillip's collar. "Who's Crystal?"

"She's a friend," Phillip answered. A friend who was willing to put herself in harm's way for a sister who wasn't even aware she existed. Best to leave it unsaid for now.

Thoughts of Leah and her abrupt departure cast a shadow over him. He must find her before she set out for the dock. There was too much happening there now. He didn't want her to walk in on the investigation.

Bill must have read the expression on his face. "Go find her, Phillip. Nadia and I won't let Jess out of our sight. We'll be right here. You need to, before it's too late."

Bill was right. Phillip was grateful for his understanding. He hated to step away from Jess so quickly after their reunion, but it would only be for a short time, and her grandparents would be by her side.

Still, he left with apprehension. It was clear Leah didn't want to be found, and the fact that she hadn't said good-bye puzzled him. If he did locate Leah, would he be able to handle the outright rejection from her?

He thought not. But he must try.
He'd rather die trying than not to try at all.

45

Phillip scoured the area for a sign of Leah. Her self-made plan was to make her appearance at the dock promptly at seven. With all the activity there now, too much was at stake for her to stumble onto the scene. There were things that needed explanation.

It was six forty-five when he rounded the corner behind the bait shop and nearly ran into her. She was sitting Indian-style on the sidewalk, her head bowed and her lips moving.

"Leah?" he called to her.

She didn't flinch. Perhaps she heard him coming. Agony and betrayal were written on her face, and the pool of tears in her eyes was full enough to drown in. He stooped down beside her. The gold chain lay on the concrete by her side. He knew instinctively she was going to abandon it, along with everything else in her life. Including him. He picked it up and fingered it in his hand.

The wall between them was high, and the thickness of it would have deterred him had he not been so determined.

"You weren't supposed to come after me."

"Nor were you supposed to leave," he challenged.

"I had no alternative." Her words were quiet and carefully chosen.

"Neither did I. Why did you leave? You broke my heart." His eyes searched hers, but she avoided his gaze.

"I need to go." When she attempted to get up, he grasped her hands. She slumped back to the ground, glaring at him with unspoken pain in her eyes. "Why are you doing this to me, Phillip?"

"What are you talking about? Why are you doing this to me?" Pain spilled from his voice. "What on earth happened to turn you so abruptly against me? At first, I assumed maybe it was the pressure of the case. But I thought we had something more, you and I. You took off without saying a word to me. You never even acknowledged me in your note."

"Look, in all honesty, I really need to go. It's time. Your daughter's life is at stake. I gave my word. I'd never forgive myself if something happened to Jess."

"You also promised me that you wouldn't leave 'til the case was over."

"Well, it will be over in a few minutes. Besides, that was before things got so complicated. Jess doesn't deserve to suffer because someone wants me dead. She has her whole life in front of her...and you have yours."

There was obviously something she wasn't saying. He sensed the hurt in her tone. "What's that supposed to mean?"

She pushed to her feet and brushed off her jeans and the tail of the oxford. "You're an intelligent man, Phillip. I think you can figure it out." She stepped past him. He didn't try to stop her.

"It's already over," he finally called when she neared the end of the building. She stopped abruptly but didn't turn around.

"What do you mean, it's over?"

"The exchange has taken place. There's no need for you to go."

She turned to face him. "How can that be? It's not seven yet."

"We changed the time. As soon as we read your note, we had no choice but to do something, so we negotiated an earlier exchange. Thank God they agreed to our request when they phoned to confirm. That's a miracle in itself. Jess is safe. We've already reunited. Nadia and Bill are keeping an eye on her while I've been out searching for you."

Leah's hands went to her face as Phillip walked toward her. He wanted to reach for her, to hold her, but instead kept his distance. To be refused by her again wasn't an option.

"How did you pull it off without me?"

Phillip pushed his hands deep into his pockets. "We used a decoy."

Leah's guard was up and rising higher as she took it in. "So, this was the arrangement from the start?"

"Pretty much, although there were a few revisions along the way."

"What happened to the decoy?"

"She got shot, but she's going to be OK. It's a long story."

"How about Mariucci and Scordino?"

"They're being apprehended offshore. On this side of the Canadian border."

"Why didn't you inform me about the plan? It would've been helpful. I might've actually gotten a little sleep."

"True," he admitted. "But there were reasons. If you stick with me, I promise I'll disclose everything to you."

"Right." She turned to walk away, hurt still evident in her voice.

This time he followed her. "You can't leave me, you know."

"There's no reason for me to stay. Not now."

He reached forward to tug at the untucked shirt that flapped with the morning breeze. "Stealing's against the law."

She stopped walking and turned abruptly. "I hardly think I've done anything that would warrant that kind of accusation." Her eyes met his with fierce intensity. The moisture lifted somewhat, but they were still pools one might drown in.

"If you'll recall, that's my shirt. I can press charges," he teased in an attempt to lighten the mood.

Her expression softened, and she lifted her hand to her forehead, rubbing her temple as if to ease the tension. "I'm sorry. I'm not in the best frame of mind right now. I haven't had any sleep…"

"Of course, I, on the other hand, slept like a baby the last couple of nights. No. Make that weeks considering the cold chill that was in the air."

As soon as he said the words, he regretted them.

A labored breath escaped her lips as her shoulders dropped their resistance.

"I'm sorry, Leah. That was wrong of me. There's so much I want to tell you. Give me a chance. Please."

She was silent a moment, and it was clear to him that a battle was going on inside. "OK. What's on your mind?" she asked.

He wasn't certain if his apology was accepted, but at least one brick in the massive wall was beginning to loosen.

Phillip urged Leah toward the side of the building. There was so much to tell her, but now that she agreed, it didn't seem like the time or the place. Jess had been away from him long enough and was waiting for him.

He leaned against the wall and reached for Leah's hands. When she resisted, he withdrew his attempt and tried to find the right words to say.

"You seem adamant on protecting yourself from me."

"I do what's necessary," she informed him.

He searched her eyes but had a hard time getting past her cold shoulder. "I don't understand. Tell me what I've done to hurt you so much."

"Look, I don't mean to be difficult, but this has been a rough couple of months. You've been through some really tough times, too, with me and this whole Jess thing. I'm grateful for what you've done. Please don't misunderstand me. But you'll be rid of me soon, and you can move on with your life. And I'll do the same with mine."

His heart sank. Is that all he meant to her? How could he possibly move on with his life, apart from her? Something was desperately wrong. He needed to tell her everything or he was going to lose her. But he didn't have a clue where to begin. Even if he did, would she listen?

"Leah, we need to sit down and talk. There's something important I need to tell you. But I don't want to do it here. I also need to get Jess checked out. Please come with me, and we'll talk this afternoon."

"I can't." Her voice was barely audible.

"You're making this really hard on me." He was growing weary. He had to keep her from leaving.

"I'm sorry. This is the way it has to be."

"I'm begging you. Come with me. I'll tell you everything, but it'll take a while. I can't let Jess wait that long. If you won't do this for me, can you at least do it for her sake?"

Leah's eyelashes flickered, and a single tear slipped down her cheek. He wanted to reach out and brush it away, but he valued his hand. And his heart.

"For Jessica," she answered. "And then I'll go."

46

Leah walked back to the vehicle with Phillip. She struggled to push aside the emotions that plagued her as she tried to mask a happy face. After all, Jess was safe, and the danger was over.

An ambulance was parked in the distance near the dock and police cars were stationed nearby. It was hard to believe the amount of activity that lurked so close to where she'd waited. No sirens were used, nor was there the sound of anything unusual, other than the chopper. Truth be told, she was overtaken in her own grief, oblivious to the world that woke around her. The southerly wind moved across the quaint town and out to the St. Lawrence Seaway, carrying the noise of the morning away from her as well.

Leah stooped to give Jess a warm hug. "You OK, sweetie?"

"Yes, thank you. Those were bad people. Are you OK? My daddy was worried 'bout you. He said he had to find you."

Sadness welled up inside, but Leah put on the bravest front possible as she pushed a loose curl from Jess's forehead. She appreciated the thought, for whatever it was worth. "I'm fine. I'm so sorry you went through all this."

"They weren't very nice. But they didn't hurt me. Daddy says I still have to get checked. He says it's pa-*se*-jur."

Leah kissed the child's cheek. "I'm sure it is

procedure. And it's good for them to check you. They want to be certain everything is OK. You'll be out of there in no time."

"Can you come visit me when I get home?"

Leah fought the pang inside. "We'll see."

"Please try. Sally and Joe aren't back from vacation, and my grandma and grandpa have to go home. My daddy wants you to come, too. He told me so."

If only it were so easy. It amazed her how simplistic a child could be. She was glad Phillip was talking with his in-laws a few steps away.

"Hey, you changed your clothes already. I just noticed," Jessica announced.

"I didn't change my clothes, silly."

"Jess trying to sweet talk you?" Phillip broke into the conversation, snatching Jess and lifting her high in the air. There was a strain in his voice that was difficult to ignore.

Phillip tousled Jess's hair, giving her a playful reprimand. Leah's throat constricted as the two of them interacted. Whatever his distress, it was clear he downplayed it for his daughter's sake. The bond between them was a beautiful thing to behold.

"Can Leah go with us to the hospital?" Jess pleaded with her dad.

"If she wants to, I think that would be real nice." Phillip smiled at Jess, then glanced at Leah with a question in his eyes. Leah noticed the familiar lines around them again. He looked tired, but the stubble on his face made him ruggedly handsome. She stopped the thoughts from forming before they took on a life of their own and turned away.

"I want you to come, Leah. Please?" Jess begged.

"Honey, Leah is very tired. Maybe she'd like to go home and rest. She can stop by and see us after that."

"I guess that's OK," Jess said with a bit of a pout. "As long as you come later."

Leah looked over at her, finding it difficult to say no. Besides, she'd promised Phillip a few minutes to talk…before she left for good. "I'll stop by later today. It'll give you both a chance to rest, too."

When she glanced back at Phillip, his eyes were on her intently. It was as if he wanted to say something, but chose not to. Thoughts stirred inside her again, like her guard was lowering. She reprimanded herself and turned away from his scrutiny. Why did he make her feel this way? To Phillip, she was just another case. She needed to move on with her life, whatever was left of it.

He broke the silence between them. "What time can you come?"

"How about four o'clock? That'll give us all a chance to catch a nap."

Jess wrestled from his arms to get down, prompting Phillip to deposit her onto the ground. As he stood up, his eyes met Leah's again, frustrating the battle even more for her. "Four is fine," he answered. "If you promise you'll come."

"I will." She thought she detected moisture in his eyes. But what did he have to be sad about now, when it was her own core that ached so profusely? She hoped the pain would stop but had little hope in that happening. How much longer could she be in his presence before she broke down entirely? "Looks like I'll need a ride home."

"Can you take my vehicle? I was going to go in the ambulance with Jess so she can get checked out. Her pediatrician is meeting us there."

"Sure, I can do that."

"I get to go in a am-lance?" Jess obviously had no idea that it wasn't the treat she imagined.

"Yes, babe. I'll be right beside you. Leah will come over later." Phillip pulled the keys from his pocket and handed them to Leah. "I appreciate it."

"See you this afternoon."

~*~

Leah drove Phillip's SUV down the street and passed by the bait shop. The public restroom was around the corner, making it convenient for the shoppers that browsed the lazy resort town. She parallel parked outside the door and went inside. One stall was occupied, so she took the one next to it.

"I'm OK, Mom—a little cold, that's all."

There was something about the tone of the woman's voice that sounded strangely familiar.

"There's no need to worry. Honestly."

Leah wished she could say the same for herself.

"Can I call you when I'm on the road?"

Leah exited the stall. The broken mirror at the sink was cloudy. Still, one glance at her reflection made her want to look away. Sure, it had been an early morning with little sleep the night before, but even through the obscurity, the circles under her eyes were evident. She needed a nap in the worst way, and it was barely daybreak. Splashes of cool water on her hands and face were refreshing. As she blotted her face with paper towels, the door of the other stall creaked open.

"Good morning," the woman said as she approached the sink and washed her hands.

Leah glanced into the cracked reflection and saw a young woman about her height with wet hair the same color as her own.

Their eyes met.

"Karina?"

Leah froze, and the damp paper towels in her hand drifted to the floor. She turned to face the woman who still stared at her through a shattered image.

"Who...who are you? Have we met?" Leah asked.

The woman's shoulders began to shake, but she said nothing as she pivoted toward Leah. Their eyes locked.

"You...you look exactly like me," Leah whispered.

"I've been searching all over for you." The woman reached toward her reluctantly, as if she wanted assurance that the embrace would be mutual.

"I...I don't understand."

"We share the same birth mother."

Leah's head started to spin, and her knees felt weak. She braced herself on the edge of the sink.

"We're sisters, Karina. But not just sisters, we're twins. My birthday is February fifth just like yours."

"How is this possible? What's your name?"

"Crystal. Our mother's name is Elizabeth."

Suddenly, so many things became clear as they stood face to face. Leah reached for her sister, just as she felt the ground move from beneath her. Steady arms lowered her to the floor, and the two clung together as the world around them faded and time stood still.

47

It took Phillip the rest of the morning and the early part of the afternoon to get Jessica thoroughly checked and settled at home. She talked non-stop until she finally drifted off to sleep. Even her pediatrician commented that her chatterbox seemed to be working particularly well.

He closed the storybook and smiled down at her. Her dark hair was spread across the pillow, and it smelled clean when he stooped to kiss her forehead. He thanked God continuously for her safe return.

And the last he heard, Crystal was going to be fine.

Now for his other request…

He was utterly helpless when it came to Leah. If only he was privy to what he'd done to cause her to turn away, he'd know how to go about fixing things with her. But he didn't have a clue.

He left Jessica's door cracked, and walked into his office to tackle the pile of mail that accumulated while he was gone. He forced himself to go through it, returning calls in the process.

He spoke with Marci. Things were going well at the hangar. It had been three days since he'd last checked in with them. Marci and Charles were the only ones there who were aware of his involvement with the marshal's office. It didn't take them long to suspect Leah's position as well.

He caught himself peering out the window of his

upstairs office, wondering about her.

A part of him feared she would leave without stopping in at all. But he must trust, no matter how difficult it seemed. He wanted to keep her within eyesight all day today, but she needed her rest as much as he needed his.

An argument battled in his mind. If she left once without saying good-bye, she could easily do it again. Her first abrupt departure was done under the condition that she'd trade her life for Jessica's. Surely Leah's commitment to Jess now should be as valid, right? She wouldn't disappear without fulfilling her promise to his daughter, would she? That Leah hadn't included him in the promise didn't go unnoticed. He pressed his fingers to his temple in an effort to ease the tension. She'd be here in less than two hours, and he was tired. He pushed the pile of bills back and went into his room to take a nap.

The effort to sleep was futile. After an hour, he got up, frustrated. He checked in on Jess who was still sound asleep. To be so carefree seemed foreign to him right now. He showered, put on a clean pair of gray sweats, and shaved. At least he would try to look presentable. The bell at the front door sounded just as the downstairs mantel clock announced the hour. It was four o'clock already.

God help me say what I need to say...

He pulled the damp towel from the back of his neck and grabbed a white t-shirt from his dresser, pulling it over his head as he hurried down the stairs.

When he saw her through the cut glass of the entryway, he was suddenly wide-awake. He unbolted the door, straightening his t-shirt in the process.

"Please, come in."

"Thanks." Her voice was quiet and controlled. Her pink sweatshirt matched the flush of her face. He took in her beauty, second-guessing why he'd agreed to be tortured with her presence only to have her leave him. She slipped past him and turned as if to wait for his direction. As well as Phillip knew Leah by now, it occurred to him that she'd never been to his home. He'd only imagined her here with him.

He forced himself to speak. "I'm so glad you came."

"Did you get some rest?" she asked.

"No, but it was not without trying. You?"

She shook her head.

The fact that she hadn't slept either made him feel a little better. Maybe he was getting to her. He felt guilty for the thought.

"How about some coffee?"

"That would be good."

The sorrowful twitch on her lip cut him inside. He took a deep breath as he led her into the kitchen.

"Tulley's French Roast, Donut Shoppe, or Black Silk?" Phillip twirled the K-cup holder for her to see.

"Tulley's, please."

"Sounds serious."

Was that a hint of a smile he detected?

Phillip took the K-cup, slipped it into the coffeemaker, and pulled a couple of mugs from a hook above his coffee station. Memories flooded him when he realized they were the souvenir mugs from the castle that he put away earlier.

She must not have noticed.

"You have a very nice place."

"Thanks. We are happy here."

She didn't say more. It seemed that the coffee took

forever to brew, like watching paint dry. He pulled the creamer from the refrigerator, put it on the counter next to the sugar bowl, then reached into the cabinet to retrieve the honey bear for her.

Finally, he handed the warm mug to her and waited for his own blend to brew, watching her from the corner of his eye. She stirred in cream and a squirt of honey, and handed the spoon off to him when his coffee finished gurgling.

"Shall we go into the family room?"

"Sure. I'll follow you."

He led her through the dining area and into the spacious room. He took the mug from her, set it on the coffee table, and urged her to the sofa. He lowered himself next to her, careful to leave a little space between them, and rested his hands on his knees as he wondered how to begin. He raked his hand through his still damp hair.

"Leah, there are a lot of things I don't understand. I've made some mistakes, and I'm sure I'll make more. I'm only human. But regardless of what you think of me and why you're intent on drawing away from me, I need you to know how I feel about you."

48

Leah struggled with Phillip's nearness. Everything around her spoke of him. To think she could enter his home, be on his turf, and push him out of her heart at the same time was ludicrous. His presence enveloped her.

But even more, her emotions were torn into a hundred pieces. She was overjoyed to learn she had a twin sister, although there was so much she didn't understand. Having two men in custody and Jessica safe was a relief beyond words. But every time she thought of Phillip, the ache surfaced.

So much had become clear. Yet there were still so many questions.

When he reached for her hand, she intended to draw away, but he gave her no chance. The familiar feelings stirred even more. She would not allow herself to be hurt again. To Phillip, she was only a case. A professional obligation. And he was in love with someone else.

His other hand reached for her chin, urging her to turn to him. His hand was warm. She was losing the battle. Sinking quickly.

Leah forced her eyes shut, trying to make sense of what was happening to her.

"I love you, Leah. Surely you know that by now?" He drew her into his arms, whispering the words again. His breath against her hair was intoxicating.

But no, he couldn't possibly mean it. Too many

things didn't add up. How could he say that to her when there was someone else? She wanted to slip free, and she tried, but his arms were warm, tender, and holding her securely.

"You don't believe me?"

He was making this much too difficult. She might have been convinced if not for the conversation that wafted through the open window the night before.

"What is it, Leah? What have I done to make you try to pull away? Please, be honest with me."

Silence settled between them, yet Phillip waited. Finally, she drew a courageous breath and spilled her feelings to free her soul. "I was outside, getting ready to come in last night from the backyard and you and AJ were talking. I didn't mean to eavesdrop, but I couldn't help it. Your words were in my airspace. You said you…" She stopped, unable to get the words out. Instead, she pulled back to face him and used a different approach. "I heard you mention how relieved you'd be after the case was over. You'd be a free man."

"Yes. Of course I'll be relieved when it's over. As will you, right? We can move on…" Uncertainty filled his eyes.

"I know you're in love with another woman and you didn't want to tell me about her." There. She finally voiced what plagued her for the past number of hours.

Utter shock was on his face. "What? What are you talking about, Leah?"

She closed her eyes and shook her head. He wasn't even denying it. She took another deep breath. "Phillip, I heard you. Don't deny it. You told AJ how much you loved her. Some officer. I've no clue who she is, but it doesn't matter. How can you possibly love two women? That's not how love works. Not for me, anyway."

"I'm not understanding, Leah. You heard me tell AJ how much I loved another woman… an officer?" He spoke as if it were puzzling to him. Like it was breaking news or something.

Phillip leaned forward and ran both hands through his hair. His shoulders rose and then lowered as he exhaled a slow, deep breath. When he finally tilted his head back toward her there was peace on his face. "I was talking about someone else who I want you to meet. Her name is Crystal, and I'll tell you more about her later. But she's not the one I love, Leah. She's a married woman. Besides, I hardly know her. You're the one who gets to me so much I can barely make it from one day to the next when you're not in my line of sight. Why do you think this has been so difficult for me? I've never loved Crystal. In fact, I didn't personally meet her until yesterday."

"You mean Crystal, my twin? You knew about her all along?" Leah threw her hands into the air. None of this was making sense.

"Wait—you knew you had a twin?" Surprise flooded Phillip's face.

"Not until we ran into each other this morning." Leah lowered her head in uncertainty. She felt a tug at the sleeve of her shirt, prompting her to look at him.

"Hold on a minute." His eyes were brighter than she'd seen them in weeks. He leaned back and captured her hands again, holding them between his own. This time, she didn't resist. Instead, she waited.

"If you met Crystal this morning, then I imagine you don't know the whole story yet. But a couple of months ago, the Miami Marshal's office received word that someone was trying to find you—someone who had nothing to do with the case at all. This person was running into continuous dead ends, because, of course, you were protected. Turns out it was Crystal."

He paused, focusing his eyes on their hands in front of him. She watched the line of his mouth as he formed his words carefully. He turned to her again. "Leah, what exactly do you know about your adoption records?"

"Very little. My parents never said a whole lot, except that my birth mother was young and from a prominent family whom she felt an obligation to protect. That's about it."

"That's what I thought."

"Crystal is an undercover officer from Texas. She was abducted by Mariucci and Scordino while she searched for you. She escaped then recovered from the ordeal. Crystal was your decoy, Leah. Your twin sister risked her life for you."

"Wait a minute. You said earlier the decoy was shot. When I met her today she seemed fine, although a bit wet."

"I'm sure she's anxious to tell you everything."

Leah's mind traveled back in time as she absorbed all Phillip said. But she needed clarification, without assumption. "So, you really don't love Crystal?"

Phillip reached up and touched her jaw line with his fingers, tracing it from her ear to her chin. His fingers were warm as he urged her to face him. When her eyes met his, she wondered how she ever doubted him.

His voice was soft and mixed with emotion. "Leah, it's not Crystal I'm in love with. It's you. Yes, I said that after this whole thing was resolved I'd be a free man, but that was because the façade would be lifted, once and for all. You've tortured me in unimaginable proportions. It would have been easier for me to bow out gracefully from being Richard, your CM. In fact, AJ offered to pull me from the case, but I refused. It was important for me to be there for you, to protect you myself. Besides, it was too late—I was smitten. On top of that, I couldn't breathe a word to you about Crystal. Not because she was my love interest, but because she was your twin sister that you weren't even aware of."

Leah dropped her face in her hands, taking it in. *He loves me.* Phillip's lips touched her hair and she reached up and circled the back of his neck with her hands, pulling him toward her while lifting her face to meet his. "You tortured me, too, you know."

He smiled mischievously and lowered his head to nuzzle the top of her forehead with his own. "That makes me happy. It was terrible being in this thing alone." His voice was low. His lips moved to hers, covering them with his warmth. When he finally spoke again, it was a whisper in her ear. His breath was even more intoxicating to her. "When you disappeared, I was frantic. I couldn't bear to lose you."

"I'm so sorry. You must have thought of me as an incompetent basket case." She laughed through her tears. "You've seen me in every mood imaginable, and I doubt competency was a characteristic in many of them."

He drew her back. "I beg to differ. Your circumstances are a bit unusual, Leah. Your reactions were understandable."

"But not excusable."

"You're much too hard on yourself." His tone was

comforting as he brushed her cheek with the back of his hand.

"For someone who's so focused, you're pretty resilient when you need to be. Your mother-in-law warned me about you."

"Oh, did she now?"

"Daddy?" Footsteps padded down the staircase.

Phillip's eyes lit up at hearing his daughter's voice. "We're in here, babe," he released Leah to go meet her. Leah's heart was full as she waited for Phillip to come back. So much had happened, it was difficult to fathom. But what did all of it mean for her future? She bowed her head and prayed for guidance.

Soon Phillip carried the sleepy-headed Jess into the room. That his daughter was safe in his arms was a treasure.

"Look who came to see you." Phillip pushed back the pillow she was clutching and kissed her cheek.

"Hi, Jess." Leah smiled at her from the sofa.

Jess grinned back.

"Good morning." Her voice was raspy.

"Morning?" Phillip teased. "It's almost dinner time. You slept a long while. Your cuckoo clock is a bit off." He wrinkled his nose at her.

"Daddy, I 'most forgot. I made a picture for Leah while I was gone. I need to get it." She wriggled free of his arms and scampered off as soon as he deposited her on the wood floor.

"When she gets something in her head, she moves on it," Phillip explained.

Leah laughed.

Jessica returned, rushed onto Leah's lap, and handed her the masterpiece. "It's a drawing of you wearing that pretty dress I like so much. The one you wore at Daddy's flying party."

Leah was overwhelmed that Jess even thought of her during her ordeal. "This is beautiful, Jess." The signature stick figure had a black dress on. Colorful flowers lined the bottom of the ivory sheet. At least that's what she thought they were. "Where did you get all these pretty colors?" Her eyes were drawn to the embossed letter that Jessica scribbled over.

"The lady at the place we stayed gave me colors to play with. She even had a toy box."

Phillip leaned forward with an intense look on his face. "What lady is this, Jessica?"

"The lady that lets people stay at her house."

"Where is this house?"

"I don't know. It's not too far, 'cause the lady says she sometimes gets pizza from Shack in the Crack. I told her we get pizza there too when Sally and Joe have plans."

Leah and Phillip were both sitting forward now.

"Do you remember the lady's name?" Leah asked.

"I don't think so, but it had a *A* like a apple."

"Were there other people there?"

"A couple people."

"Did the lady ask you what you were doing there?"

"The one bad man told her he was my grandpa, and the other man was my daddy. They told her they were porters."

Phillip frowned at her. "Porters?"

"Yep. The porters that write stories 'bout plane axe-dints."

Realization dawned on them at the same time. "So...she would never have known to report anything odd," Phillip breathed out quietly.

"It's got to be Addington's Attic," Leah reasoned. "It's a B & B, but Mrs. Addington also does a little catering. I stopped by there to get prices on a couple party plates for the open house. We ended up not using her services, but I'll bet that's where Jess was. Mrs. Addington probably had no idea who those guys were. I can't believe I didn't think of it before, with the embossed A on the note and everything."

"Miss Addy...uh huh, that's the name," Jessica said proudly.

"We'd better check it out," Phillip said as he reached over and love-pinched his daughter's cheek. "AJ and Riley should be finishing up their paperwork soon. I'll give AJ a call. They'll want to search her place and trace any phone calls the men made from there. This might be the break we need to locate anyone else who might've been involved." He turned his full attention to Jessica. "Honey, when AJ was asking you questions this morning, why didn't you say something?"

"I don't know, Daddy. I guess I just forgot. I didn't know it was 'portant. You tell me I talk too much anyway."

Leah laughed at the look of shock that skirted Phillip's face. She held up her hands in a mock attempt to stay out of it. He was on his own on this one.

Phillip shook his head with an apologetic grin. "I'm sorry, Jess." He scooped her up from Leah's lap and planted a kiss on her forehead. "I'll try to be more careful in the future."

"It's OK, Daddy. None of us is perfect."

49

Leah was nervous the next day when Phillip drove her to meet Crystal and Michael for an official introduction. He reached for her hand as if to calm her down. Still, the uneasiness was real.

"Relax. I'm sure she's as anxious as you."

"Yeah, but she's known about me for how many months? And I only found out yesterday?" She pulled down the mirrored visor and touched up her lipstick.

"You look fantastic, Leah." From the corner of her eye she saw him watching her.

"Thanks, but I looked horrid when I met her yesterday. I'm surprised she recognized me."

"I'm telling you, she's probably doing the same thing you are right now. Besides, you don't think she knows what you really look like?" He winked at her.

Leah put her lipstick away. "Pray for me?"

"I will. And for the record, I've prayed for you ever since the day you nearly rammed me over in the hall by my office."

"The way I remember it, you weren't looking either." Her thoughts turned more serious. "Really? Even back then?"

"Yes, even then. When I told you that you tortured me, I wasn't kidding."

A smile of satisfaction crept to her face. She had a few things to confront him on as well—like when he egged her on to keep talking about her fascination with *the aviator*. She'd find a way to get him back. The thought gave her pleasure. She watched him for several miles as he concentrated on the road ahead of them.

"I love you, Phillip." She broke the silence.

His lips curved into a huge smile as his eyes stayed focused on the traffic situation ahead. "I've dreamed of hearing you say that, and now you tell me when I can't even take you into my arms and hear it up close."

"It's called leverage. It gives me the upper hand."

He shot her a quick glare, but the longing in his expression was obvious.

"We're here. Ready?" he announced a few minutes later.

Leah took a deep breath and closed her eyes, silently asking God for strength.

He pulled into a parking spot and turned off the ignition. "Still want me to come in with you?"

"Absolutely." She needed someone to hold her hand and could think of no one she preferred over Phillip.

He moved to her side of the vehicle, opened the door, and offered his hand. He pulled her toward him, his mouth dangerously close to hers. She felt his warmth, only a breath away, but he was silent and made no move to kiss her. He turned before she had a chance to respond, but not before she caught the mischievous expression in his eyes.

His lack of contact left her flustered. "I guess one good turn deserves another," she admitted with a hint of cynicism.

In a moment, they were at the hotel room door, and he'd managed to completely take her mind off the tension she felt earlier. "Thanks, Phillip." She squeezed his hand.

His grip tightened on hers in return.

The door opened, and a split second later, Crystal and Leah were in each other's arms.

"It's so good to see you. I could hardly wait," Crystal said.

"I could hardly wait either," Leah stammered.

"You look rested."

"And you look wonderful—and dry." Both women laughed and hugged again.

"Hi, Phillip," Crystal greeted him.

"Good to see you, Crystal. Glad you're all right."

"Aren't you going to introduce us?" The voice spoke from behind Crystal. A nice-looking man made his appearance and extended his hand.

"Where are my manners? Come in, please. Karina, this is my husband, Michael Robbins. Michael, Karina Rubenski—my sister." Her shaky voice held a touch of pride.

"It's so good to finally meet you, Karina." Michael offered his hand and pulled her into a warm embrace instead.

"The pleasure is mine. But you can call me Leah. I've kind of gotten used to it."

"Leah it is." Michael turned to Phillip and reached for his hand. "How are you, Phillip?"

"Doing great, Michael. It's good to see you again."

Leah's heart warmed at their easy exchange. They moved to the patio table on the hotel balcony. Crystal poured sodas for each of them as they continued talking.

"I don't know how we would have made it had it not been for you and AJ." Michael directed his gratitude to Phillip. "And I'm afraid we never would have found you alive, Leah." Michael turned to her.

Leah's eyes met Phillip's. "He kept pretty good tabs on me."

"More so than she realized," Phillip admitted, his hand covering hers protectively. She'd never felt more secure in her life.

"You went through a tough day yesterday, didn't you Michael?" Phillip asked.

"It was gut-wrenching to say the least, sitting on the sidelines and waiting for word. But, obviously, Crystal took the brunt of it. Quite literally. I'm glad AJ had such good aim when she was locked in his crosshairs."

Leah turned to her sister, dumbfounded. "It was AJ who shot you?" She hadn't heard the full story yet, and she was eager to get the details.

"It was an alternate plan," Crystal explained as she turned to Phillip. "You didn't tell her?"

"No. I thought I'd give you two something to talk about."

"As if that would be difficult," Crystal teased. She went on to explain. "AJ's a sniper. The best. He was on the roof when I walked out for the exchange. Kevin was in scuba gear under the dock, waiting. We were all wired on audio together. The plan was for Kevin to surface and overtake the men, pulling me away before I got on the boat. AJ wanted Kevin as close to me as possible without being visible. If worse came to worse, AJ's plan was to take them out from the roof, but then it might have been hard for him to get to me. It seemed like a great plan until Kevin's transmitter died and he didn't hear the countdown. AJ had to do something, because by that time, Mariucci was already holding me with a gun to my neck. Since I had a bulletproof vest on and was standing near the edge of the boat, AJ made an executive decision and shot me to force me overboard. Evidently, I passed out for a few seconds under the water, but I remember that it felt like a lifetime. Then Kevin grabbed me. From all their years of working together, Kevin knew to hold me under the dock until it was safe for us to surface. It was pretty chilly without a wet suit, but I survived. Then AJ fired at the boat motor, and the rest is history."

"Unbelievable!" Leah shook her head in bewilderment.

"It was a little scary when the plan got changed at the last second. But I'm fine. I guess I'm out of practice."

"Out of practice?" Leah asked, trying to understand.

"Crystal is an undercover cop for the city of Dallas," Michael explained.

"Oh, of course." Now she remembered. Phillip told her the decoy was an undercover. He'd earlier referred to her as officer. There had been so much to absorb in such a short time.

"She put her career on hold to raise our two-year-old son, Trevor."

Leah bit her lip. *I have a nephew.* She looked forward to meeting him.

"Which reminds me; we need to call home. I'm sure Mom has Trevor up by now," Crystal said to Michael.

A twinge of apprehension pierced Leah. What on earth was her birth mother like? And as wonderful as it all seemed, was she ready to face her? Would their meeting detract from the memory of her own adoptive mother who spent the best years of her life raising her?

There was so much to think about.

Phillip squeezed her hand. He must have noticed her sudden unease, but more importantly, he understood.

50

Phillip didn't want to date her long. Perhaps it was eagerness, or maybe pure selfishness. He admired her from across the table at the Shack in the Crack as she cut though her calzone and dipped her forkful into their signature marinara. She looked up and caught him off guard.

"What?" she asked. "Too much sauce?"

"You can have all of it you'd like."

"Thanks for your permission." Leah laughed.

"Sometimes Daddy tells me I take too much sauce," Jess offered.

"What, are you two ganging up on me now? I feel thoroughly picked on."

Phillip reached over to help Jess cut her bite into a smaller one. He stabbed it with a fork. "Go ahead, drown it, Jess."

She did.

Several days had passed since the exchange. Jessica's informative comments added a great deal of substance to the case. Addington's Attic was scoured for information and clues. AJ returned to Miami and already confirmed the arrest of a third accomplice. Sam Canali's charges would likely be reduced providing his story proved correct. He acknowledged, more than expected, including Officer Patrick's involvement along with the identity of the messenger who'd been paid off. It amazed Phillip how easily criminals stabbed each other in the back when it came time to save their own skin. All three hearings were set for two weeks from today.

Meanwhile, Mariucci and Scordino, battered, bruised, and recovering, would soon be transferred to Miami to face charges when they were stable enough to be transported the distance.

Loose ends still needed to be tied up, but for all practical purposes, it appeared the finishing stitches were being sewn on Leah's wings of freedom.

Crystal and Michael left that morning. Phillip valued the newfound friendship. Leah was adjusting nicely to the idea of a twin sister and a brother-in-law. He wondered how she might respond to the idea of having a husband and daughter in the near future.

He forced himself not to bring it up to her yet. So many other things were on her mind. For him to offer a marriage proposal on top of everything else was beyond what she could absorb right now.

When they returned to his place later, he went upstairs to help Jess get ready for bed while Leah waited on the porch swing at the back deck. Jess, donned in her princess pajamas, bounded down the stairs to say good night to Leah. He was pleased at the bond developing between them, despite their efforts to gang up on him.

He'd suffer through the trauma.

"I'll be back shortly," he called to Leah as he lifted Jess into his arms.

"You won't go anywhere tonight, will you, Daddy?" Jess asked him a few minutes later as he tucked her in.

"Of course not, babe. Where do you think I'd go?"

"I don't know..." Jess twisted her lip. Phillip detected her subtle insecurities over the past couple of days.

"Does it bother you that Leah is here to visit tonight?"

"No," she answered. Her small brow was furrowed. "But what if Leah goes somewhere? I heard you and her talking 'bout her home at the dolphin place."

"The dolphin place?" Phillip asked as he brushed a tear from her face.

"You know, the place the men tackle each other."

Miami Dolphins. His smile was meant to reassure her. "I don't want her to go to the dolphin place either, Jess. I'd like Leah to stay here. Maybe I'll ask her. For now, it'll be our little secret. But you can pray she'll say yes when I finally ask her, OK?"

Jess nodded, thrilled to be a part of the covert operation.

"But even if she says no, it'll still be you and me, exactly as it's always been, OK? I'm not going anywhere."

Jessica pressed her lips together and a newfound determination crept to her face. Her eyes lit up. "I could even share my room with her."

Phillip smiled at her offer. She had no idea what it was like to have a mother in the house. "Thanks, Jess, but I doubt that'll be necessary. You need to get to sleep now, OK?"

"Good night, Daddy."

He kissed her cheek. "Night, babe. Sweet dreams."

"You, too."

Phillip turned the light off and flipped the night-light on, leaving her door open a crack. Her thought process amazed him at times.

Leah was seated in the swing when he returned.

"Got her settled?"

"For now," he answered as he sat next to her, thinking about his conversation with Jess.

The night around them was quiet. It would be a great opportunity to ask. He forced his thoughts elsewhere. "Now that Crystal and Michael are gone, what do you think? Did you have a good time with them?"

"Did I ever. Crystal and I talked in depth at breakfast this morning."

"I'll bet you did."

"It's amazing how much alike we are, not only in our physical appearance, but in our thoughts and actions. In everything. It's cool to have a sister, but the fact that we're twins makes it even more special."

"Did she tell you a lot about your mother?"

"She told me some things, showed me a picture of her. She's beautiful."

"Like mother, like daughters." Phillip's hand brushed her arm.

"She's a Christian. I'm thrilled about that."

"I'm so happy for you."

"There are some things that confuse me though." She turned to face him.

He searched her eyes.

"Crystal invited me to Dallas in a few weeks, depending on the outcome of the case. But I'm so apprehensive to meet my birth mother. Is that normal?"

He pulled her toward him, drawing her into the crook of his neck. He felt her relax. "I would think that you're very normal. This is a lot to take in. You've had huge things thrown at you lately."

"But I'm afraid for other reasons, too." Leah's

voice was barely a whisper.

He rubbed her hair between his fingertips. It was soft and silky as he touched it to his face.

"What do you fear?"

She sat forward, pulling herself from his embrace. She started to say something, and then stopped.

"Are you afraid you might not like her? Or that you won't get along?" Phillip asked, choosing to give her the space she needed.

"No, it's not that. According to Crystal, she's a wonderful person. They have a great relationship, especially now. But I'm afraid…that I'll love her."

"Loving her is a good thing, isn't it?"

"Not at the expense of the memory of my mother who raised me."

He understood. All too well.

"Believe it or not, I had nearly this same conversation with Joe not long ago." That night was still so vivid to him.

"Go on."

"When I realized I was in too deep with you, I went to him. Told him everything…including my guilt over loving you."

She glanced at him in confusion.

"Because of my growing feelings for you, guilt became my companion. We were pretty tight," he smiled. "I was so afraid that if I allowed myself to love you, it might negate my love and memory for Daria. Joe explained to me that God would expect me to move on with my life when the time was right. He went through the same thing with Sally."

"Really?"

"Yes. Joe was married before. His first wife left him, but the feeling wasn't mutual. He loved her and wanted her back more than anything. It was a terrible situation. Two weeks after she left, she was killed in a car crash. For years, Joe suffered emotionally. Finally, he got help. With God's love and mercy, he pulled through. He met Sally while I was protecting her."

"What? You protected Sally?"

"She was the whistle blower in a corporate scandal in the District of Columbia. WITSEC relocated her here. She got a job at the Kraft Plant where Joe happened to work at the time. He was smitten from the beginning. With fear and trepidation, he eventually asked her out. She accepted, and they've been married nearly four years now. They've been like family to me. After Sally's case was over, she didn't want her old life back."

"I had no idea."

He stroked her hair. "You have every right to meet your birth mother, Leah. She made some mistakes, but she needs to experience your forgiveness. Meeting her won't take away a single thing from your adoptive mother and father. They will forever be the ones who raised you as their own. That was their calling. You'll always have the memories of growing up a Rubenski. It doesn't negate who you are."

"I guess you're right."

"In the same way, when I say I love you, it doesn't diminish the fact that I will always love Daria. But it's time for me to move on. My memories with her are incredible. Undeniable. But I can't live in the past, afraid to find love in the future. Besides, I'll bet your parents are giving me a thumbs-up right now. From what you told me, I think they'd approve of you learning to know your birth mother. If they were alive today, they'd probably want to meet her, too, so they could thank her for the pleasure of raising you as their own. Keep in mind, they wanted you pretty badly."

"So, you're saying I get a double blessing in a way?"

"Exactly. God allowed you to be raised by a wonderful couple. You experienced things as a Rubenski you'd never have experienced otherwise."

"True."

"You realize if you hadn't been in Miami and in need of a new identity and a case manager, I'd never have met you, at least not that I can figure out in my human reasoning. That should alleviate any doubt about your part in joining the WITSEC program as well."

"Ultimately"—Leah paused to think a minute— "you're saying that if I negate my past by dwelling on what I believe to be my failures, it's like I'm negating my present?"

"Kind of. When we question God and walk in regret, we're second-guessing His purpose for our life. We are to trust in Him with all our heart, and refuse to lean on our own understanding. Most often we create our own problems. That's why His mercy is new every morning. Because He knew we'd need it. You should give it all up to Him, trusting that He'll make something beautiful out of you, no matter the past."

"So, don't refute the fact that I'd like to meet my birth mother, don't worry if I end up loving her and wanting to develop a relationship with her, and don't question my adoptive parents' role in my life and my love for them, nor theirs for me, and—"

"Exactly. When you meet your birth mother, be thankful she chose your parents to raise you. What a blessing you've been given."

She looked as if she understood.

He hoped one day soon, if she said yes to him, he might enjoy her as an added blessing in his own life. He opened his mouth to tell her. But, no, he needed to allow her to conquer her own battles first.

He remained silent and forced the words to wait.

51

Leah flew into the Dallas Fort Worth International Airport. As she walked through the expandable jet-walk, her thoughts raced. Phillip offered to come with her, but this was something she needed to do for herself. She pushed back a stray piece of hair and took a deep breath as she traveled through the terminal toward baggage claim and the curbside pickup area.

God help me.

Crystal met her at the loading zone and gave her a warm embrace. They talked the whole way to the house, and Leah started to relax until they pulled up to the gated drive.

Crystal punched a number into the electronic panel and the gate lifted. She reached for Leah's hand and squeezed it. Leah appreciated the reassurance, but she was still apprehensive. Phillip's reminder to stop, take a deep breath, and know that God was right at her side came to her thoughts.

Crystal's arm was firmly around her as they walked up the front path. The fragrance of flowers penetrated Leah's senses, but she didn't notice the blooms. Her gaze was fully glued to the door. She was about to meet Elizabeth Cabo, the woman who'd given her up at birth.

When the opened, she broke.

She didn't even get a good look at her mother before their arms encircled one another. The woman who'd given birth to her trembled with an emotion that matched her own. Leah tried to catch her breath. Her face was wet, and her tears fell onto the soft, pale sweater of the one whose arms she belonged in at that moment. Finally, they drew back and looked at one another.

"I hear they call you Leah." Elizabeth's voice was a stuttered whisper.

Unable to speak, Leah nodded. She couldn't take her eyes from her mother's face.

"You are so beautiful. I've dreamed of this day for so long."

Crystal encouraged them over the threshold, closing the door behind them.

"I have so much I want to say to you," Elizabeth continued.

"Thanks for inviting me." Leah forced control to her voice. Leah took in her surroundings. Her mother was obviously upper crust. The home was well-decorated but not overdone. "You have a lovely home."

"We'll be having brunch in a few minutes. Are you hungry?"

"Yes. That sounds lovely." Leah hadn't had the stomach to eat when she left her house at six this morning. Now that the introductions were over, she was famished.

Her nerves relaxed even more as they moved into a comfortable breakfast room. Within minutes, Elizabeth set an exquisite array of food on the table, including a variety of fruits and croissants on a crystal platter.

"What type of juice would you lovely ladies care for?" Elizabeth asked, motioning to two Depression glass pitchers on the table.

"Orange, please," Leah replied, reasoning it might not be appropriate to swirl her special blend here.

"Yes, orange for me as well," Crystal answered.

Elizabeth nodded and filled their glasses then poured a fifty-fifty combination of juices into her own glass and took a swallow. Leah's heart surged.

"You mind if I ask the blessing?"

"Not at all," Leah and Crystal spoke in unison and bowed their heads.

"Thank you, Father," Elizabeth began. "Words cannot begin to express my gratitude to You for allowing us this special time. Please bless this food, and watch over our conversation. We give You thanks for all You have done. We pray this in Jesus' most revered name. Amen."

During the last cup of coffee, Elizabeth's eyes teared. The initial resemblances had all been compared, and a lot of laughter was shared over the clink of breakfast dishes. But Leah sensed the heaviness that etched its way to her mother's eyes.

"Leah, I must apologize to you for…giving you up." Elizabeth lifted the linen napkin to cover her face, but she couldn't hide the trembling.

Leah took a deep breath, anticipating her next words.

"I was only nineteen. My parents didn't know what was happening in my life. We had an argument about something, and I left in a huff without realizing I was pregnant, let alone with twins." She drew a shallow breath and wiped her eyes before continuing. "We didn't speak for a long while."

Elizabeth's voice calmed as the story unfolded. "There was a friend who helped me during that time. I had no idea what prenatal care was. I moved into an apartment with her about five hours away. She was a few years older and had already given up one child for adoption. But that wasn't something I'd considered. I wanted to raise my baby, even if it meant sacrificing my relationship with my family forever. We were estranged anyway, so it didn't matter to me at the time. I went into labor late one night, and my friend coached me through the transitions in the apartment. It was tough, and I was scared spitless. I was convinced we needed to call for help, but finally, I delivered."

Leah sat spellbound, taking in every word.

"Crystal came first, and you appeared twelve minutes later. I was so shocked, so naïve. I had no clue I was pregnant with twins, and there was no way I could care for two babies. I struggled with the thought of adoption for a couple of reasons. First, I couldn't tell anyone, because I didn't think they would let me separate you girls, knowing you were identical twins. I felt stuck. I didn't want to give you both away, but I knew I couldn't keep you both either."

Leah sat in silence, her pulse racing.

Elizabeth blew her nose and sat up a little straighter. "I came up with a plan. Since no doctor was present, I figured no one would ever know. I had my friend look after Crystal while I took you, Leah, to the local health department to get a birth certificate for a single birth home delivery. Two days later, I left you in my friend's care and I took Crystal in, telling the health department that I lost the original certificate. Since they remembered me bringing a baby in, they believed me and gave me a certified copy. But it only duplicated the name Karina Cabo."

Leah held her breath as she waited for the rest of the story.

"I took you to an adoption agency, Leah, to start the proceedings to give you up. It seemed the least likely offense since you were the one I named Karina to begin with. On top of that, I knew I'd be the one to deal with the fact that I had another daughter who, according to the certified copy, was also named Karina. I figured I'd take care of that later and have her name changed to Crystal, which was the name I'd chosen for your sister at birth."

She paused to catch her breath, and closed her eyes with the painful memories. "It was only a few days later when I got word that a physician and his wife were eager to adopt you. They'd been on the waiting list for quite some time. They obviously had no clue what I had done. I turned over the original birth certificate to them. They liked the name Karina, so they kept it, took you home, and you legally became a Rubenski." Elizabeth opened her eyes and faced her.

Leah gave her a weak smile as her mind replayed the confession. What had she been thinking? Where had her mother been coming from?

Elizabeth smiled ruefully and continued. "The moment I signed the papers it was clear to me that I made a dreadful mistake. The following week, my intention was to return to the agency to spill it all out and get you back, but I chickened out. Walt and Doris Rubenski wanted a child so badly. I couldn't bear to tell them the truth."

Crystal moved her chair closer to her mother and placed a hand on her shoulder. "Are you OK to go on, Mom? I know how hard this is for you. Maybe we need to wait and finish later."

Leah agreed, but Elizabeth insisted she needed to get it all out in the open. She forced a smile that didn't quite reach her eyes and searched Leah's face as if trying to gain permission to go on.

"I poured myself into raising Crystal by myself, but it was hard. After a year, I ate crow and returned home to my parents. We reconciled. They graciously forgave me for running, and they accepted me as a single mom who needed help. But it broke my heart even more, because I realized that, had they known about you, they would gladly have helped me raise the two of you together. Not long after that, I discovered the Rubenskis had moved away, and I lost all hope of ever being reunited with you. I pushed it aside, but burying it only led to misery. I never told my parents about you. They died last year without knowing they had twin granddaughters. Crystal was the first person I ever told, apart from my childhood friend who helped deliver you. Turns out she's now a pastor's wife. What a remarkable woman she's become through all she has struggled with. I'm so glad God's mercies are new every morning to anyone who asks, without partiality or preference."

Leah searched for words.

Crystal reached for her hand.

Leah bit her lower lip as she fought the urge to break down completely. "What happened to our...father?"

"Your father disappeared as soon as I told him I was pregnant. We haven't spoken since. I have no idea where he is."

"How difficult for you," Leah said.

"It was. Please understand. I gave you up, and shouldn't have, Leah. It was the biggest mistake of my life. But I didn't choose to abandon you over Crystal for any reason other than the fact that it was your name on the original birth certificate. You've had an original certificate all your life, although I lied about the single birth. I'm sure you've had to deal with questions in your life because you were adopted. That dynamic is tangible. But you had a real father to look up to and an adoptive mother, and I'm certain they loved you as their very own. You had a good family. I remember the Rubenskis. They seemed like a remarkable couple."

Leah's emotion ached with their memory. "Yes, they were amazing parents."

"Crystal has had other challenges. She spent her life dealing with the fact that she never had a father. You've both won in some respects, yet you've both lost considerably because of what I took from you. The loss that has been my companion over the years has been phenomenal. I've suffered daily for my mistakes. Here I am, twenty-seven years later, spilling it all. Where do I fit in now? I've no doubt lost your respect due to my foolishness."

Tears fell freely as Leah absorbed the truth of the past. Crystal was crying openly. Elizabeth's head was bowed low over the table. Everyone's emotions were torn. She didn't understand the irresponsible actions her mother had taken. Yet she'd been young and afraid. Wouldn't she have done the same thing if she'd have been in her shoes?

Let the person without a fault cast the first stone.

The verse was a warning. It didn't matter why her mother had done any of the things she'd done. Leah had made her own share of mistakes. What right did she have to be upset? To be angry now would be like negating all the circumstances that made up the fabric of her life now.

It was time to get out of the past and move on. What if David and Bathsheba had held onto their mistakes and refused to move forward? There would have been no Solomon, nor would there have been a Joseph, the husband of Mary, who was handpicked by God to be an earthly father to raise His only begotten Son.

No, she couldn't be angry for the mistakes of the past—hers or her mother's.

God's love and mercy reached beyond that, and so should hers.

Leah rose to her feet and moved over to kneel at her mother's side. She reached for her and pulled her into a warm embrace.

Elizabeth's face was tear-stained. "Can you ever forgive me for what I've done?"

"I forgive you for every bit of it, and I respect you fully. It must have been tough for you to tell me this, but let's move on. Don't feel bad for me. I've had a wonderful life, and I believe God has great plans for my future. I'd be thrilled if you and Crystal would be a part of it, and I'd love to be a part of your lives as well."

"You would?" The expression on her mother's face was one of surprise.

"I would. We'll start from here," Leah assured her as she rubbed her arm tenderly.

Crystal moved over to join them, kneeling on the other side. Leah was overwhelmed as she and her mirror image encircled their mother in love and forgiveness.

Leah sensed an overwhelming presence in the room—so much so that she imagined she might look up and the Sun of Righteousness Himself would be standing there with His arms outstretched as He ministered life to them. She had already felt the healing in His wings.

52

The refined restaurant exuded life. Tall windows circled up to a dome ceiling, and a large waterfall flowed down, surrounded by a bed of lush greenery. Real doves added to the atmosphere as they glided peacefully from a live tree perched near the central fountain.

Phillip watched Leah closely as she sat across from him. The four days she was away seemed much longer. She was the picture of grace and beauty as her gaze moved over the menu. Her ivory, angora dress fit her perfectly and complemented her every detail. He forced his attention to his own menu, forming his selection in case his mind wandered again before the waiter returned.

"This is such a beautiful place." Leah's voice was quiet as she looked about her. He liked the way a few strands of her hair fell from the elegant twist to frame her face.

"I'm glad you like it."

Leah's dark eyes twinkled in the candlelight as she took it in.

"So, tell me about your trip. How was it?" Phillip questioned after the waiter brought their beverages.

"Wonderful. I learned a lot about my birth mother. The three of us spent so much time together doing what mothers and daughters do." She laughed as if she were carefree. "We shopped, ate pizza, got our nails done, looked at old photos, and did everything imaginable in between."

"A great time to bond. Like a bunch of guys at a hockey game."

"Yeah, probably so." Her smile warmed him from head to toe. "It truly was amazing. At first, I was apprehensive. But after she spilled her life story to me, it became easy to forgive. I feel completely accepted by everyone, and I know they sensed my acceptance of them as well."

"And how are Crystal and Michael?"

"They're good. We had a barbeque at their place last night. They live about twenty minutes away. My little nephew, Trevor, is a real charmer. You should've seen his confusion when he laid eyes on me for the first time. It was epic."

"I'm sure."

"We still have a lot of getting acquainted to do, but I think we've made a positive start."

Phillip could hardly take his eyes off her as they conversed quietly over the delectable meal.

Through the glass ceiling above their table, the sky became a blanket of color as the sun settled in the distance while they shared a black forest cheesecake for dessert.

"I missed you." He reached for her hand across the linen tablecloth and covered it with his own.

Her gaze met his. "I missed you, too. It seemed like so long."

"Longer for me than for you."

"How so?"

"You were the one out having a good time, traipsing off to get acquainted with your roots. I worked doggedly while you were gone, trying to catch up on all the work you distracted me from."

"So now it's my fault?"

"Basically, yes. It was difficult for me to get anything done with you at the hangar when I was forced to keep my identity a secret."

"I didn't solicit the job at the hangar—you offered it," she teased.

"I know. But I wasn't aware of the consequences."

"That'll teach you."

"No sweat. I wouldn't trade the outcome for anything. I love you, you know."

The reflection of the candle between them flickered in her eyes, illuminating a look of regret on her face. "Sometimes I feel so bad."

Her comment took him by surprise, and he grew apprehensive. "What are you talking about?"

"You're so focused. And together. During the past few months, I've scaled the spectrum of emotions in every area of my life. I love you, too, but how can you accept me when I've been so flighty and emotional, and even difficult with you? I don't deserve your love, and I'm embarrassed over my actions."

"Oh, Leah, let it go. None of that matters now."

"I'm serious. I've blown it so often. When we were at the lake I treated you terribly."

"Trust me—that was probably a good thing." His gaze held hers. He noticed the flush that crept up her neck and colored her face. He gathered that she understood.

"But then I just left you—"

"I understand your reasons. I'm sure they seemed valid to you at the time."

"Thank you, but that's no excuse. I'm so sorry for what I did to you. I took the situation upon myself and refused to put my trust in God. I did believe He would work things out, but I couldn't wait for His timing. I have a bad habit of that."

"You're human...and you're precious, Leah. I forgive you completely. It's tough to wait on Him when we're looking through a glass darkly. He understands. He made us, remember? But we learn from our mistakes, and eventually things become clearer as we trust Him to see beyond the darkened glass. If we miss it, we correct it and move on. That's what being a vessel of honor is about. God uses the circumstances in our lives to purge us of the things that are not pleasing to Him. In your case, you felt like your trust in Him failed. When you're willing to make the little corrections and adjustments He brings to your mind, you become that much closer to being an instrument of grace. It doesn't happen overnight. It's through faith and patience that we receive the promise. You've learned a valuable lesson of trust."

"Sometimes I still question the whole WITSEC thing."

Her honesty was refreshing. "OK, worst case scenario—you really made a mistake when you allowed fear to rule you. You threw yourself to the mercy of the system and became another person. But He already had a back-up plan mapped out for you, and found a way to turn your mistake into good. You were instrumental with your involvement in WITSEC. Remember, we live in a cruel world. Count yourself privileged that you were used to administer justice. The guys have been caught. The operation was a success. And even in the midst of it, God put his finger on your human fear, taught you a valuable lesson, and still managed to see that justice was served. He won. You won. And the network of people who surround you have been impacted. The element of faith in each one of us was built up. Don't you understand? You and Crystal were both so instrumental. God used you both despite your own misgivings."

"Trust, huh?" Leah's eyes searched his.

"Yes. Even now, resist the doubts. Leave them in God's hands and move on. One more chance to lean on His understanding instead of your own." He lifted his eyebrows in an unspoken challenge.

Assurance moved across her face. "Thanks. Thanks for listening, encouraging me, and forgiving me."

His eyes took her in, and the desire to be closer to her got the better of him. "Let's go for a walk. There's a great park nearby."

"Sounds nice."

He left cash and a generous tip on the table, stood and took her hand. "I found something of yours I'd like to return to you," he told her nearly ten minutes later as they walked the landscaped path.

"Oh?"

He reached inside his jacket and pulled out a long gold chain. Relief was on her face at the sight of her vintage pocket watch. The panic chip that was installed on it was a direct link to him, day or night.

"I can't believe I was going to leave it." She fingered it in his hand.

He lifted it over her head, and his fingers lingered at the nape of her neck. He pulled her toward him, touching his forehead to hers. He felt her shoulders rise under his arms with her soft rhythmic breathing. Every beat of his heart longed for her.

"From the very beginning, you knew you had access to me at the touch of a button. You've never used that option. But I'm asking you now to be bonded to me forever. I can't afford to lose you, Leah. I don't want you to leave me again, ever."

Her eyes met his with uncertainty. "What exactly do you mean?"

"Open it and you'll see."

He waited as she unlatched the antique piece. Her open hand moved to her mouth and she gasped when she saw the diamond that glistened under the dimly lit lamppost. "Oh, Phillip…" She lifted her face to him again.

"I'm asking you to be my wife. This is the bond I want to nurture between us forever. To be connected to you in spirit, soul, mind, and body is my every desire."

Warmth flooded her eyes. "I would love to be your forever wife, Phillip Richard Zellmer."

He breathed a sigh of relief. *She said yes!*

"Where do I sign?"

He frowned. *What was she talking about?*

"Never mind. You already have my heart for collateral."

Phillip laughed at her playfulness. He'd certainly sacrificed his to her a long time ago before she ever knew it.

The ring glistened as he slipped it on her finger. Phillip drew her into a deep embrace and felt her pulse quicken against him. It was difficult to imagine the barrier of ice that was between them only a few short weeks ago.

If the warmth of her mouth was any indication of what he could anticipate in the future, he would be one satisfied man. He planned to spend a lifetime proving their love was mutual.

He could hardly wait to get started.

53

Leah closed her eyes and breathed in the fresh scent of the bouquet in front of her. Soft music played in the background as the final guests were ushered in. A tear tried to push its way to the corner of her eye. Joe nudged her and extended his left arm to escort her down the aisle.

"Ready, my dear?"

She nodded and took his arm. Phillip was already at the front of the church waiting for her. He stood tall and handsome, his black tux complementing his appealing frame. She warmed at the thought of him.

AJ waited beside Phillip as his best man, and Michael and two other friends were next in the lineup. Leah viewed her row of attendants. Marci and two girlfriends from Miami were already in position. Crystal had just moved into place as her identical matron of honor. Jessica and Trevor marched proudly to the front of the church.

At Leah's immediate right was a whole group of pilots, marshals, relatives, and friends of Phillip's she had yet to meet. She spotted the group from the hangar toward the middle. She was thrilled to see ex-SEAL Kevin sitting next to Special Agent Tom Riley. Phillip's in-laws, Bill and Nadia Clepole sat at the front with Sally, who'd left an empty spot for Joe when his "giving away" duty was complete.

To her left were some friends from Miami who'd traveled the distance to New York to witness the occasion. At the center aisle about halfway down, she spotted Albert and Sylvie Stewart, and she was thrilled her Miami neighbors were able to come. Behind them, Mrs. Yancey, her tomato-growing New York neighbor sat, whispering to the woman beside her. Rubenski aunts and uncles and newfound Dallas relatives were given the honor of the first several rows. Seeing her birth mother front and center brought an indescribable sense of joy. She only wished her adoptive parents could have celebrated with her and Phillip as well.

The "Wedding March" began.

Joe nudged her. "It's time."

Her mother rose and turned around, prompting the crowd of guests to follow suit. Leah moved toward the front of the church, eyes locked on Phillip's with every step she took. She winked at him playfully. He smiled and winked back.

Joe fulfilled his duties and gave her away with a kiss on her cheek. She took Phillip's arm and moved forward with him. Thirty minutes later, the announcement came from their pastor.

"By the authority given me in the State of New York, I now pronounce you husband and wife. Ladies and gentlemen, I present to you Mr. and Mrs. Phillip Richard Zellmer. Mr. Zellmer, you may kiss your bride."

He did.

The audience exploded in applause.

As they pulled away from each other, Phillip reached into his jacket for his cell phone. "Ready?"

"Let's do it."

More applause broke out as they took their first marital selfie with their friends and family all behind them. The sounds of celebration spilled through the church as they made their way down the aisle. Jessica, Trevor, and the attendants followed behind.

Phillip lifted Leah off her feet when they reached the privacy of the foyer. His lips parted into an award-winning smile as he brought her back down and pulled her to himself. His emerald eyes spoke of his longing for her and he pressed his lips over hers. It didn't matter that the foyer was filling quickly with the bridal party eager to congratulate them. All Leah knew was that she wanted to drown beneath his embrace forever.

He pulled away and whispered in her ear. "Mrs. Phillip Zellmer...Leah Karina Zellmer. It has a nice ring to it."

She tugged at the lapel of his tux and pulled him in closer, the warmth of his breath stirring within her. "Leah Karina Zellmer," she spoke her new name aloud. "It does have a nice ring to it."

She may as well get used to it. There was still a lifetime to go.

Leah's Blueberry Braid with Lavender-Infused Lemon Sauce

Dough
¾ cup warm water
2 ¼ teaspoon active dry yeast
2 Tablespoons white sugar
1 egg
½ teaspoon salt
2/3 cup softened butter
3 cups all-purpose flour, + or – as needed
2 Tablespoons melted butter (hold for last step just before baking)

In glass measuring cup, combine warm water, yeast, and sugar. Let sit approximately ten minutes to test the integrity of the yeast. It should froth and double in size. Meanwhile, in a mixing bowl, combine egg, salt, softened butter, and flour. Add the yeast liquid and knead together by hand or with a dough hook. When completely mixed, cover with a thin cloth and let rise in a warm place until at least double in size (about 1 1/2 hours). While it's rising, continue to make the other fillings until the dough has risen.

Blueberry Filling
2 ½ cups fresh or frozen blueberries
1/3 cup white sugar
2 Tablespoons cornstarch
½ cup water

While waiting for dough to rise, combine all ingredients for blueberry filling into a small saucepan.

Cook over medium heat until thickened and bubbly, and blueberries begin to pop open. Set aside to cool.

Cheese Filling
8 ounces softened cream cheese
8 ounces part-skim Ricotta Cheese
1 egg
¼ cup white sugar
½ teaspoon Haitian or other concentrated vanilla
1 tablespoon cornstarch
2 tablespoons all-purpose flour

In a small mixing bowl, beat the cheeses and add egg to combine. Add rest of cheese filling ingredients. Cover and set aside.

Lavender-Lemon Glaze
¼ cup boiling water
1 to 2 tablespoons culinary lavender as desired for strength
1 to 2 teaspoons lemon juice, as desired for flavor
2 to 2½ cups powdered sugar
2 tablespoons cream or half-n-half

Steep lavender in boiling water for approximately ten minutes. Strain pulp and discard. Add lemon juice to the lavender tea. (If it tastes too strong, add a very small amount of water to dilute, but you'll want to be careful to only use approximately ¼ cup of the infused liquid for the next step.) Add powdered sugar to the lavender tea, and add cream. Add additional powdered sugar if needed to get a thickened but pourable consistency. Set aside to cool.

To Assemble Braid:

Determine if you want to make one large braid or two smaller ones. For smaller braids, divide the dough into two parts. Below, only one large rectangle will be referenced.

On a large sheet of parchment paper, sprinkle additional flour and lightly knead, then roll dough into a large rectangle. On right and left side (long sides), with a kitchen shears, snip the dough into approximately three-inch snips, each one inch wide. Leave the center section uncut, as the filling will be placed on the center section. Depending on how long the rectangle is, you will have approximately ten one-inch strips of dough on each side of the rectangle. Carefully transfer the parchment paper and dough onto a baking sheet.

Spoon blueberry mixture onto the center third of the dough from the top of the rectangle to the bottom, and spread evenly. Dollop the cream mixture on top of the blueberry mixture. (You may have leftover fillings, depending on how much filling you add.)

To make the braid, start at the top edge of the rectangle and bring the first right strip over the center filling on an angle, then bring the first left strip over the center filling atop the filling and first strip. Alternate right and left strips to form the braid the length of the dough. Cover and let rise for one hour.

When risen, brush melted butter over the dough.

Bake at 350° for 30-40 minutes or until golden brown and filling has set. Remove from oven and let cool for about ten minutes. Drizzle lavender glaze over top. Serve warm.

Fall in love with the person you're sharing it with. ☺

ACKNOWLEDGEMENTS

It's always interesting to learn who an author credits for various tasks associated with the publication of their work. To adequately express my gratitude to the handful of faithful friends, family members, and professionals who played a part in this final product is no small feat.

Darlene, Kathy, and Jacque: Thank you for taking the time to read a draft of this book in its very early stages. You kept reading even though deep inside you knew how much work it needed. The feedback you offered was invaluable, and your belief in me and in this project meant the world to me, and still does. For that I am grateful. To Bonnie, thank you for your efforts in proofreading my manuscript and for providing feedback.

Andrea: From the moment we arrived at our first writer's conference in 2008, we knew this craft was something we wanted to pursue as we rubbed shoulders with authors, publishers, and editors alike. You encouraged me, and fed the dream inside me. Years later, your professional editing skills polished this piece for submission. Thank you from the bottom of my heart.

Cecil Murphey: You paid it forward by offering a scholarship to attend the 2008 Blue Ridge Mountain Christian Writer's Conference. I was one of those fortunate recipients, and I am forever grateful for the opportunity you provided.

Prism Book Group and Pelican Book Group: Thank you for believing in me and in this project. Paula and Susan, you read my submission and saw hope between the lines. You gave me a chance, and I am so appreciative. Susan, you're a pleasure to work with as my editor. Your commitment to preserve the integrity of my voice and message means a lot to me.

Nicola, Editor-in-chief and publisher, you are a blessing. Your leadership, commitment, and selfless ministry at Pelican are admirable. All that, and you are an amazing graphic artist, too! You have accurately captured my vision for this cover. For that and for the opportunity you provide to writers like me, thank you.

To those who worked feverishly behind the scenes to make this book the best it can be, thank you.

Keith: What a representation you are of a godly husband. Truly. You're my best friend and soul mate. Thank you for never, ever giving up on me. You read my first draft and offered me fresh ideas. You take an interest in my projects and your eyes light up when we flesh out new stories together, particularly after a couple cups of your wicked coffee. I can't wait to continue this journey with you by my side.

And finally, to the Author and Finisher of my faith, thank You, Lord, for creating the dream in me to write. May the parables I pen be a reflection of Your love, offering words of life to move the soul.

BIOGRAPHY

Linda Widrick's desire is to be a beacon of light in a dark world, sharing God's love and grace through her writing. A dreamer at heart, she loves to pull her inspiration for stories from snippets of everyday life. She enjoys kayaking, traveling, treasure hunting, and spending time with family and friends over a good cup of coffee. She and her husband Keith live on Florida's west coast, but enjoy spending time on their farmland near the Tug Hill region of New York, the setting for much of her first published novel.

Thank you

We appreciate you reading this Prism title. For other
Christian fiction and clean-and-wholesome stories,
please visit our on-line bookstore at
www.prismbookgroup.com.

For questions or more information, contact us at
customer@pelicanbookgroup.com.

Prism is an imprint of
Pelican Book Group
www.PelicanBookGroup.com

Connect with Us
www.facebook.com/Pelicanbookgroup
www.twitter.com/pelicanbookgrp

To receive news and specials, subscribe to our bulletin
http://pelink.us/bulletin

May God's glory shine through
this inspirational work of fiction.

AMDG

You Can Help!

At Pelican Book Group it is our mission to entertain readers with fiction that uplifts the Gospel. It is our privilege to spend time with you awhile as you read our stories.

We believe you can help us to bring Christ into the lives of people across the globe. And you don't have to open your wallet or even leave your house!

Here are 3 simple things you can do to help us bring illuminating fiction™ to people everywhere.

1) If you enjoyed this book, write a positive review. Post it at online retailers and websites where readers gather. And share your review with us at reviews@pelicanbookgroup.com (this does give us permission to reprint your review in whole or in part.)

2) If you enjoyed this book, recommend it to a friend in person, at a book club or on social media.

3) If you have suggestions on how we can improve or expand our selection, let us know. We value your opinion. Use the contact form on our web site or e-mail us at customer@pelicanbookgroup.com

God Can Help!

Are you in need? The Almighty can do great things for you. Holy is His Name! He has mercy in every generation. He can lift up the lowly and accomplish all things. Reach out today.

Do not fear: I am with you; do not be anxious: I am your God. I will strengthen you, I will help you, I will uphold you with my victorious right hand.
~Isaiah 41:10 (NAB)

We pray daily, and we especially pray for everyone connected to Pelican Book Group—that includes you! If you have a specific need, we welcome the opportunity to pray for you. Share your needs or praise reports at http://pelink.us/pray4us

Free Book Offer

We're looking for booklovers like you to partner with us! Join our team of influencers today and periodically receive free eBooks and exclusive offers.

For more information
Visit http://pelicanbookgroup.com/booklovers